Come up a Cloud

Ron D Smith

Copyright © 2016 Ron D Smith

All rights reserved.

ISBN-13: *978-1537132358*
ISBN-10: *1537132350*

"Before you embark on a journey of revenge, dig two graves."

A saying commonly attributed to Confucius

Prologue

    The bald tires on the bucket-of-bolts truck whined as it rattled past Sandstrum's Machine Shop on Route 4. Out of the corner of his eye, the farmer behind the wheel glimpsed a plump figure in camouflage pants loitering near the back corner of the corrugated tin building. The old man would have assumed it was one of the machinists taking a smoke break, except the person wore an odd headpiece. It looked like a Viking helmet, like the ones you saw at Minnesota football games. The other odd thing: The Viking held a rifle canted downward. The gun looked like one of those fancy Bushmasters, which copied M-16s like the one the farmer had carried in the jungle.

    The farmer rummaged his brain for any hunting season starting in early August. Squirrel season wouldn't kick off for a few more weeks, not that a flimsy law stopped anyone who craved pan-fried rodent. He'd heard Bushmaster made a .22, which wasn't much more than a peashooter dressed up like a serious piece of work. Anything more powerful would rip a squirrel to thunder. And wearing desert camo to hunt squirrels? That was even less necessary than an assault rifle, unless squirrels had gotten a lot smarter than they used to be.

    The farmer decided the hunter was one of Sandstrum's friends, a city fool who had come up to pretend-hunt. That didn't explain the helmet, but lots of things city people did were hard to explain. He headed down the road to Snoots for a lunch of ham sandwich and PBR. He would give the camoed figure no more thought until he heard the sirens thirty minutes later.

1

  The last satellite truck packed up and headed out of town. It had only been two days since Tommy killed us, and already we were being forgotten. I used to watch cable news in the morning before work, so I knew how these events went. Mass shootings like ours had become as predictable as the phases of the moon. We would be important for one twenty-four-hour news cycle, long enough to see our pre-massacre smiling faces up on CNN's website. Though Tommy would receive most of the attention, even he wouldn't get much. I wish I could say the guy who killed us was a little interesting. Maybe the story would be more titillating if he had some dark hatred he couldn't suppress. But Tommy was just Tommy. A little strange maybe, but who isn't? He stepped into the machine shop like it was no big deal and, BAM, turned the place into an abattoir. Lunch break was just starting. I was twenty pages into Norwood *by Charles Portis (my second time reading the novel) when he pointed his gun at me. In case you're wondering, I was dead before I felt any pain. Least ways, I don't remember any.*

  Tommy's parents are holed up in their house like frightened gophers. And who could blame them? Because Tommy's not around to punish, the town will take it out on Bob and Patsy. My dad will be at the front of that line. Maesie Mattsen will take some heat, too, because everyone wants to know how she escaped the machine shop alive. They won't believe Tommy just let her go. What Tommy did was not Maesie's fault, but that won't matter to my dad, who could give a one-hour PowerPoint on how to be a vengeful asshole.

  I always had a small thing for Maesie. I remember how she liked to read a lot in school, just like me. And you know how some girls are ugly in a kind of cute way? Like if you took each part of her face individually, you'd say not good, not good, not good. But when you put all the parts together, they add up to something nice. It never bothered me that she was tiny. Maybe we could have had some good times together if I had got off my ass and done something about it. But I was barely twenty-one and felt no urgency.

COME UP A CLOUD

A pearl of sweat streamed down the bridge of Maesie's nose and hung at the tip like a water balloon. She had taken a moment from spading the widening hole in the chicory and wild onion sod to inhale the earthy fragrance of her work. This was the eighth hole so far in her back yard. The others haphazardly pocked the sod like test pits for an archeological dig. The latest and deepest hole sunk a foot and nearly twice that in width. Maesie had worked at this hole for nearly an hour, the work slow because of sandstone chunks that comprised much of the topsoil. No matter. Leaning against the spade, she admired the mound of gravelly clay and rocks she had created. If she could make the hole slightly bigger, she might search for an old piece of garden hose to use as a breathing tube. She would lie down in the hole and blanket herself with loose dirt. It would be pleasant down there, she imagined. Quiet, too. No one would bother her.

Maesie wondered how long she could live in a hole like that, covered up, before she began to starve or had to pee. Something to think about. Something else to distract her. If Maesie wanted a distraction, however, she could have thought of something better than boring holes like a frenetic gopher. The embalmed bodies of six men were lined up at the funeral home like mannequins ready for display at Macy's. They awaited burial in their own fresh holes. Maesie needed no reminding of that.

She jerked her head and tracked the sweat bead as it released from her nose and flew into the pit. She resumed digging, making the hole wider and oval so that it would look less like a grave.

Maesie had not ventured from her weedy backyard sanctuary since the law let her go. Hugging a dusty gravel road on the southwest corner of town, the decrepit clapboard one-story where she lived her twenty-one years had no close neighbors. The back yard was its own enclosed world. No one could easily enter it but through the back door. Century-old, gnarled cedars and blackberry scrub on three sides abutted the back corners of the house and created an opaque perimeter. The back yard, quiet most of the time except for an occasional interruption by redwing blackbirds and the drone of cicadas, was the only place Maesie felt safe following the bloodshed. Here, she was free from the accusing eyes of the town. Indoors was no good, though. Too shut up, like the machine shop.

The back screen door squeaked open. Maesie would have peed her pants from fright had she not expected Cahill Renfrew, who maneuvered around a couple of shallow holes as he approached her.

"Struck oil?" Cahill asked, as if he had expected such a scene.

"Not unless it's hiding inside these stones," Maesie said.

Cahill, whose skin was bleached and his hair light and thin to the point it took on a sky blue hue, kept his chambray shirt buttoned to the collar to guard against the sun's rays. He kept his sleeves similarly secured around his wrists. He was not an albino, but he was within spitting distance of one. Cahill never went without a seed cap perched on his bony head. Today, he wore a camouflage cap with a DeKalb logo, the bill pulled down to eye level. His narrow head looked like the top of a bowling pin. In consequence, his cap always seemed too big for him, like his ears were all that kept it from dropping to his jaw line.

If Cahill had any ambition, it was to be known as a town tough, following in a tradition that included Skunk Olstad, and, to a lesser extent, Maesie's father. He saw the fear those men elicited, which he identified as respect, and wanted that for himself. But Cahill did not have it in him to be like them. Besides being left wanting in physical attributes, Cahill did not possess the required maliciousness. Nature had instead given him empathy.

He grabbed a rusty metal lawn chair and clanked it down beside Maesie. It was the same chair where Maesie's father parked himself the rare evenings he came off the road.

"I tried calling, but I guess you run out of minutes again," he said.

Maesie jabbed the spade and hit another rock in the bottom of the hole. She reached in to dislodge it. It was twice the size of her fist.

"Get on with it," she said, examining the rock as though it were a valuable ingot.

Cahill raised his hands in a faux gesture of innocence. "Get on with what? I just dropped by to see how you was holding up."

Cahill did odd jobs for the Sandstrums and others when his mother's government check came up short. Maesie knew Sharon Sandstrum would waste no time sending Cahill to kick Maesie off the property. Roger Sandstrum, owner of the machine shop as well as the house where Maesie lived, had rented the place to the Mattsens since before Maesie was born. Nearly all of Smackdab was poor, but the Mattsens were among the white-trashiest in Sharon Sandstrum's opinion. She had never liked that her husband rented to them, as if a long line of middle-income families waited to rent the four-room hovel. After her mother died, Maesie quickly became behind on rent. Sharon had sent her husband to evict Maesie. Instead, Roger hired her to work in the shop office three mornings a week to help pay off what she owed. She had worked there less than two weeks when Tommy Klimp turned the shop into Tarantino blood porn, killing everyone but her. Roger was the last of the victims to die of *multiple ballistic traumas*, as it was listed in the official cause of death.

Cahill, feigning nonchalance, leaned back and interlocked his hands behind his head. No sooner had he settled in that position than he loosened his hands and moved forward again. Maesie knew from the way he fidgeted she had accurately identified the purpose of his visit. She coaxed him toward his objective. "Sharon is paying you Judas money to kick me out of here," Maesie said. "Don't insult my intelligence by pretending otherwise."

Cahill kicked at the loose dirt from the hole with the heel of his boot. "She says you ain't up to date on rent, and she's got every right to boot you. And, hell, I got a right to make a buck as much as the next guy."

"I can think of better ways," Maesie said. "But they all involve work."

Cahill scratched a spot behind his right ear. "Like this ain't gonna be an effort," he said. "You're so damn stubborn I'll likely have to carry you out of here."

"I'll land a foot to your scrotum if you try."

"Big talk from a runt," he said.

Maesie unconsciously licked her lower lip. When Tommy put a gun to his head to punctuate his deeds, a rocketed driblet of his temporal lobe landed there. She had wiped off the globule immediately, but not before she had felt it rapidly cooling from its original ninety-eight-point-six degrees. Since then, she repeatedly scrubbed her lips to the point they had become cracked and bloody. She could feel that speck of wet, warm brain matter now as if it were still there, quickly cooling again and again.

Cahill crossed one jeaned leg over the other. Producing a three-inch folding knife from his shirt pocket, he chipped off dirt that clung to his Durango boot. He held the blade up to his nose and whiffed it curiously like it was the unfamiliar odor of honest labor. "You can stay at our house, if you want," he said. "Until you find some place permanent."

Maesie wanted to say hired thugs aren't supposed to offer the evictee a place to stay. She knew Cahill made the offer only because he expected her to decline it. Cahill lived with his mother on the other side of Smackdab. Becky Renfrew did not like Maesie for reasons never clear to her.

"I'm sure your mom would love to have me over, but I'll take a pass," Maesie said.

"You've got to go someplace, because you can't stay here," Cahill said, like a bartender announcing last call.

Maesie could not imagine stepping outside her yard again. She needed to think of a good excuse to remain.

"Who's standing in line to rent this worm-eaten lump of lumber?" she asked. "Sharon ought to let me stay to guard her property. I could keep vandals from messing up the house." As if it weren't already in such a condition.

"No need. This eyesore will be gone in no time anyway," Cahill said. "She's gonna have it dozed. She thinks she can sell the whole twenty better if the house ain't on it."

Maesie pictured a scene from *The Grapes of Wrath*, a bulldozer brought in to mash her history into splinters. And for what? The rocky ground had never produced much besides weeds. Maesie knew the real reason Sharon Sandstrum wanted to take the house down.

"Roger's not even in the ground yet," she said, "which means Sharon must be hurrying to hide the family jewels."

Cahill nodded. "Once the six are buried, you can bet all the survivors will be hunting up a lawyer. They'll go after Roger's money for failure to provide a safe place to work. Mom's already talking about it, even though her and Denver weren't legal."

"Seems like you're being a little shortsighted, chasing a quick buck when it goes against your mom's long-term interests."

Cahill grinned and shrugged, as though that sufficed to explain his thinking.

Maesie lay back and looked at the sky. Though clear of all but a few light clouds, she felt the firmament could fall and crush her at any moment. She believed no one cared what happened to her. No one would lose a second of sleep if she had to set up house in a road-side ditch somewhere.

Maesie reached to pat Cahill's boot. "Just let me stay here and don't tell Sharon." She tried to give her voice a sweet lilt, but it squeaked like a hinge in need of WD-40.

Maesie thought she could see compassion in Cahill's eyes, but his hands were clinched in resistance. "I don't get paid until you're gone," he said. "And I need that money."

"I have a paycheck coming from the machine shop," Maesie said. "I could lend you some."

Cahill shook his head. "Sharon said you might bring that up. She says it's been garnished, or whatever the hell it's called."

Neither spoke for a moment. A cicada revved near one of the cedars on the east side of the yard.

"What about Rolf?" Cahill said. "Him and Skunk will be back soon, sure as shit. Rolf could find you a new place."

Maesie shook her head. "The last two times my daddy came back, he asked me for money."

Cahill finger-flicked a fat grasshopper that had landed on his knee. He stood to leave. "I ain't got time for your problems," he said. "I got my own pressing in on me. So start packing. I'll be back later to check on your progress."

As he opened the back screen door, he said: "This ain't a bluff, Maesie. Don't make things hard on yourself."

Maesie knew he was serious, but she wasn't leaving.

2

Skunk hated coming off the road, and Mom and I hated having him back home. The house felt so small and stifling with him in it. You could see the disappointment on his face each time he walked through the door again and laid eyes on me. I don't know what he expected, but something far different than what I was. I thought I turned out all right, so I tried not to let it bother me.

Skunk never hit me, and that wasn't just because I outweighed him by fifty pounds by the time I was fourteen. I'm wondering now if it was because he knew I wouldn't hit back. The disappointment would have been more than he could stand. He wouldn't hit Mom either. She would have given him as good as he gave. She was the only person who scared him.

I don't know why he bothered to come back to Smackdab at all, except he liked to see the fear he put in people. This time, he'll think he has no choice but to return to town. He'll be drawn back like a hyena catching a whiff of a fresh kill. It will be bad for the Klimps and for Maesie, and Mom won't be much help. She's too broken down to stand up to him right now.

Eight hundred and sixty-five miles from Smackdab, Skunk Olstad had turned peevish. Three days with no sleep did that to him. A similar bout of insomnia occurred in Southern Utah a few months earlier. The name of the dung heap of a town along U.S. 191 escaped him, but he remembered the woman's name: Sheila, or maybe Sheena. She claimed she was half Navajo, but her skin was lighter than Skunk's.

Sheena was something else. She wouldn't stop talking. In the sack, toilet, everywhere. Skunk didn't mind a little sex talk, but Sheena clattered on like an old chainsaw, most of the time complaining about the bastard she married.

"Search that Wikipedia thing for 'worthless son of a bitch' and swear to God you'll see Hernan's picture," Sheena said.

Skunk responded with a grunt, not to agree that Hernan's mother was a bitch, for how would Skunk know? But to indicate Skunk had heard Sheena and that she did not need to elaborate further. Skunk did not want to encourage the woman's yammering.

"He's a helluva cook, though, ain't he?" she had said, meaning Hernan.

Yes, he was, Skunk thought. Sheena had stolen Hernan's meth product and was steadily working her way through it when she showed up at the tavern where Skunk and Rolf Mattsen bellowed *Are You Sure Hank Done It This Way* and similar songs their crowds always wanted to hear. Sheena wasn't much to look at. Nine-year-old boys had more curves than she did, and her acne scars produced pinprick shadows across her face in the dim bar light. But she had the crank going for her, which she offered Skunk a taste of during a set break.

"I guess you'll be wanting something for it," Skunk had said, halfway hoping the price was above his pay grade.

"I'd sure like to get the smell of my old man off me," Sheena said. "I was thinking a good soul cleansing fuck ought to cover it, and I kind of like the dirty cowboy type. All in all, a win-win for both of us."

Skunk wasn't so sure.

"The cans in this joint ain't exactly sanitary," he said.

"Neither is my room back at the motel," she said. "But that's the place I had in mind. I don't like parking my ass on the floor of a public toilet any more than the next gal."

Skunk had that effect on ugly women, where they would offer a screw before offering their name. He hadn't had much sex drive since prostate surgery two years earlier, but the crystal was too tempting. Meth was not Skunk's primary inebriate of choice, but he wasn't picky when a hump was the one thing required of him to get it. Free was extra good considering the state of Skunk and Rolf's financial situation, which was so bleak that "situation" was almost too big a word for it.

After the guitar duo warbled their way through *Mamas Don't Let Your Babies Grow up to Be Cowboys*, which was always their closing song, Skunk rode with Sheena back to the motor lodge. She had paid for a week, and she had stored enough Stoli and bags of nacho cheese Doritos to eliminate any compelling reason to leave the room the remainder of her stay. Skunk had planned only a quick hump and dump. Instead, Rolf would have to go solo through his repertoire of Hank Williams and Ferlin Husky tunes the next two nights while Skunk's attention was drawn elsewhere.

Despite dedicated efforts, a large portion of Hernan's product remained after forty-eight hours of partying. Sheena hit it harder than Skunk. On the third day, she did not rise. Kind of like the anti-Jesus. Skunk unknowingly had spent the night sipping vodka and watching *Law & Order* re-runs with a corpse. He took heart he wasn't much of a spooner.

After wiping the room clean, he collected all but a small portion of the remaining meth, plus all the cash he found in Sheena's purse. He hurried four doors down to Rolf's room to roust him. The time had come to depart. Skunk figured if blame fell on anyone for Sheena's death, it would land on Hernan, particularly when the cops found the small sample of potent meth Skunk left behind. If the authorities wanted to talk to Skunk, they would have a hard time finding him. He and Rolf were paid in cash and spent it in the same form. After driving to Colorado, they sold Skunk's old Nissan pickup with three hundred thousand on the odometer to a wannabe silver miner. Selling price: two hundred dollars' cash and four buy-one-get-one-free Dairy Queen Blizzard coupons.

Now, Skunk and Rolf were in Aspen. The state of Colorado had been good to them in the past. A couple of two-bit crooners like them fit the ambience rich tourists expected when they went tavern slumming. But the economy was in a down cycle that summer, and there wasn't much work to be had. They hadn't played a gig in more than a week, and they had taken to busking five minutes here and there in between roustings by the cops.

Looking back on it now, Utah was where Rolf began to steadily deteriorate. Loopy seemed like a good word for it, like Rolf experienced a perpetual four-beer buzz. Skunk had an uncle who suffered dementia and lived in a nursing home where someone who didn't get paid nearly enough wiped the old man's ass twice a day. But the uncle was in his nineties when he died; Rolf was fifty-four, two years younger than Skunk. Rolf hadn't gotten so bad he needed his butt wiped, yet. But Skunk made sure to remind him to use the can to avoid an accident. If he'd had the money, Skunk would have put his partner on a bus back to Smackdab weeks ago.

Skunk was wide-awake at five a.m. in the rustic ski hostel, the cheapest lodgings they could find. Occasionally, he could fall asleep for a few minutes just before dawn, but it wasn't going to happen this time. He had been hitting the rum and Cokes pretty hard in a wasted effort to inebriate himself to sleep. He would give just about anything for a few minutes of slumber.

Skunk turned on the television, which was set to cable news. He was about to turn to something else when the talking head said something about Smackdab. A high school picture of a chubby Tommy Klimp popped on the screen. It looked like it had been scanned from a high school yearbook. That photo was followed quickly by one of Luke. The photo was a duplicate of the one Skunk carried in his wallet.

Skunk turned off the set and lit a cigarette. So Luke was dead. He and the boy hadn't had much to do with each other for years, but Skunk imagined what he felt was love for his son. Skunk wondered how Diane was holding up. She would be planted on that stool of hers at Snoots, knocking back vodka sours as quickly as Billie could mix them. Even with their only child killed, that part wouldn't change.

Skunk had reached the point in life where the quality of his morning dump dictated more than anything the type of day he hoped to have. He would like to keep things that simple. He would like to stay out of the mess in Smackdab, stay right where he was and try to get some rest. But he knew what would be expected of him. The whole town would be waiting, looking for him to return home like an Old Testament angel with a serious bone to pick. That's what Skunk Olstad was good for, everyone thought. He settled scores.

Rolf Mattsen slept on the top bunk, fully clothed and snoring loudly as usual. Skunk envied the man's simple-mindedness. And his sleep.

Skunk slapped the snoozing man on the legs.

"Get up," Skunk said. "We're going home."

3

I didn't know Coach too well. He didn't teach or coach in Smackdab when I was in high school. The Olstads do not set foot inside sacred spaces as a general rule, so I never heard him preach when he came back to town and took over the church pulpit. But I can see from here the bloodbath that got us killed has not made life easy for Coach. He can't come to terms with why God allowed us to get cut to pieces just as we sat down to our ham sandwiches and Funyuns. As if it were possible to justify. Much of the town—those that believe in that stuff—need Coach to explain the greater purpose of the event. They yearn for anyone to give them something they can buy into that will allow them to sleep through the night again. They want a reason beyond how God works in mysterious ways. They don't want to hear how they should simply accept God's will without question. The preacher does not believe everything happens for a reason. He does not believe God had a Grand Plan that required six of us to be eviscerated by semi-automatic weapons. But Coach doesn't know what to believe anymore.

Let me tell you, Coach. You've got to lead the memorial service for us tomorrow, because who else is going to do it? Nobody in town expected much ministering from you before this, just someone to call on the sick and pray over the dying. But Tommy changed the landscape, and now you've got to do your job. Nut up and avoid saying anything that would screw even more with the fractured psyche of the town. If you're successful, you can fade into retirement, this time for good. Live the rest of your life in comfortable tedium, your mind free of the theological questions gnawing at you. But first, just get everyone through the next thirty-six hours.

Lemuel Hunney, known to everyone as Coach, came down the back stairs by the tavern's service counter. The usual smells greeted him: cooking oil competing with decades of stale beer and vomit soaked into the joint's creaky pine floorboards. He took his late breakfast at the bar, as he had for six years since returning to Smackdab after failing at the college coaching level. Two eggs and white toast, because Billie Quirk didn't stock anything exotic like rye or wheat. Her clientele didn't frequent Snoots for the food.

A huge red- and gold-bordered Miller High Life sign centered over the bar bathed the area in a red glow like a foundry smelter. Otherwise, Billie kept the tavern so dark her patrons located their drinks by touch.

Coach nodded to Jordy Wakefield, the only other person in the bar besides Billie. He sat at a yellowed Formica table against the far wall. Coach lived above the tavern, but Wakefield practically lived *in* it. By all appearances, his fulltime job was avoiding physical labor beyond the repetition of lifting a pilsner glass to his whiskered face. Anytime a person suggested Wakefield lend a hand with any task requiring him to get off his butt, he would wince and begin rubbing his back, saying: "Sorry, but my sciatica's really barking at me today."

Wakefield's wife, Brenda Sue, who had married down when she chose Jordy as her life mate, worked days at the local GasGo convenience store. The three Wakefield rug rats, all under nine or ten, were left in Jordy's charge during the day, which meant leaving them to their own devices at home. As long as their tetanus shots were up to date, Jordy didn't worry much about his offspring.

Billie already had the eggs on the griddle.

"Sleep tight?" the tavern's owner asked her upstairs tenant.

"Like King Tut," Coach said, perching himself on a stool at the bar. As Billie turned away from him to salt the nearly cooked eggs, Coach observed her ass. She still wore Levi's pretty well for a woman her age.

Get your mind out of the gutter, old fart, Coach thought. A minister shouldn't think about his landlady that way. It embarrassed him. He absently felt the top of his head. He always went to bed with a wet shock of hair because he preferred night showers. The tradeoff was getting up the next day looking like a biker gang had partied on his scalp. It didn't matter much. His hair, the color of a pile of dirty nickels, had been more or less untamable since he hit sixty. He had never cared before, but he now wondered how Billie saw him.

Billie owned the only drinking establishment in Smackdab, and she put little of her profit into upkeep. Two four-pane windows fronted the tavern on either side of the entrance. Billie had masked the glass with black latex paint so the inside of the bar always looked like nighttime even on the brightest days. The primary source of light and decoration, besides the Miller light, was a string of white Christmas lights that circumnavigated the interior walls.

In the back of the bar behind six four-top tables, a much-used Brunswick pool table took up space near a jukebox. The green felt on the table had worn down to the slate in the two places where open break shots were taken.

A few years younger than Coach, Billie was as much a spouse as he would have again. She fed him breakfast, conversed a little, but not too much, and otherwise left him alone. If she judged him, she did not make it obvious. The opposite of his ex-wife. However, Coach had never thought of her *that way* until now.

She filled Coach's coffee mug. "Ready for tomorrow?" she asked.

"Getting there," he said, though any eulogy he had tried to put to paper thus far had read like a pack of lies. He needed to find a tack that wasn't as wishy-washy as "God is hurting right along with us."

When the entrance door behind him squeaked open, Coach saw a large silhouette back-lighted in the doorway. Though the arrival's face was in shadows, Coach could identify him easily by his physique. Harp Denbo was built like a fifty-five-gallon drum with spaghetti straws for legs. He had no butt to speak of. It was like whatever he ate and drank couldn't squeeze past his belt into his lower extremities. Coach had never before seen Denbo in the tavern, because Denbo did not associate with the locals.

The large man nodded to Coach as he approached the bar. He took a thick wad of clipped paper money from his front jeans pocket and pulled a five off the top. To Billie: "How much for a mug of hot water?" He pronounced it *wudder*.

"Not a thing," Billie said, just as perplexed as Coach at the man's presence.

"Thank you," Denbo said, returning the wad to his pocket. He nodded toward Wakefield. "I'll be sitting at that table when it's ready."

"I'll get it for you just as soon as I serve this man his breakfast," she said, nodding at Coach.

Coach waved her off. "No rush," he said. "Get the man's water."

Despite his barrel shape, Denbo could afford to dress in a way that deemphasized certain physical characteristics. He was the only man in the area who wore professionally pressed shirts every day. The shirts were tailored to Denbo's torso so that they did not hang off his shoulders like ponchos. He belted his jeans up around his belly button so his paunch did not lap over his belt. The dry cleaner put sharp creases in every pair of jeans. On cool days, Denbo wore a butterscotch calfskin jacket that cost more than most people in Smackdab made in a month. This summer morning, however, he was in shirtsleeves; his pale yellow oxford looked as though it had been taken off its hanger moments earlier. None of that, however, could cover up the man's inherent roughness. Replace the clothes with something soiled and one could imagine Denbo coming off an overnight shift unloading ship containers from Shanghai.

Like Coach, Denbo was not a Smackdab native. A year earlier, Denbo and his wife had moved to the area from Pennsylvania or someplace in that part of the country. They had bought a farm five miles northeast of town. The Denbos had the farm's colonial-style house renovated before they arrived, and they rented out every square foot of the cropland and pasture. Mrs. Denbo never came to town; she went to West Fork or farther when she wanted or needed anything.

No one in Smackdab knew much else about the Denbos, so gaps were filled in without regard to facts. Some speculated Denbo was a former mafia assassin now in witness protection, but Coach doubted the federal government had the budget to buy a three-hundred-acre farm for a witness. A more plausible theory was Denbo had made a fortune in business and sold out while he was still young enough to enjoy life. And where better to enjoy it than the Midwest among good God-fearing people? A more prosaic guess was Denbo's wife had inherited a gob of money. Whatever the reason, Denbo would only smile if anyone asked about his past.

After Billie delivered Denbo his mug of hot water, he removed a tea bag from his shirt pocket and plopped it in. Coach could not make sense of why Denbo would come to Snoots now. And to have what looked like a serious conversation with Wakefield? They made an unlikely pair. Coach doubted Wakefield had ever been farther than West Fork, and his fashion style could be described as Carhartt clearance rack. What little Coach knew about Denbo did not gel with his coming to Snoots to talk to Wakefield. Denbo seemed—Coach hated to use the word—*moral*. Too moral if there was such a thing. It was like he didn't want to be soiled on the outside or inside by Smackdab.

Billie set a plate of eggs and toast in front of Coach. She reached under the bar for a bottle of hot sauce, which had never been refrigerated. If Smackdab had a health department, a room temperature bottle of Texas Pete would be a minor infraction compared to many other issues in Snoots. A person had to have serious gastrointestinal issues to sit on the men's toilet.

Coach nodded toward the men at the far table. "What do you make of that?"

Billie leaned close enough that Coach could smell the shampoo in her hair.

Vanilla bean.

"They stopped talking when I brought his highness his water, but I heard them mention Roger Sandstrum. And I swear Skunk Olstad's name came up, too."

Coach began to eat his eggs. Denbo said something inaudible. Coach took another bite when he sensed Denbo and Wakefield had quit talking and were looking at him. Coach put down his fork and returned their gazes with a questioning one of his own.

"I said I'd like to talk something over with you," Denbo said. Though he sat fifteen feet from Coach, his voice was no louder than when he spoke to Wakefield. Denbo's voice and face were pleasant enough, but he repeatedly clinched and unclenched his beefy right fist like he held an invisible exercise grip.

Coach shrugged. "I'm listening," he said, taking a bite of toast.

"What do you think happens now?"

Coach assumed Denbo was talking about the aftermath of the slaughter, but what did he expect Coach to say? The government now would come and take their guns? That there was now a shortage of good welders in town? That someone would burn down the Klimp's house? What?

"Healing happens now," Coach said with a wad of bread in his mouth. It was a mealy response, he knew, but he could not conjure up anything better at the moment.

Denbo scoffed. "You don't really believe that, do you? That Smackdab will just bounce back and before long no one will remember the events of last week? You wouldn't be that naïve." He pronounced it *wudden*.

"All right," Coach said, swiveling his stool to face Denbo. "What happens now?"

Denbo smiled, revealing browned teeth.

"That's up to us, isn't it?" Denbo said.

Us who? Coach wondered.

Denbo balanced his teacup on his skinny knee. He said: "Down in the southern part of my home state, part of Appalachia, there's a small town with hard-working people like you have here. Coal miners mostly. But there is always a bug in every salad. And there was this one guy who was nothing more than a bully. He'd harass and steal from his neighbors any time the mood struck.

"He was too slick and smart for the sheriff to ever pin anything on him. And then the bully threatened his neighbors with a shotgun if they didn't quit calling the law on him. Everyone took him seriously because they assumed he was half-crazy. The man knew he had free reign, so he robbed, bullied, kicked tail, and did as he pleased. He even shot a guy in the back with buckshot. The guy lived, but he never told the authorities who shot him. The townspeople eventually could endure no more and took matters into their own hands. A dozen or so of his neighbors went to his place one night—some of them still hadn't cleaned the coal dust from their faces—and set fire to his house. The man was found the next morning blackened like Cajun chicken. Everyone who was at that house covered for everyone else, and no one was ever arrested. The sheriff did not try too hard to solve the case either.

"Anyway, the town acquired a reputation as being... weird, for lack of a better word. A place where people closed ranks, killed one of their own, and then kept their mouths shut about it."

"I can't quite make the connection with our situation," Coach said. "There's been no vigilantism here."

"Bear with me," Denbo said. "That coal mining town seemed to recover, but not really. You'd think, with the law of averages, a small town like that would never experience anything else that notorious. But no more than a year later, a coal miner garroted his wife and three kids. When the law showed up, the man was sitting on the linoleum floor of his kitchen in a pool of his family's blood, singing *Here We Go Round the Mulberry Bush*. Just the title over and over. Some believed he was one of the fire starters."

Coach began to speak, but Denbo held up his hand to stop him. "There were other minor happenings here and there. Then, fast forward another year or two. Some two-bit traveling evangelist-slash-con man came to town promising to rid the place of all the evil that plagued it. He arrived with a lot of fanfare, set up his revival tent on the edge of town and had a big prayer meeting the first night. A lot of townspeople showed up. Some took the man seriously, but most came just because they were curious. The evangelist said he could tell as soon as he crossed the city limits that the community was overrun with demons. He started pointing his finger at people in the crowd and saying he could see the devil in their eyes. Those poor folks—the ones that took it seriously—started to get all worked up and scared. Others just got angry. The preacher paid no attention, going on with his shtick. He read some scripture, hopped around a little, prayed a lot and so on. He collected a few coins for his act and said he'd be back the next evening for another show—though he didn't call it that—because he said the town was in even worse shape than he thought. The next night, though, the preacher was nowhere to be seen. No one in town showed up for the revival either. It was like everyone *knew* he wasn't going to be there. He had just disappeared. The tent was still there, and so was his old minivan. But no preacher. After a couple of weeks, someone finally took the tent down and hauled it to the dump. I don't know what happened to the van, but I do know the evangelist hasn't been seen since. It's like he got swallowed up by a hole." Denbo paused and smiled. "More likely an old mine shaft."

He put his mug back on the table and leaned back as if he were finished. Coach wondered if Denbo had read the story somewhere, or if his information came firsthand.

"Interesting story," Coach said, "but still..."

Denbo cut him off. "Let me get at this another way. Say you have a tiny pain in your upper abdomen. It seems like nothing serious until one day you notice your skin is starting to yellow. Maybe you just need to get out in the sun more. But what if it's something worse? What if it's cancer eating into your pancreas? Maybe you should take those symptoms more seriously, but you won't know for sure until you go to your doctor six months from now. And by then it will be too late."

Coach couldn't help but rest a hand on his stomach. "First a story about a bad-luck mining town and now we're talking cancer?" he asked.

"Smackdab has cancer," Denbo said. "Its ailments seemed minor until last week. Now we can see clearly the town is diseased. I'm telling you as straight as I can, those killings will lead to more tragedy if we don't wake up. What we have to do now is cut out the evil."

"Evil? We?"

"Anyone who cares about the community's future," Denbo said. "You, as the only minister in Smackdab, should be at the forefront of efforts to root out evil and all that goes with it. That includes complacency, sloth…"

Coach glanced at Wakefield, the laziest man in Smackdab, who seemed oblivious to any irony. More important, though, Coach did not believe a cancer bedeviled Smackdab, even if he had any desire to root it out.

Before Coach could think of how best to argue that, Diane Olstad pushed through the front door, pausing as her eyes adjusted from the harsh morning light to the interior dimness. Billie began to mix Diane's first vodka sour of the day. Coach saw it as a good time to turn away from Denbo and finish his breakfast.

Diane sat two stools down from Coach without acknowledging him. She looked like she hadn't slept for days. She wore the same navy blue pantsuit she had on four days earlier, the night of the shootings, when Coach had gone to her house to console her. The outfit hung like a gown on her spindly frame.

Diane worked for an insurance agent in West Fork, but she had not returned there since her son and the five other men were murdered. Despite her alcoholism, she was a good worker, from what Coach knew. Her boss told her to take as much time as she needed.

Waiting to see if she would acknowledge him, Coach studied Diane's deterioration. Not just what had occurred in the past several days, but since he had known her. Her caramel-colored hair, dyed so many times it had lost all natural body, hung from her scalp like clumps of uncooked spaghetti sticking out of a pot. Her face bore the wrinkled markings of a lifetime of smoking. The tip of her aquiline nose was permanently red.

Diane had been something approaching beautiful in the not too distant past. But years of marriage to Skunk, plus an ocean's worth of chemical abuse, had wrested nearly all remnants of beauty from her severe face.

Conversations about Diane Olstad's decline often included a single hopeful statement:

The boy seems to have turned out all right.

The boy who was casketed five blocks away at the funeral home.

"How you holding up?" Coach asked.

"Passable," Diane said without looking up from the iced drink Billie brought her. She was seldom sociable when she visited the bar. Coach wondered why she bothered to come. She could buy a bottle of vodka and stay at home if she didn't like company. It would be cheaper. But Diane showed up at Snoots nearly every evening, ready to medicate herself at two-fifty a pop. Since the massacre, she had begun coming in earlier and staying longer.

If she started early the next day, Coach guessed Diane would be nearly comatose by the time of the community service.

"Could I offer you a ride to the service tomorrow?" Coach asked.

"You can offer if it moves you, but I don't plan to go," Diane said, already taking her third gulp.

"You have to," Coach said. "There'll be a chair in the front row for you right along with the other families."

"Someone else can have my seat," Diane said, taking the final half of the liquid and swishing it around her mouth. "Maybe I'll sell it to the highest bidder. Plenty of people would love to have a front row seat for that show, huh?"

She signaled for another round.

"I wouldn't call it a show," Coach said. "It's a chance for the community to mourn together."

"I'll do my mourning right here on this stool," Diane said.

Out of the corner of his eye, Coach had noticed Denbo resituate himself in his chair so he could look directly at Diane. Wakefield mimicked his move.

"I'd like to have a word with you." Denbo said. He looked at his hands as he spoke, inspecting his fingernails. Coach knew he was talking to Diane. She knew it, too.

"Free country," she said, taking a drink.

Denbo reached behind him and took a chair from table next to his. He set it between him and Wakefield. "Over here," he said.

Diane did not move.

Coach did not look at Denbo, but he could guess the large man was seething. Coach assumed he was not used to having his requests rejected. After a moment, Denbo stood and approached Diane. He leaned against the bar on the other side of her. He brought his tea with him and set it on the bar.

"Has your ex-husband returned to town yet?" Denbo asked.

"I guess you don't understand the meaning of 'ex,'" Diane said, focusing on her drink. "I don't keep tabs on his whereabouts."

"There is a rumor that the famous Mr. Olstad has fallen on hard times." Denbo smiled, revealing a lateral incisor out of alignment with its neighbors. At that moment Coach would give a Ben Franklin for a pair of Vise-Grips to latch onto the tooth and yank hard.

Without looking up from her drink, Diane took her phone from her purse and held it up as if to offer it to Denbo. "Here. Call someone who gives a royal shit," she said.

Ignoring the phone, Denbo went on. "From what I understand, your husband and Rolf Mattsen are just the same as homeless. They have to beg for money just to get something to eat."

The source of the rumor, Wakefield, cackled as he watched from his table.

Denbo continued: "Smackdab is as down as it's ever going to be. From now on, things will get better. I promise you that. But we cannot keep allowing it to be influenced by a bad element. We need to cleanse the community of its lesser kind. Forgive me for saying so, but that would include your husband and his cohort. If your spouse needs to return to pay his respects, I understand that. But he should not plan to stay."

Diane took a white napkin square from a stack on the bar and wiped a moisture ring left by her glass. "We live in a free country," she said. "For all I care, Skunk can hold a parade in memory of Luke, if he makes up his mind to."

"Just bear in mind my words," Denbo said. He punctuated his warning with another smile. Coach couldn't look at anything but the crooked incisor. He once owned a dog with tooth like that. It had been an ugly mutt, but loveable. Denbo was something different.

Diane said nothing more. She took a final gulp of her drink, put six wadded dollar bills on the bar and exited. It was her shortest stay at Snoots in years.

4

"Windmill" Bob Klimp wanted only to be known as a decent man. "There goes a good fella," he wanted people to say. Everything he did—hard work, loyalty to family, paying bills on time—was born out of that wish. Such a simple ideal, he thought, but it was no longer within reach. It had been gutted the second his son fired the first shot.

Guess it wasn't meant to be, he thought.

Such was the extent of reflection Bob wanted to give the subject. Bob did not like to overanalyze. What was, was. Such as how he got his nickname. It was not because he looked like a windmill. There was some resemblance, though. He stood medium tall, narrow-shouldered and perceptibly bowlegged as though he'd had a fondness for horse riding as a child. If he strode in a hurry, his arms flung back and forth like a speed walker.

Instead, Windmill Bob earned his nickname when he put up two wind turbines on the low ridge south of his house. They were his babies, each with a rotor diameter of six feet mounted on a forty-foot tower. The turbines powered half the appliances in the Klimp household, and, until the executions, Bob had plans to erect two more as soon he could afford it. If people wanted to call him Windmill Bob for that reason, it was fine by him. They could call him whatever they wanted, as long as they applauded him for harnessing some of the wind that picked up over the prairie and whipped around Smackdab like a squall most of the year.

Bob sat on the ridge now, between his babies, and listened to the slow whir of the motors in the nearly still breeze of August. Five minutes to noon, and Patsy would be preparing his sandwich down at the house, which he had built by himself. The house that had taken him three years to construct piece by piece while the family lived in the old one that used to front the new one before he tore it down. His hands and arms were flecked with a thousand tiny scars from lumber and nails, just so he could imagine people saying: *That Klimp fella's building that whole damn thing by himself. By God, there's a helluva man.*

That was back when Bob still had a sliver of dignity. Life had to go on, though. That's why Patsy was making his sandwich for lunch, even now, as she did every weekday before the bloodbath. That's why Bob would sit at the kitchen table and eat it, just like he did every day. Like Thursday of last week, at the same moment their son was rampaging through the machine shop. That day, his birthday, the aroma of vinegar and fresh-cut cucumbers had welcomed him into the kitchen. Patsy was pickling again.

Bob did not greet his wife, who stood at the counter with her back to him. She returned the favor. They had been married that long. Bob eased himself gently into a chair at the kitchen table, anticipating the cracking of his painful joints.

"I can stick a few cucumber slices on your plate, if you want," Patsy Klimp said, still not turning from her work. Her husband came home for lunch every day. She served him, she said, because she enjoyed it.

As he waited for her, Bob admired his wife's tanned legs. She had defined calf muscles the size of baseballs, like those on an athlete. He had not seen her run in years, though, except the time she scared up a rat snake in the garden.

"Stick them all you want," he said, just realizing what Patsy had said. "But I won't stick them in my mouth."

"Oh now," Patsy said, continuing to slice. "It wouldn't kill you to have a fresh vegetable once in a while."

"It might," Bob said. "Then you'd be sorry."

The summer garden was Patsy's idea. He never made peace with cucumbers, green beans, or, for that matter, anything green, particularly steamed broccoli. That stuff had the aroma of rotted road kill. For Bob, the only edible green was mint ice cream.

Instead of a perfunctory sandwich, Patsy set before him a store-bought honey bun. A yellow unlighted birthday candle stuck in the middle of it. Bob guessed the pastry was past its expiration date, one Patsy had gotten half off at the GasGo where she worked nights.

"Sorry for this poor excuse for a birthday cake," she said. "I'll make a real one Saturday."

"That's all right," Bob said. "It's the thought that counts."

Bob did not like a fuss on his birthday. He did not like the attention he got just for being born. All he wanted was a day absent of drama. His job as head custodian at the high school, which required copious bending and kneeling, was doing a serious number on his back, knees, and most every other part of his body. When he came home, all he wanted was to sit a few minutes.

"You want the candle lit?" Patsy asked.

Bob wondered what good a birthday candle was unless a man got to blow it out.

"Guess not," he said.

"I'll sing *Happy Birthday* if you want," Patsy said, patting her husband's shoulder.

"Rest your vocal chords," Bob said.

He put his hand on the waistband of his wife's khaki shorts, letting the hand drop lightly onto her butt. She smelled like dryer sheets.

Laundry day.

Knowing some activities were worth enduring arthritis, Bob said: "Instead, how about we go into the bedroom and get naked so you can give me my special present?"

Still embarrassed by such talk after nearly three decades of marriage, Patsy stepped out of her husband's reach. "You know I don't like doing anything when Tommy's in his room. But if you play your cards right, I might let you unwrap something special this weekend."

When isn't that boy in his room?

"Can you let me know what the right cards are?" Bob asked. "If I knew, I'd play more often."

"I don't think you've got that many hands in you, you geezer."

"Tough talk coming from a woman four months older than me."

Patsy clanked down a porcelain plate with a white-bread sandwich and baby carrots next to the untouched honey bun.

Bob lifted the bread to reveal a slice of American cheese over baloney.

"No turkey?"

"Not until I get to the store," Patsy said. "That's Tommy's lunchmeat, but I'm hoping he doesn't count the slices."

"Hell, we bought the damn baloney anyway," Bob said.

Patsy studied her husband, hands on her hips. "Are you pouting?" she asked.

He was. It was bad enough turning a year older without having to suffer a baloney sandwich, too.

"No," he said. He took a mirthless bite of the sandwich.

Since his promotion at the high school, Bob came home every weekday for lunch at one o'clock. He had simple culinary tastes, and he ate the same thing every day: a turkey sandwich with American cheese. On Friday, to cap off the workweek, he celebrated with an egg salad sandwich prepared from an egg Patsy boiled that morning. Every day was predictable, just the way Bob liked it.

Patsy's nightly shift at the GasGo began at four. The thirty-minute lunch was the sole time during the week they saw each other awake. Any important conversations had to be squeezed in during lunch or wait till the weekend. Those conversations were usually about their son.

"Have you seen him yet?" Bob asked.

Patsy dried her hands on a kitchen towel and sat beside her husband. "Not a peep."

"He ought to be up by now," he said, focusing on his sandwich rather than his wife. "He needs to keep regular hours like the rest of us."

"Help yourself, if you want to try to get him up," Patsy said.

"I'm not putting this on you," Bob said. "I just wish he'd show more initiative."

It was a familiar refrain. Something about Tommy had never been right. Bob knew it like he knew the backyard walnut tree would soon drop its fruit and gum up the lawnmower. Some things you could set a Timex by. Patsy didn't see Tommy the same way Bob did. Lots of boys were reclusive, she said. The issue festered between the couple like a canker.

Hell, Tommy was no longer a boy, Bob thought. He was twenty-one. Normal adults didn't stay in their rooms all day. Normal folks got out and made something of themselves. Went to school. Got jobs. Met people. Formed relationships. Tried to better themselves. Not Tommy. Patsy had been too easy on him.

Tommy made an occasional appearance outside his room, but seldom for any positive reason. Recently, he had been drawn out to offer an opinion on the brand of underwear Patsy had bought him. Tommy tore open the package of offending briefs and stuffed them down the garbage disposal. It took Bob two hours to unclog it. Patsy then bought three different brands of underwear and asked Tommy to choose one. Later, she laughed off the incident.

"I didn't realize tag-less underwear was such a big deal," she said. "And all this time I've been using the tags to tell me where my butt should go."

Another time, the scent of laundry detergent, the same brand Patsy had used many times before, enraged Tommy. He refused to wear any clothes, locking himself in his room, naked, until Patsy bought new detergent and re-washed everything. She did so with no complaint.

A few months ago, when the credit card bill arrived, Bob ran out of patience. Tommy had ordered hundreds of dollars in of junk online, including a Made-in-China samurai sword replica and a long sleeve athletic shirt the color of a clear autumn sky. That was a good one, Bob thought at the time. Tommy hadn't done anything athletic since middle school.

His parents had never given Tommy the credit card number, but he had plenty of opportunities to locate it. He was at home alone often enough.

One day when the credit card statement arrived, Bob banged on his son's door with his fist. "Get out here right now and explain this," Bob said, as if Tommy could see the statement through the door. Bob assailed the door again, waiting for a response he wouldn't receive. He had lost any authority over his son. Bob had nothing to threaten Tommy with, short of kicking him out of the house. He had fantasized plenty about that, but Patsy wouldn't let him. As he banged on the door, she stood behind him, looking worried the door would break loose from its hinges.

"All right then," Bob said to the door. "If that's the way you want to play it, we're cancelling the credit cards. And we'll start keeping our money where you can't find it."

Bob looked behind him at Patsy, because his speech was as much for her as Tommy. "None of that junk food you like. Nothing until you get off your ass and start doing something with your life. Start looking for work. Anything, even if it's part time. Get out of your room and make an effort. I don't care how small it is. Just show me you're trying to do something. If you do, we'll see about revising the punishment."

Bob never knew if it was his ultimatum or something else. A week later, however, Tommy had the first date of his life. The woman was Maesie Mattsen, the dwarf. Bob thought Tommy could have done better than Rolf Mattsen's child, but that was all right. It was a good first step. Social interaction of any kind was encouraging.

At first, Patsy and Bob assumed the date had gone well. Tommy started to show a little more interest in his appearance, combing his hair and using deodorant. He left the house more often during the day. But each time he returned home, he had nothing to say. He hurried to his room and slammed the door. Had Maesie rebuffed him? If Tommy couldn't make a go of it with her, Bob wondered, what hope was there?

"I'd like to try again to get him into see a doctor," Bob said, peeling a strip of crust from the bread of his birthday sandwich.

Patsy pursed her lips and leaned back with her arms crossed.

"We're not getting into that again," she said. "I thought we agreed he's acting better lately."

Bob glanced over his shoulder at his wife. "You can't tell me there's nothing off kilter with him," he said. "Whatever happened with the Mattsen girl, I think it's made him worse."

Bob pushed the baby carrots around the plate with his index finger, wondering if he needed to eat all five. On occasion, if Patsy was distracted, he sneaked them into the kitchen wastebasket.

"If she broke his heart, she'll have me to contend with," Patsy said. It didn't sound to Bob like a joke. "And, you know, lots of boys go through an awkward stage," she said.

"He's not a boy anymore, Patsy. It's time you realized that."

Patsy stood from the table and began to slice more cucumbers. "I admit he's a little different, but different is not always bad. Different can actually be beneficial. We don't all have to be like everyone else, do we? You've got your windmills."

"Turbines," Bob corrected her.

"We had him checked out that one time," Patsy said, beginning the same litany of points she drew on every time they talked about Tommy. "The doctor said there was nothing wrong with him."

"That was what? Fifteen years ago? And that was for autism."

"If there was something else wrong with him, the doctor would have caught it," Patsy said.

"Then let's send him to a therapist, if he'll agree to it," Bob said. "They've got one or two in West Fork."

"You think Tommy's crazy?"

"You don't have to be crazy to see a therapist. Lots of regular people do it."

"Such as?"

Bob thought for a moment. He was sure a few people around town sought psychological help. But that was not the kind of thing people flapped their gums about. Not in Smackdab.

"I'm going to roust him," Bob said, standing.

"Don't get all riled up on your birthday," Patsy said, putting her hand gently on his shoulder. "Don't ruin the day."

Bob said nothing and went to Tommy's room to bang on the door. "Tommy?" he said. "Get out here now."

No answer.

"Either open the door, or I'll get my tools and take the door down. And it'll stay down."

Still no answer.

Tommy was otherwise engaged at the machine shop.

5

Maesie felt secure, or as close to it as she had since the murders. Why hadn't she thought of this earlier? Rolf would spit and grumble if he knew where she was, but piss on him, she thought. The ground was still frozen the last time Maesie saw her father. He still carried on as if he needed to be out on the road, as if Skunk and he were still in great demand. The duo had cut a few singles back in the early eighties when radio stations were not yet totally beholden to corporate suits that programmed pabulum. Deejays occasionally played something they chose.

One of Skunk and Rolf's recordings, *Get Outta My Dodge*, had caught the attention of a morning drive-time jock in Colorado Springs. He played it weekday mornings at ten minutes past seven for several weeks. The single's popularity spread to a few other country stations in the Rockies, creating a small buzz for Olstad & Mattsen. There was scuttlebutt, though never confirmed by anyone in Smackdab, that *Get Outta My Dodge* enjoyed an underground following behind the Iron Curtain in the waning days of Ceausescu's Romania.

Olstad & Mattsen spent half of each year or more on the road out west. Neither man was a wonderful singer by himself, but they harmonized in a lonesome, pitiful way that traditional country music fans loved. Still, Skunk and Rolf were no longer overrun with gig offers. Mostly, they whored, fought, and God knows what else for gas and booze money. No one in Smackdab cared as long as they stayed away, given the duo's penchant for causing trouble when they came off the road.

Cahill's Crown Vic rolled to a stop in the driveway. Maesie knew he would soon figure out where she was, but he couldn't do anything about it other than kick and scream a little. He would report back to Sharon Sandstrum, who would call the authorities to finish the job Cahill failed. She wasn't sure what she would do then. Play it by ear, she guessed. At least she had delayed the inevitable.

Maesie listened quietly as Cahill entered the front door without knocking. He clomped through the house, calling her name. The sound of his voice carried between the floorboards. Maesie knew he was looking in her bedroom, where he would see she hadn't begun packing her things. "What the f... You mean to tell me... I can't fu...."

The sound of his steps carried into the kitchen. The back screen door opened and slammed again after a pause. Cahill returned to the front of the house.

"Goddammit, Maesie," he yelled. "You ain't packed shit yet. Where the hell are you?"

He paused at the front door for several seconds before stepping off the porch. He got down on his hands and knees and looked under the porch. "You under there?"

Maesie didn't answer.

"So help me God, woman, don't make me come in there after you."

"Come on then," Maesie said from farther back beneath the house. She knew he wouldn't. She had invited him under the house when they were younger, but Cahill was too afraid of darkness and tight spaces.

"You haven't done shit since I was here last," Cahill said. The disappointment in his voice nearly made Maesie feel bad for him.

"What do you mean? Didn't you see those holes out back?" Maesie asked. "I dug a bunch more after you left. Even dug up half an old planter. If you haul it to the scrap yard in West Fork, I'll split the profits with you."

"That ain't the junk you need to be focused on," Cahill said, sounding like he was close to busting a valve. "You got to get the stuff in your house packed up and ready to get out of here."

"I can't leave. I told you that already."

Cahill lowered himself from his hands to his elbows, but he still couldn't see Maesie in the darkness. "And I told you already you ain't got no choice. There's a Caterpillar coming."

Like anyone would miss her, Maesie thought. She had always felt like a stray dog that sauntered perennially around town, one that could disappear weeks before anyone noticed its absence. She believed her small size was equal to the value most of the town placed on her existence. After what happened, Maesie had expected the town to pay her attention, if only to blame her for what Tommy Klimp did.

In late spring, Maesie had agreed to take in an Adam Sandler movie with Tommy at the West Fork Cinema Four-Plex. Tommy was nobody's idea of a great date, but Maesie hadn't been to a movie theater in forever. Besides, the line of eligible men in Smackdab asking out a dwarf was a short one. She used to hope Luke Olstad would ask her out. Folly for sure, but she had caught him once looking at her in a way other men did not. A girl could hope, right? But nothing happened with Luke, and so there was Tommy.

One date was enough. Tommy paid for the movie and Skittles, but the night was otherwise a bust. The guy still had a thing for Viking culture, just as he had in high school. He talked most of the night—Viking this and Viking that—even through the movie previews. Tommy believed he was descended from Viking royalty, and he spoke occasionally in a language he said was ancient Viking. He also wore a horned helmet, which looked like the real deal.

Tommy convinced himself they were in a relationship after their sole outing. He came by Maesie's house each day for a week, though Maesie never answered the door. When Maesie started her job, he began skulking outside the machine shop, waiting for her to arrive for work each morning and again later when she left.

At first, Tommy seemed meekly nonplussed when Maesie asked him to quit bothering her. His mien turned gloomier, and then more intimidating. The shop employees saw how uneasy Tommy made Maesie feel, and they made a few half-hearted attempts to shoo him away. When that didn't work, Luke Olstad talked to Tommy and suggested he quit coming around the shop because he made Maesie uncomfortable. Tommy did not return for two days, giving Maesie a sliver of hope he had gotten the message. On the third day, he busted through the back door of the building with an arsenal large enough to make the Belize army envious.

Maesie felt a sting on her elbow. Something in the dirt let her know she had invaded its territory. She hoped it wasn't a brown recluse.

"I bet everybody's trying to figure out why Tommy did it," she said, trying to subtly draw information from Cahill.

Cahill had calmed down a little and leaned against the edge of the porch. "What's there to say? There ain't no amount of words to describe that kind of crazy," he said. "I've been hearing a lot about Skunk, though. About how he's gonna come whirling into town like a cyclone and go Old Testament on the Klimps because Luke got killed. Your dad will be right there with him."

Maesie should have guessed. Even with the deaths of seven, counting Tommy, the town was talking about Skunk, a combination of celebrity and thug whose reputation hovered over Smackdab like a malevolent phantasm. Cahill considered Skunk the ideal of what a man should be, and he deluded himself into thinking the town considered him in the same league with Skunk.

Cahill deluded himself if he thought he would ever be regarded the same as Skunk. Cahill was no paragon, nor did his lack of ambition indicate a bright future. But who was Maesie to talk? She knew goodness existed under his faded shirt and combustible temperament. Her fondness for him stretched back to their early days in school. He had never teased her about her size, though he could have been excused for knowing no better.

Cahill tried to deny his inherent goodness, which Maesie suspected was one reason for his temper. But anyone who bothered to notice could see that Cahill cared deeply. He felt protective of anything that he considered his, which included his town. This baffled Maesie. Smackdab had never benefited Cahill any more than it had benefited her.

He was raised—one would be generous to call it that—by a lush of a mother and a creep of a father. Becky and Scooter Renfrew were too busy trying to kill each other every night over a meal of boiled potatoes and PBR to have time to nurture their child. "Nurture" found no more footing in their lexicon than "temperance." The finest contribution the Renfrews made to society was ceasing to procreate following Cahill. The most propitious event in Cahill's life occurred when his dad was chased out of town for using his school janitor's job to spy on the girl's locker room.

Free of his father's physical presence and his mother's emotional one, Cahill practically raised himself. Though he hadn't done a stellar job of it, he did the best he could with the tools and examples available to him. Maesie believed he had been more successful than his parents would have been. Still, Cahill was "that Renfrew" in Smackdab, as though nothing else needed to be said.

When Cahill kept his temper in check, he could be as nice as anyone around. Maesie believed niceness was an underappreciated asset. Someday, given the right influences and a decent bi-polar pharmaceutical, she thought Cahill could become a regular human being.

Cahill did not interest Maesie romantically. She did not need a man to make her feel worthwhile. She had experienced independence long enough to prove she could get along by herself. But the shootings had crystallized a few thoughts, when she wasn't fretting over her own guilt. For example, how pleasant it would be to have someone miss her when she was gone. She could think of no one currently who fit that category, but Cahill held some potential.

Maesie readjusted herself in the loose dirt, which hadn't seen daylight in one hundred years. "Anytime there's a mass shooting in a city, everyone climbs over each other claiming a connection to the victims or the killer," she said. "Like they're really suffering, because they had their nails done by the second cousin of one of the victims. I wish it was like that here, where none of us really knew each other. Where it didn't have to hurt so much and so directly."

Cahill took out his folding knife and jabbed it in a dandelion plant. "Mom ain't stopped bawling," he said.

Denver Moss off and on kept house with Becky Renfrew. Cahill felt bad for his mother, but he wouldn't miss Denver. Cahill, half the size of the older man, had sent him one night to the emergency room in West Fork with a knife slash through his forearm flexor tendon. Cahill never talked about it. According to semi-informed sources, however, the argument started when Denver said he liked Lucky Charms in a pinch, but they didn't rise to the level of magically delicious. Cahill took offense.

Cahill mourned for Luke Olstad more than his mother's boyfriend. They weren't friends, but everyone liked Luke despite his parentage. Luke was one of the few people in town who didn't turn away when he saw Cahill coming. Misfit toys like Cahill and Maesie, and even Tommy, could count on cordiality from Luke.

"I wonder where they'll bury *him*," Cahill said.

"Tommy? In the ground more than likely," Maesie said.

"They better not go and put him in the Masonic where everyone else'll be put."

"Not my concern," Maesie said.

"Your mom's buried there, ain't she? What if they plant him next to her?"

"She wouldn't have much to say on the issue, being dead and all. But if she could talk, which would be pretty interesting to see, mind you, she'd say one hole in the ground is as good as any other."

"I guess we'll see what everyone else has to say about it," Cahill said. "I sure wish they'd get him buried soon, though. You can't let a guy like that lay around too long."

"I think caskets are airtight by design," Maesie said, though she knew it wasn't putrefying remains that bothered Cahill. He had always been jittery about death and what became of souls when they left their human vessels.

"Don't tease me," he said. "You know it ain't the smell I'm worried about."

Maesie made an *ooooo* sound like a cartoon ghost. "Cahill's afraid of Tommy's ghost," she said.

Cahill blinked. "I'm not afraid of nothing," he said. "But you never know about the spirit world. You can't take the chance on him getting loose before he's buried."

Maesie laughed. "I don't think that's the way it works. The spirit leaves the body at the time of death, doesn't it? Tommy would've started floating around the moment he plugged…" Maesie stopped abruptly. "Wait a minute," she said. "I just sensed Tommy's presence. Do you see him out there?"

"Quit fucking with me," Cahill said, now angry. He stood up and brushed loose dirt from the seat of his jeans. Maesie heard him walk away, but not toward his car.

A long moment later, she heard him return. Something made of metal clanked and snaked toward her. She lay on her back and did not know what it was until the pole jabbed into her ribs.

"Dammit, Cahill, stop it," she yelled.

"Then get the hell out of there," he said. "I got to get paid." He rammed the pole at her again. Because Maesie could not see, it was by luck she grabbed the pole just before it struck home again. She yanked it from Cahill's grip. Before he could react, she thrust the pole back toward him and struck home on the front of his ankle. Cahill's boot took the brunt of the jab, but the quick turn in Maesie's favor was enough to unnerve and frustrate him. He retreated several feet.

"I can keep finding more poles," he said. He did not know what else to say.

"You've got me terrified now."

Cahill paced and muttered to himself. Maesie could not make out what he was saying. He returned to the porch, but not too close should the pole come his way again. "For shit's sake, Maesie. Help me out here, will you? I need that money, and you're going to have to leave here one way or another."

"I told you I can't leave here. I just can't."

Cahill stomped the ground like a small child. "You're the most stubbornest..." he began muttering again and headed to his car. Over his shoulder he said, "The dozer comes two days from now, and it'll push this shack down on top of you. If you think I'm bluffing, you're in for a surprise."

6

I knew Skunk couldn't stay away. I could feel my dad being drawn back to Smackdab as if our murders created a huge swirl of chum in the water meant just for him to bathe in. It's not preordained as though God is yanking his strings, but he just can't help himself. Let's not kid ourselves that this has anything to do with me. It's all about my dad's need to be at the top of the dung heap. He has to be the one everyone else looks up to, even if they look on him with fear and derision. So, let it be. Let Skunk come back, if that's what he believes he has to do. And he'll bring Rolf Mattsen with him. The more the better. But Skunk won't like what he finds here. His days at the top are coming to an end.

    The car Skunk had acquired earlier that day in Pueblo, Colorado died on a two-lane forty miles west of Scott City, Kansas. While Rolf lolled with their gear a few blocks away in a Safeway parking lot, Skunk trolled the backyards of a nearby neighborhood for accessible vehicles. He didn't know how to hotwire a car, but he knew how to check for keys. The worse the vehicle, the more likely the owner was to keep the key under the seat. After checking just four cars, he found an ancient Monaco sedan with its key in the ignition. Judging from the grime and the indentations left by the tires where it had been parked in the backyard dirt, the car hadn't been driven in years. Skunk reasoned that no one would be too put out if he used it for a while.

    He was pleasantly surprised the engine turned over, and even more so that the gas gauge indicated the tank was nearly full. From the way the Dodge sputtered, however, Skunk figured a good deal of the tank's contents was water. A lawn sprinkler would have made a good suspect but for the lack of any grass in the yard. Whatever the fuel mixture had been, the Dodge had burned through it or given up trying, and left Skunk and Rolf stranded in the middle of flat-ass nowhere.

They would try hitching for a while, but Skunk hadn't seen any signs recently indicating a town was nearby. Unlike interstates, which Skunk felt wise to avoid in the borrowed car, two-laners running parallel to the bigger roads often carried people more inclined to chance it with hitchhikers. The men had hitched plenty of times before. Truckers and other frequent flyers tired of hearing their own voices would slow down to give Skunk and Rolf a good look. The guitars the two carried bolstered their chances. Some folks had romantic notions about rough-looking troubadours.

Skunk stepped from the stalled Monaco and looked east and west. An occasional vehicle passed, but he saw nothing but fields in either direction. The southwest Kansas cauldron showed no mercy. He took off his straw Stetson Llano and slung away the accumulated flop sweat. He wouldn't bear up in the Kansas heat for long unless he got some liquid in him to replace his breakfast of rum and Cokes. His head pounded.

"What'd we stop for?" Rolf asked, still seated in the car.

"We run out of gas, Buddy."

Rolf seemed satisfied by the answer for a moment. Then he said, "Why don't we drive on to the next gas station? There ought to be one close. There always is."

"We got no gas to get there," Skunk said. "And we're as broke as an old man's pecker. We'll have to hoof it for a while, and maybe get someone to pick us up." He retrieved the two guitar cases and duffle bags from the back seat. Rolf still hadn't moved. He clutched a bundle composed of two soiled motel pillows, sans cases, secured by bungee cords. Whatever was sandwiched between the pillows, Rolf kept it a secret. For weeks, he had slept snuggled with the mysterious pillow bundle like it was a precious teddy bear. If Skunk had wanted, he could not have looked in the bundle without waking Rolf.

"Well?" Skunk said. "Smackdab ain't coming to us."

Rolf pulled himself slowly from the car. He looked around like he had forgotten how they got there. Skunk had set his friend's guitar and bag on the shoulder in front of the Monaco. "Grab your kit," he said. "And let's move on down the road some away from this car."

Rolf hooked the pillow bundle to his bag, hoisted it and his guitar, and followed behind his partner. Skunk looked back often to ensure Rolf kept up. Both men raised their right thumbs any time they heard a vehicle come behind them from the west.

Skunk wished he knew what was going on in Smackdab and when the funerals were planned. The only thing in the Dodge that seemed to be in decent working order was the AM radio, but he had caught no more news about the shootings. The big story was an earthquake in California that buckled a section of freeway north of L.A. Three motorists died, including an actor who appeared a few times as a kid on *Growing Pains*. Skunk wondered who besides west-coasters gave a rat's ass about that.

Skunk had tried to call his ex-wife twice since morning to get more information, but Diane had not answered or called back. That was predictable. She likely had already worked up some scenario in her pickled brain that put the blame for the whole thing on Skunk. He tried a third call, but his phone had run out of juice.

Five minutes into their trek, Rolf had dropped twenty yards behind his partner. "Where we headed, Skunk?" Rolf yelled.

Rolf was sweating so much that wet spots below the armpits of his pale pink western shirt had become the size of a squash and the color of watermelon. Skunk waited for him to catch up. "I told you where we're going four times already," Skunk said. "Home. To Smackdab."

Rolf nodded as though he remembered, but Skunk doubted he knew why they were returning home. Skunk had told him about the shootings, but he hadn't wasted time with details.

He reached for Rolf's bags, but Rolf recoiled, swinging his gear behind him.

"What're you after?" Rolf asked with the look of a badger protecting its young.

"You're lagging, so I thought I'd carry your bags for a bit," Skunk said.

Rolf paused, and then unhooked the pillows and their secret contents from the other bag. He kept the pillows and handed the bag to Skunk, who draped it over the same shoulder with his.

"How long do you think we'll be staying there?" Rolf asked.

"Don't know. I'd like to get there first before I start thinking about leaving again."

The reason for returning to Smackdab was only marginally less fuzzy to Skunk than it was to Rolf, except that Skunk knew it was anticipated. The town would expect him to show up soon because hell had to be paid.

A Ford Explorer hitting on five cylinders passed the hitchhikers and skidded to a halt on the road. It idled there, sounding like it was about to cough up a lung, until Skunk and Rolf could catch up to it. A skinny boy of sixteen or seventeen occupied the driver's seat, tapping his thumbs on the steering wheel. The boy's face was covered with so many freckles that he looked olive-skinned from a distance. He had the dried sweat smell of a person who worked outdoors.

"How far you guys going?" he asked.

"As far as you are, so long as you're headed east," Skunk said, throwing his and Rolf's bags in the back before hopping in the passenger's side with his guitar case between his legs.

Rolf climbed in behind with his guitar case and pillows. "Obliged, young dude," he said. "You reckon you could turn up the air some?" he asked.

"It don't work," the kid said.

"How's about a beer or something wet?" Rolf asked.

"If I had a beer, it'd pretty much be boiling hot, based on the information I just shared," the boy said.

Rolf leaned forward with a hand on each front seat. "How much we getting paid for this gig?" Rolf asked. "They don't even throw in beer."

The boy looked in the rearview mirror before turning to Skunk. "What's his deal?"

"Don't mind him," Skunk said. "He's kinda loopy. The sun, I reckon. I don't suppose you got a water jug or anything? We're as dry as sandpaper right now."

The kid reached between his legs and pulled up a gallon milk jug from the floorboard.

"Not much left," he said, shaking the jug to prove his point. "Mostly my spit, but I ain't got no Ebola or nothing."

"You sure?" Skunk asked. "I'd hate to take your last few drops."

"Go ahead," the kid said. "I'll be someplace soon where I can refill it."

Skunk twisted off the red cap and took three quick swallows. The water was so warm Skunk knew it had been sitting in the sun awhile. Still, the water beat having nothing to drink. He handed the jug to Rolf, who finished the contents and let go an "Ahhh," as if he had just drunk pure ambrosia.

"Just sit back and relax and think about how you ain't walking right now," Skunk said to Rolf.

Easily assuaged, Rolf pulled his hat over his face and tried to nap.

"I guess that was your car back there," the boy said to Skunk. "I saw you were from Colorado. Run out of gas, huh? I never cared much for Coloradoans. You all think your shit don't stink."

Skunk said nothing.

"I always make sure I got plenty of gas in the tank," the kid said. "Common sense, you know? Where you trying to get to anyway?"

"Any place that ain't here as long as it's east of it," Skunk said.

One hundred yards ahead, a lanky mutt, white with butterscotch splotches, sauntered across the road right to left. The kid veered into the left lane as the dog crossed to that side. He would have nipped the dog's ass with the left corner of the Explorer, spinning the mutt like a top, but the dog skipped over the shoulder and into a weedy ditch at the last moment.

The driver laughed.

"Woo boy," he said. "That's one lucky sonofabitch today."

Skunk considered the condition of the SUV, particularly the sorry state of the engine. He moved his hand along the lapel of his Manuel short jacket and felt the outline of the modified chainsaw file. He kept the file in a hidden pocket of the lining. He had shortened the shaft slightly, and sharpened the end so that it was like an ice pick, but with a stronger shaft. Skunk had used the file to get out of a few jams and to get into twice as many.

Skunk wasn't keen on sticking the kid, who wasn't much younger than Luke. But the driver was already making his headache worse. Plus, it would be nice to dispense with hitching and get the hell through Kansas as soon as possible. The only question was whether the Explorer was up to the challenge. He wished a person driving a late-model sedan, say a Lexus, would occasionally pick up hitchhikers. But it always seemed to be people driving clunkers.

"I guess you guys're some kind of music outfit?" the boy asked.

"Something like that," Skunk said.

"You look like you play country music. I bet I'm right, ain't I?" Without waiting for an answer, he said: "Must not be too good at it, which is why you were driving that piece of junk back there."

Skunk was too intent on thinking about the durability of the vehicle to respond to the insult. "What's wrong with your machine here anyway?" he asked. "Sounds more like an Exploder than an Explorer."

"It does better than it sounds," the driver said. "At least I ain't run out of gas in it. And I burn a lot of it. I just got done with a job for a fella west of here, and now I'm headed to do the same for another fella. I spend half of what I make on gas going from one place to another."

"Maybe you ought to reassess your business strategy," Skunk said.

"At least I work for a living," the boy said.

Skunk wondered if the kid had a decent wad of cash on him.

"Did the first dude pay you?" he asked.

"Not so far," the kid said. "He wants me back again tomorrow."

"Sounds like you're just as broke as we are," Skunk said.

"I'll be flush at the end of the week, and you two hillbillies will still be thumbing rides."

"Boy's got a bit of a mouth on him, don't he?" Rolf said from the back seat. His eyes remained closed.

Skunk peaked at the gas gauge. It showed empty. He took his hand off the lump in his pocket.

"I thought you said you never let the gas get down to empty," Skunk said.

"Damn, you ask a lot of questions," the kid said, his face hardening. "The gas gauge don't work, but believe me, I know within a pint how much the tank's got."

Rolf had given up napping and now looked out his window. "Where we at, Skunk?"

"Southwest Kansas," the driver answered instead.

"It don't look like Smackdab," Rolf said.

"I don't know where Smackdab is," the boy said. "But you're about five miles on down the road from where I picked you up." Then to Skunk: "Is he always this dumb?"

"Kansas, huh?" Rolf said, peering out his window as though he was seeing his surroundings for the first time. "Why don't you people plant a goddamn tree once in a while?"

"You can't plant wheat on a tree," the boy said, slowly, like a teacher repeating a basic fact to a thick student. He slowed to a stop on the highway's shoulder. "This is where we part company," he said.

Skunk saw nothing but wheat fields on either side of the road. "Where's your turnoff?" he asked.

"On down a ways, but this is close enough. You both smell, and you ask too many annoying questions."

Skunk felt the chainsaw file again, but he concluded the Explorer was not worth the effort. Also, the highway was too exposed and too busy. A large town must be up ahead.

Just before shutting his door, Skunk stuck his head back in. "Sometimes a lucky day can be real obvious, you know?" He said. "Like you get laid without having to beg for it. Or you find a dollar stuck down in the crack of your car seat. But sometimes, the luckiest days are ones you don't realize. Like a shot from a deer rifle misses your skull by a centimeter and you don't even know it. You just hear the crack of a distant rifle a second later. Now, let's say a young fella might be such an asshole that he makes another guy want to take something long and sharp and make a new hole in kid's nostril. But the guy is so tired he decides to let it pass. You know what I mean?"

The boy scrunched his face. "I sure don't."

Skunk hard-slapped the door with his open hand. "I'm saying you're one lucky sonofabitch today."

7

The morning of the memorial service, Coach decided to again visit Jean Pankin. She had been his first visit following the rampage. He hadn't known her husband Pink well, but Jean had attended church faithfully since her childhood, first at a small Lutheran church on the prairie, then at First Baptist in Smackdab, and finally Community Fellowship Church, which the three Smackdab churches folded into when none of them could survive separately.

Because Jean Pankin was the only one of the victims' immediate families who attended Coach's church, not counting the Klimps, he would stop by her house ahead of the memorial service. The visit would come more from obligation than want. Coach liked Jean Pankin—he liked all his church members more or less—but he preferred aloneness to human interaction in almost any situation. Why then had he chosen teaching, coaching and now ministry, all of which required a lot of human contact? He did not know, except that he thought he would be good at each. He assumed he would be a dynamic preacher without knowing why. He fantasized the sanctuary, usually half empty on Sundays, would soon begin to fill with townspeople who came to hear the wonderful Reverend Hunney proclaim the Word. Instead, attendance dropped even further during his tenure.

Jean Pankin lived in a modest frame house three blocks south of Route 4, the main east-west street through town. Her Ford Taurus was parked in the open-air car shelter attached to the left side of the house. Two cars Coach did not recognize were parked behind it. The front yard and the driveway were so short that the rear of the third vehicle protruded into the street.

Jean Pankin collected rooster art. The postage stamp front yard was overrun with cockerel lawn ornaments of various sizes and materials. Pink, a master welder, had accommodated his wife's poultry zeal by fabricating a three-foot rooster from scrap iron, which was positioned in the grass between the street and sidewalk. The rooster had not been painted, and its surface had oxidized to the color of ochre.

But it was not the rusty rooster that first caught a visitor's eye. The Pankins had planted a banana tree in their small front yard. The growing season for tropical vegetation was brief. Subsequently, the tree never bore fruit. To Coach, it always looked sickly, though it stood six feet high, because half its broad leaves were the color of summer squash rather than emerald. Each fall, Pink dug up the pitiful tree, wrapped it, and hibernated it on their enclosed back porch until the following spring. The best times of the tree's life, Coach imagined, were on the porch.

Coach parked on the opposite side of the street. Two men, middle-aged and unfamiliar to Coach, stood in the front yard. They stared at the tree like they expected it to produce a banana for their amusement. One of the two smoked a cigarette. Both looked uncomfortable in short sleeve buttoned shirts, one blue plaid and the other pale green. The green-shirted man wore a lime green tie with daisies, which seemed incongruous to the occasion. Both were small and angular like Pink. His side of the family, Coach guessed.

The men nodded at Coach as he walked past them to the door. Coach wished them a good morning, but neither man spoke or smiled.

Jean's fortyish daughter, who lived in Omaha, answered the door. Like her mother, Chelsea Pankin was nearly as wide as she was tall. But she had the same hospitable smile, which she could not stanch, even with her father's death so fresh.

"Come in, Mister Hunney," Chelsea said. "Mom will be glad you stopped by."

"You haven't changed much in twenty-five years," Coach said.

Chelsea patted her round hips. "There are two ways a woman could take that," she said.

Chelsea had never married. If Coach remembered correctly, she taught kindergarten. Even as a teenager, she looked like a teacher of small children, with a big lap and pillowy arms that provided a perfect fit for five-year-olds. Like many others who had grown up in Smackdab and moved away, Chelsea had taken History from Coach. He assumed she had been a good student, but he didn't remember much about her academically. He tended to remember poorer students better because they required most of his attention.

"Mom's in the kitchen with my aunt," Chelsea said, leading the way. "She has to stay busy to avoid breaking down. This morning, she's making rolls."

The house smelled of yeast, something much different from the minister's apartment above the bar. Coach had been to the Pankins once before the murders, for dinner. It was a comfortable home, though the furniture must have pre-dated the Pankin offspring. Like most families in Smackdab, the Pankins did not replace furniture or appliances as long as they remained functional, as long as duct tape kept them in service.

You wouldn't have known Jean Pankin had recently lost her husband to violence. Other than being dressed as if for church, she looked the same as always. She bent over a mat of dough on the floured kitchen table, flattening the dough with a rolling pin. Though she wore a peach-colored apron, a small bit of flour showed on the sleeve of her brown print dress.

"Coach," she said, setting down the pin. "Nice of you to stop by." Coach could now see that her eyes were glassy, bloodshot.

A bony woman with a severe face peered over Jean's shoulder, as though she were there to supervise.

"You know Pink's sister-in-law, Betty?" Jean said, motioning behind her with the pin. "Her and Pink's little brother, Jim, live in West Fork."

Coach now remembered he had met the other woman once when she came to worship with Jean at church.

"I could have called, but I wanted to see with my own eyes how you're holding up," Coach said.

"I was just wondering this morning about that poor Maesie Mattsen," Jean said, deflecting the question as she set the rolling pin aside. "What's going to come of her?"

"She's had to be pretty resilient in her life," Coach said, knowing that wasn't much of an answer. "But I came here to see how *you're* holding up, Jean."

"Oh, you know," she said, her voice trailing off. "We'll all get through it."

Coach knew that was as revealing as Jean would get. Smackdabbers, many of them of Scandinavian descent, saw showy feelings as weakness. There would be a tear or two during the service, a few sniffles, but that would be the extent. Smackdab weeded out weepy types and sent them someplace else where shows of emotion were more acceptable.

The oven timer dinged. Without waiting for Jean's go-ahead, Betty threw on a mitt and removed a tray of rolls from the oven. She set them on the counter to cool.

"We're baking rolls for all the families," Jean said. "I can't just sit around and mope all the time."

Jean motioned everyone into the living room to sit. Coach took a seat on the largest easy chair. People always wanted the minister to take the nicest seat. He had been sitting on a lot of similar chairs in recent days.

Coach had sat in the Pankin living room before, and it made him uncomfortable again. Ceramic roosters occupied every available flat surface: bookshelves, end tables, and windowsills. A half dozen glass ornamental roosters with blood-red combs and brilliant teal tail feathers hung from a potted fern in one corner. From every angle, dozens of beady eyes stared at Coach as though he was a threat to their mistress.

Betty and Chelsea bookended Jean on the couch. Jean's sister-in-law snaked her arm inside Jean's arm. "She's got people that love her," Betty said. "We'll be here as long as she wants us. Won't we Chelsea?"

"You bet we will," Chelsea said.

Jean smiled.

"I've been telling people who've called on us that Pink loved his job so much, he always said Roger would have to fire him if he wanted to get rid of him," she said. "We never imagined there was a third way."

It struck Coach as an odd thing to say, and he didn't know if he should smile, nod, or ignore it. He opted for a weak smile.

"God doesn't give us any more than we can handle," Betty said.

Coach loathed that maxim, one he had heard often since the killings. It was as though God shoveled shit on people until they nearly reached a breaking point. Then God would sit back and see how they dealt with it. The idea of it had never made sense to Coach, but he knew enough to keep his mouth shut. People thought preachers did a lot of talking. Often, the job was more about what a pastor did not say.

Jean studied her minister's face. Coach worried she could read his thoughts. If anyone had the ability, it was Jean Pankin.

"I'm a little worried about us," she said.

"It's a lot of sorrow for you to contend with," Coach said. "I agree."

Jean waved her hand like Coach's comment was superfluous.

"No, we'll manage. No, I'm worried about the town," she said as she waved her hand again in a broad sweep. "Everyone will think we're a bunch of crazies. A murder town. I don't care so much what others think about us, but I do care what we think about ourselves. People in Smackdab have always had a tiny inferiority complex, you know? And now this? I fear we'll get so down on ourselves that we'll never get back up."

"Um hmm," Betty said, using a tone like she was sitting in the front pew of an apostolic church. "People in Washington and New York

City and places like that will come in here and try to take our guns away. You just watch."

Unsure what Betty's prediction had in common with Jean's concern, no one responded.

"I wish I could do more for you than offer words and prayers," Coach said, making sure he kept his eyes on Jean and away from her sister-in-law.

"There's nothing more important than prayer," Jean said.

Coach remained silent. It would be foolhardy to argue the point with a woman whose husband was so recently butchered by an assault rifle.

The three women, staring at him like owls on a limb, may have detected something in his silence. Coach realized that, having mentioned prayer, he was expected to say one.

"You believe that, don't you, Reverend?" Betty asked. "About prayer? And praying that God will take care of Jean and the others? That poor man's family needs the Lord's healing, too, even though I believe with all my heart God will have to punish them first."

"I do sometimes wonder if God is listening," Coach said before he could catch himself.

"Of course He is," Betty said. "Maybe we don't always like the answer."

Now that he had started, Coach had to continue.

"Do you believe God's answer to someone's prayer was to kill six innocent men, including your husband's brother?" he asked.

"Sometimes we're not to know God's will," Betty said. "Only to accept it."

Coach noticed that Jean and Chelsea remained impassive, their hands folded on their laps like matching corpulent china dolls.

"Well, God is a mystery," he said, rising to leave. "Be sure to call if I can do anything at all," he said to Jean. He left without saying a prayer.

8

Maesie did not sleep well enough to have dreams, but nighttime made memories of the shooting scene more vivid. When Maesie heard the loud pops coming from the shop, she knew what they meant. She hid under her desk. She did not see anyone killed but Tommy, who had come into her office after he aerated Roger Sandstrum. As soon as Tommy called her name, she wet her pants.

They'll see I peed my pants when they find my body. That'll give them a good laugh.

She had to quit thinking about that day, though she did not know how that would be possible. Still, she had other problems pushing in on her, like how to make money to pay for food and shelter while remaining a hermit. In Smackdab, a dwarf with limited skills was as worthless as a cracked straw in a Coke can. The Internet was supposed to offer all sorts of ways to get rich from home, but she'd never known anyone who had done it. Besides, she had cancelled her web connection around the same time she lost her cell phone service. Her computer was so old it had whined like a wounded retriever anytime she fired it up.

Maesie had done well to make it as long as she did after a 2003 Camaro had launched her mother into the afterlife four months earlier. Charmin Mattsen had been walking along Route 4 to her job at Poulsen's drug store when the Camaro came up behind her and pitched her thirty feet across a ditch and into a row of box elders that lined the parking lot at First State Bank. Instantly, she was as dead as a road-killed cat. The driver, a seventeen-year-old boy Maesie vaguely remembered from a few grades behind her at school, had dropped a lighted cigarette in the floorboard between his legs. He was trying to fish it out when the car veered to the right and splintered Charmin's pelvis into hundreds of bits and pieces.

Her mother had been the most important person in Maesie's life, but she had no time to mourn. She made some effort to generate funds to pay the most pressing bills. One Sunday, she crafted a sign for a fake organization called Little People for a Better Tomorrow and stood at the caution light at Broadway and Route 4 to collect money in a KFC bucket. She had found a reflective vest among her father's things like the ones worn by road workers.

Maesie collected nearly thirty dollars, enough to purchase several boxes of macaroni and cheese, peanut butter and other food items that wouldn't go bad in her lifetime. Maesie went out again the following Sunday and collected twenty dollars more, just a fraction required to pay the power bill. When she went back out a third time, the town constable, Bennie Duroque, told her to seek another means of income. Little People for a Better Tomorrow dissolved.

Roger Sandstrum hired her to do clerical work four hours a day at the machine shop. If he had lived, Maesie imagined Roger would have regretted that HR decision.

The day of the service for the six murdered men, Maesie set her mind to walk into town to put in her application at the GasGo. The idea of leaving the house made her palms sweaty; she repeatedly licked her upper lip. But she knew she had to do something. She couldn't live under the house forever, especially since there would be no house soon enough. Now that Patsy Klimp had quit, the convenience store had a late-shift opening. The store was usually quiet after ten o'clock at night, with little human interaction required, which made Patsy a good fit for it. Maesie had already practiced how she thought the interview would go with Brenda Sue Wakefield, the store's manager:

I recently lost my position at a manufacturing concern due to unforeseen circumstances. You may have heard about it. Kind of a big deal around these parts. Anyway, I'm here about the job opening.

You? You're too short to reach the top of the shelves.

That's why God invented step stools. I can provide my own, if you don't have a spare. Besides, think how clean I'll keep the floors. From my vantage point, no speck of dirt will escape detection.

Customers may take advantage of you.

I guess there's a first for everything. But unless you're running a basketball team, it shouldn't make a difference. I'll be the best worker you have.

Maesie made it as far as the edge of the yard before paralysis overtook her. She felt her chest constrict and her breathing labor. It was too soon to be out in the open. She thrice wiped the phantom brain matter from her lip before she scurried back inside.

Cahill had not yet returned for a third time to try again to evict her, but he would appear soon enough. But even if Maesie could think of somewhere else to go, she wasn't sure she could force herself to leave. There was little about the house she would miss. It looked like it had been picked up by a twister and dropped back on its cinder block foundation at an odd angle. Her father cursed the low-slung structure the rare times he returned home. He was also fond of maligning the place during his occasional phone calls.

"Sandstrum ought to be ashamed of himself," Rolf said. "Taking rent money for that turd."

"Technically, he's not," Maesie said. "I came up short on cash again this month."

Still, Rolf cursed the house like doing so was the one thing that could make him happy. "This hovel is so goddamn lopsided," he said once. "I swear I could set a marble on the floor before hitting the sack, and it would still be rolling when I got up the next morning."

Maesie's father never admitted the connection between his career choice and the sorry state of the Mattsen living arrangements. His job—and to call it such was being generous—was meant for his personal gratification, and not for domestic preservation. He felt no guilt each time he returned to see the house in worse shape than he left it. He even seemed somewhat insulted that Charmin and Maesie hadn't found better digs during his absence.

"At least it's shelter," said Charmin, who rarely complained about anything. "Keeps us dry most of the time."

Rolf grunted. "As long as it don't rain hard," he said. "Sometimes I think we'd be better off pitching a tent out by Dead Lake."

Maesie believed her father had a point. True, the house would never be featured in *Southern Living*. But Roger Sandstrum had been patient when Maesie had gotten behind on rent following Charmin's death. And so that's what made it the best home in Smackdab.

Roger Sandstrum thought the same. He had dropped by occasionally to ask permission to step through the house to the back yard. Maesie's mother always said of course he could. Maesie wondered why he needed to ask to survey his own property, but what did she know? She followed him out back once, just to see what drew him there. He stood in the yard a few minutes as though he were revering the Lincoln Memorial. He told Maesie the house, where his grandparents lived and died, used to front a one-hundred-twenty-acre patch of rocky soil that kept a small herd of Angus cattle fed in hay and pasture grass. Roger said he loved that place with its interwoven smells of cow shit and sneezeweed. When he was a boy, there had been a rope swing with a bald truck tire hanging from a mammoth elm near the back corner of the yard. Best swing ever, he said.

But business was business. When Roger inherited the land, he sold five-sixths of it in twenty-acre parcels, and he took down all the outbuildings but the one closest to the house. The elm, crippled from disease, got the ax, too.

    Maesie tried to come to terms with surrendering her sanctuary. If she had to, she could get by until late October or early November by sleeping outside, as long as she had a couple quilts for chilly nights. It would be nearly ideal if she could find a place to stay out of sight. She might head out to the prairie around Dead Lake, like Rolf had talked about. Few people went there. Her dad had once promised to take her camping under the stars. He had bought some camping equipment at an estate sale, but he had never gotten around to taking her. The camping gear was still stored in a plastic bin in her parents' bedroom.

    Maesie could not prevent her mind from wandering back to the shooting. She had spent two hours sitting in the front passenger seat of a police cruiser, sprinkled with bits of brain splatter, as she recounted events with an investigator. The cop was about her father's age, with a large belly that pushed determinedly against the buttons on his shirt. His tie, with illustrations of Tabasco sauce bottles, twisted wrong side out. He reeked of garlic fries he had been lunching on when he got the call to haul tail to Smackdab.

    She could not remember the cop's last name, but he insisted she call him Isaiah, instead of Detective Whatever, to help her feel more at ease. Isaiah seemed nice enough. He kept his car idling to maintain the cabin temperature at sixty-eight degrees, and he had retrieved wet wipes from an EMT so she could clean the mess from her face.

    "I've got a pretty good handle on what you've told me," the cop had said after she told her story three times. "Anything else you might have forgotten?"

    Maesie licked her lower lip for the first time to feel if she had gotten all the brain matter. "Not really," she said.

    Isaiah stared her down, like her mother used to do when a young Maesie was caught lying. "I've been doing this a lot of years," the detective said. "And I know when I'm being lied to. So I want you to tell me right now, point blank, looking me square in the eyes, if you were mixed up in any of this."

    Maesie held his gaze, trying not to look guilty. "Mixed up how?" she asked.

    "Did you know he was coming here to today loaded up like the Second Army? Did you help plan it?"

"No sir, I did not," Maesie said. She thought she kept from blinking, but she wasn't sure. "At first, I thought all the noise was just normal shop sounds. But I guessed pretty quickly it was gunfire, and I knew just as quickly who it was. The front door wouldn't open, like I already said, so I couldn't get out that way."

Maesie held her breath as the detective studied her. After a long moment, his stone expression softened. "Yeah," he said. "He used a piece of scrap metal to jam the front door. You would've needed a battering ram to get out that way."

From his side, the cop cracked Maesie's window an inch. Maesie knew why. Her urine soaked jean shorts were starting to dry, adding a pungent smell that did not mix well with garlic fries.

She knew she was taking chances, but she couldn't keep herself from saying more. "I went and hid under my desk. Tommy found me, ordered me to come out and face him. I did, closing my eyes so I wouldn't see him shoot me."

Maesie paused, remembering the moment.

"I was thinking, wondering, if the bullet would strike me before I heard the gun fire. Maybe I wouldn't feel it."

She shrugged like she was wrapping up a review of a regular workday. "Anyway, Tommy shot himself instead of me. End of story. I had no idea he'd do anything like that. None at all."

"And he never said a word to you?" the detective asked.

Maesie shook her head. "Nope. Just shot himself, and fell backwards onto the floor like a sack of russets."

Isaiah seemed satisfied with everything she told him.

"If there were no conspirators, there won't be a trial. So, you may not hear from me again," he said, turning off the mini-recorder that lay on the seat between them. He folded the cover on a leather binder in which he had taken pages of notes. "But you should keep ready just in case. And if you think of anything else, be sure to call me."

"I won't think of anything else," Maesie said. "The whole thing happened so fast, just like you always hear. It was a big shock. No idea he would do that."

Isaiah offered to drive her home, which she accepted.

"Give me a call anyway," the cop said when they reached her house. "I'd like to hear how you're doing. You can get counseling through social services if you need. That's what taxes pay for."

"I'll be fine," Maesie said, getting out of the coolness of the cruiser into the blistering heat of the mid-afternoon.

Maesie crawled under the front porch one last time. The black dirt under the structure's foundation was cool, dry and contoured to her body in a way that her ancient mattress never could.

She had tasted the dirt a few times; it wasn't so bad. It had the vaguest hint of sweetness. Maesie knew the soil contained a dose of bug parts, but no more than the average hot dog, she imagined.

The area beneath the porch had become Maesie's sanctuary when she was five or six, when she realized she wouldn't grow like other people. Charmin had held her daughter out of kindergarten because she didn't want the other kids to make fun of her. Charmin would have home schooled Maesie the rest of her school years if she could have afforded it. But having Rolf as the sole family breadwinner was like counting on a piece of gravel for one's water supply. Charmin took a job as cashier at the drug store.

"I want you to know I love you just the way you are," Charmin had said the day before first grade started. "You're just the right size."

"Okay," Maesie said, not sure what her mother's point was. She had never worried much about her size.

"You're not going to catch up with the other kids," Charmin said. "You're always going to be smaller. You'll make up for it in other ways."

"Okay," Maesie repeated.

"What I'm trying to say is, you're going to be extra small. Okay? You'll always have to climb up on chairs instead of sitting down in them like your mama does. Kids will look at you funny at first, but you'll get used to it. And they'll get used to you. I just want you to understand you're perfect, and I love you very much."

Her mother had told Maesie she was perfect every day of her life, so the gravity of those words this time did not sink in for Maesie until she arrived at school. The other kids, except for a few, made it clear Maesie was not like them. At the end of that first day, when she got off the bus in front of the house, Charmin wasn't yet home from work. Instead of entering the house, Maesie looked for the quickest place to hide and pout, which was beneath the front porch.

She did not crawl out until the next morning, though Charmin had pleaded with her through the night. Maesie spent a lot more time under the house until she was about fourteen, when she decided she needed to get over herself.

Sometime around then, Rolf returned home from the road with an old fiddle. He gave it to Maesie.

"That's a damn good fiddle," Rolf had said, though it could have been a twenty-dollar cheapie for all Maesie knew.

"I got it off an old boy in Arkansas," he said. "Paid a lot more than I should have, but I figured you could learn to play it."

Maesie guessed her father stole the instrument or won it gambling. Her money was on theft, which would explain why it came with no bow.

"What do you want me to do with it?" Maesie asked.

When something annoyed Rolf, he scratched the cleft of his chin like he was trying to eradicate an ink stain. The more annoyed he became, the harder he scratched. "Play it," he said, his fingers working furiously beneath his mouth. "What the hell else you think it's for?"

"Not much without the bow, I'd say."

"Well, hell. Ain't you ever heard of im-PRO-vising?" he said, emphasizing the middle syllable of the word. "It's a piss-poor carpenter who blames her tools. I played a whole night one time without the high E string on my guitar. You ought to be able to im-PRO-vise without a bow."

Maesie had. First, she learned to pluck the strings while holding the fiddle upright between her legs as she sat on the ground. Later, her mother found her a used bow in West Fork. The fiddle was somewhat cumbersome to hold the traditional way, so she continued to straddle it, playing the fiddle like a cello.

It was a decent fiddle, Maesie surmised, because she wouldn't give herself credit for making the thing sound sweet. But it did sound good in Maesie's hands. She played a few bluegrass tunes she knew by ear from listening to her father. Mostly though, she made her own music, playing the fiddle in a lonesome way that would make a dog howl. She never played for anyone but herself and her mother. Not even Rolf got to hear the music she made with his gift.

The fiddle was with her now, wrapped up in an old baby blanket, under the porch. She doubted she would ever feel called to play it again.

9

I feel sorrier for the Klimps than I do anyone else. How would you feel if you had to live the rest of your life knowing you parented a notorious killer? That it was a cocktail of your genes that produced a monster? Nature or nurture? Either way, you're fucked. You'd wake up every morning and your first thought would be you're the parent of a mass murderer. You'd be sitting on the toilet and between grunts you'd think MASS MURDERER MASS MURDERER. *You'd be sitting on the divan watching a cop show, and you'd be hoping the fictional killer accumulated more fictional victims than your child did in real victims, as if that would make your kid not seem like Satan's spawn or quite as evil as a make-believe villain.*

It sucks to be dead, but it would suck to infinity to be the Klimps right now.

After his visit to Jean Pankin, Coach still had time to kill before the service. Though he should have focused on tightening his eulogy, he wanted to do anything but that. Perhaps he would drop in on the Mattsen girl. It wasn't technically necessary. She wasn't related to any of the deceased, she wasn't harmed in the shooting, and she had never gone to church. Still, he told himself he would check in on her when the dust settled a little more. If he got the time. If he felt up to it. If he was still the preacher.

Smackdab wasn't much of a church-going town. Coach sometimes wondered if he should take evangelism more seriously, but it wasn't his way to get in people's faces about Jesus and the rest of it. Still, he felt some pride—before the guilt tamped it down again—when the little sanctuary was packed the Sunday after the murders. Deacons brought in folding chairs from classrooms to handle the overflow.

Happy as he was to have so many people in the service that morning, the large crowd caught Coach off guard. He expected a few of the irregulars to attend, adding to the usual number of sixty or so, but nothing like the crowd that showed up. He had taken his sermon text from the end of Lamentations, which seemed appropriate at the time.

> *The joy of our hearts has ceased;*
> *Our dancing has been turned to mourning...*
> *For this our heart has become sick...*
> *But you, O LORD, reign forever;*
> *Your throne endures to all generations.*

He might have chosen something a little less obscure had he known he'd have so many listeners. He wasn't at his best that day, because he could think of few comforting words to offer. If everyone had come to hear a vengeance sermon, that wasn't in him either. He expected the numbers to drop back to normal the following Sunday.

As the only licensed pastor of the only church in town, everyone looked to Coach to assuage their shock and guilt over the shootings. He had already faced the usual questions about what was God's will and how He could have let such a thing happen. Coach didn't have a good answer, but his stock response had been something about the mystery of God. That didn't satisfy anyone, but what would? Life was a bitch, but saying so wasn't going to make anyone feel better.

Since the carnage, Coach had fantasized about the old days when he taught History and coached at Smackdab High. Fresh off his divorce, he had moved to Smackdab, taking the job farthest from east Texas he could find. Coach had never been much more than a mediocre teacher, but his football teams had been something else for a few years in a row. They won the small school state championship one year and came close again the following year. That got him a job as head coach at a little liberal arts college, but those teams only won three games in two seasons. Coach returned, humbled, to Smackdab, the one place where he had approached being somebody.

And although he had fancied himself being regarded as something of a sage to the town, he would never offer his opinion unless he was asked. And when asked, he would phrase his response as a question. But he could imagine how it would go:

I was thinking about running for school board this next time, Coach. What do you think?

Rick Larsen has that seat now, doesn't he? How do your qualifications compare?

Yeah, you're right. I don't have a chance.

To strengthen his gravitas, Coach took New Testament classes in the city, got licensed as a minister, and took the open position at

Community Christian for twenty-two grand a year, plus a small housing stipend. Not much, but plenty in a town like Smackdab, even before adding in his teaching pension.

Coach still had his ancient Volvo 240, a pea-green machine he bought used twenty-five years earlier. No mechanic in Smackdab knew much about Swedish cars, but the Volvo had cooperated for the most part, like an old man with only minor arthritis and mild cataracts. He rented the room above Snoots when he returned to Smackdab from his college coaching failure, joking with church members that a minister living above a bar was like a doctor taking a room at the hospital. In truth, it was the cheapest room he could find, and so spare of furnishings that he could convince himself he was living like a penitent, cloistered monk.

As for the part about being regarded as a sage, Coach was still waiting for that to happen.

He thought again about Billie Quick. What would everyone think if the only pastor in town began courting the proprietor of its only tavern? *Courting*. Now there was a word. And not one Billie was likely to take seriously. If she had any fondness for Coach, and there was no indication she did, using a word like *courting* would kill it.

Coach pulled into the church parking lot, intending to put together the sermon for the memorial service, when he realized he wanted to do anything but that. He thought about returning to his apartment, but he knew he would accomplish nothing there except taking an unnecessary nap.

He had put off the inevitable long enough. It was time to visit the Klimps. He had dreaded the thought of it, the notion of being pastoral to *those people* at this time. But it was his job. He didn't have to feel good about it, though, as he often said when his natural feelings overtook his spiritual wishes:

I'm only human.

The Klimps lived in a faux brick one-story on a small acreage west of town. The land had belonged to Bob's grandparents, and it used to be fronted by a mess of a farmhouse with cement shingle siding that had cracked and broken and yielded easily to bitter prairie winds. Bob had built the new house snug up behind the original before tearing it down.

The new house sat on a low ridge. The grounds sloped behind the house, the back yard, and a small lot to a creek, which was more of a ditch carved by runoff. Depending on rainfall, the creek might be dry eight months of the year. The ground beyond the yard was peppered with creek stone – good for little besides sheep or goat raising. The Klimps did neither.

Past the creek, the acreage rose again half the length of a football field to the end of the Klimp's property line. That's where Bob had installed two wind turbines. If he put another one up there, it would look like the three crosses on Golgotha.

A half-minute after Coach knocked on the front door, Patsy Klimp peeked suspiciously through the small diamond-shaped portal on the wood laminate front door. She saw the familiar face of her minister and unlocked the door to let him enter. Coach never regarded Patsy as particularly uppity like some folks did. Laconic, maybe. Sure of her opinions. But that described the majority of Smackdab's population.

It was mid-morning, and Patsy was still in her bathrobe. Her face was dry, though puffy. Coach wondered if she had just gotten out of bed, or if she had been crying earlier. Coach did not like to be reminded that seven men died in the spree, the last one being Patsy's son.

"Nice of you to take the time, Pastor," she said. Coach thought he detected a hint of sarcasm. She had never called him Pastor.

"I hope this doesn't look bad on you, visiting us like this," she said. "No one else has bothered, except for all the news people. Not even folks we've known our whole lives."

The edge in Patsy's voice hit Coach the wrong way. He considered saying he'd come back another time, and then not come back at all. Still, he was there...

"I heard those crime lab people were out here for a couple of days," he said. "I thought they might not allow anyone on the property."

Patsy winced.

"So... Now they're gone, obviously. I just wanted to see what I could do for you," he said.

"Do? Such as?" Patsy asked. "All the doing's been done. But you can come in, if you feel you should." She stepped aside. Coach hesitated, even more sure this visit was a mistake. He reluctantly stepped in.

Unlike the Pankin house, the Klimp home smelled stale, almost like death, as though a huge exhaust fan had sucked out anything that had once been alive about it–anything that made it a home rather than a structure.

Usual sounds that no one would notice until they disappeared, such as clocks ticking and appliances whirring, were absent. It was as if the house knew it had harbored a mass murderer, and was as ashamed as the humans who still occupied it.

The Klimps had no family in Smackdab. Their daughter, Emmalynn, attended college someplace in Illinois. If Coach remembered the story right, Bob's father had died when he had a seizure while discing a field. The tractor's wheels were cut hard to the left when the elder Klimp fell off at the end of a row. The tractor and disc, going in a continuous circle, cut the man into mush before anyone came upon the scene.

A couple years later, Bob's mother and older sister died when their car collided with a stock truck a few miles east of town. The driver of the truck wasn't hurt, but the car was crushed like a Coke can. Bob was riding in the back. Rescue workers used the Jaws of Life to extract him. Bob escaped with a few scrapes. He was raised by grandparents, now dead.

That was a lot of bad to happen to one person, but Bob never acted like he had more bad luck growing up than any other man. Bob's emotions never swung far one way or the other. If he had any deep philsopical thoughts, he hid them well. His one obvious weakness was capacious worry about what other people thought of him. Coach considered that a very minor flaw.

Patsy's parents were gone, too. She had family in another part of the state, but she wasn't close to them. Coach did not know her story well, but he remembered hearing once about an uncle, or maybe it was a cousin, who served time in prison for manslaughter. Coach wondered if whatever triggered Tommy's rage came from that side of the family.

"Bob's in the pasture watching his windmills," Patsy said. "He prefers their company to humans. Have a seat while I go yell at him."

When he entered the front room a few minutes later, Bob Klimp was fully dressed in an army-style olive pocket tee and jeans. The armpits of the T-shirt were darkened with sweat. He looked as though he had shrunk since the last time Coach saw him. This newest tragedy had finally diminished him.

"Might come up a cloud later," Bob said as a greeting. "We could use a little rain."

"I guess so," Coach said.

"Did Patsy offer you some coffee?" Bob asked. "Or maybe you'd like something iced?"

"He didn't come for a drink," Patsy said. "He just came to do his job. We better let him do it before people find out he's here and get on him about it."

The Klimps sat down on the high end of a leather sofa that sloped to one end.

"Sorry you have to do this, Coach," Bob said. "But we appreciate you coming by. You may be it for the time being as far as visitors go."

Patsy shook her head.

"Why us?" she asked, not expecting an answer. "What did we do to deserve this? We've stayed married, we've always worked, we go to church most Sundays, and we tried to raise our children the right way. We've never had much money, but we haven't lived above our means. Look around town. How many other people can say all that?"

Coach did not offer a response. Patsy seemed to be angered more than grief-stricken. Nobody spoke for a moment, though it seemed to Coach like a very long one.

"That Mattsen girl..." Patsy said with no elaboration. She stared at the floor in front of her with eyes glazed, as though Maesie scuttered at her feet like a roach.

Coach would not encourage Patsy to go on about Maesie; Bob looked away like he felt the same as Coach.

"Anything I can do to help with the arrangements?" Coach asked.

The Klimps did not answer. Neither looked at their visitor.

"It would be best to keep the service private," Coach continued. "No announcements in the paper. I hope you can understand why."

Patsy's reverie seemed to snap at that. "Who knows what he would want," she said, as though that was what Coach was asking. "Maybe we could find something in his room that would give us some clue about what to do for him. But I just can't bear to go in there. Not yet."

As she spoke, Patsy stared at the far wall. Coach followed her gaze to the portrait of Tommy, his senior picture, next to one taken a year later of his sister. The photo of Emmalynn, most likely taken at the town park, showed a girl who looked confident enough to do anything. Her chin was bit sharp, like that of a Disney witch, but Emmalynn was beautiful, with straight, shoulder-length blond hair and pale eyes like her father's.

The framed photo of Tommy was nothing like the one next to it. He had his mother's darker features. The photographer would have told him to look natural. Instead, the teenager looked like he was minutes away from his execution. His mouth was slightly agape and his teeth showed, as though he had attempted to smile. It looked like a pained grimace instead.

In the picture, Tommy leaned against the rear tire of a cabbed John Deere tractor. Farm equipment was a popular backdrop for boys getting their senior portraits taken, but the Klimps did not farm. As far as Coach knew, Tommy had never done farm work for anyone else. He wore a Viking helmet in the portrait, which made him look even more out of place.

"He had his peculiarities," Patsy said, reading Coach's mind. "He wasn't a bad boy, though."

Coach thought killing six unarmed men during their lunch break was the dead-on definition of bad, but this was no time to quibble.

"Here's something you could do for us," Bob said, leaning forward with hands on knees. "Here in a week or so, I'd like to express our regrets to the town. I thought about writing a letter to the West Fork paper, but that strikes me as kind of weak. So then I was thinking we could ask families of the victims, and anyone else who wanted to come, to show up at the church some night so I could talk to everyone face to face. To tell them how truly sorry we are."

"I don't know, Bob," Coach began.

"You'd be a complete fool to do that," Patsy said. She continued to stare impassively at her son's portrait, but Coach could see her ears reddening. "We need to do just the opposite. We need to stay out of sight and deal with our shame in private."

"I'd disagree…" Bob began, but Patsy cut him off.

"No," she said with firmness that Coach assumed Bob had heard many times. Her tone indicated the discussion was over.

The three sat silently for another minute.

"Well, how about if I take care of things with the funeral home?" Coach asked. "I'm over there quite a bit anyway."

Bob flinched. Coach knew his words had hit home, as they aroused the image of six dead men freshly embalmed. But Coach felt no sympathy. The Klimps had a right to mourn, and Coach would help them the best he could with that. But their son had committed a horrific act. And for that the Klimps had to feel pain. Lots of it. At some point in the future, they could be redeemed. That was the way these things were supposed to work, Coach believed. He didn't make the rules.

"We appreciate the offer to help with the funeral," Bob said. "But you don't need to be involved. You got your hands full helping the others."

"I can still say a few words at the burial site, if that's what you need," Coach said. He hoped the Klimps would decline his offer.

"There won't be a site," Bob said. "We've decided to have him cremated. It would be for the best if folks around here didn't have to be reminded of what he did every time they saw his grave."

"That's a wise choice," Coach said, feeling some relief. "I've already heard some grumbling about burying him in the town cemetery. You know how folks can be."

The three sat silently for a moment.

"Is Emmalynn on her way back?" Coach asked.

"We told her to stay away awhile," Bob said.

Patsy snorted. "She didn't need a lot of convincing," she said. "She's humiliated. Ashamed of us."

"Do you blame her?" Bob asked.

Coach felt he had stayed the minimum required time and stood to leave. "Be sure to call if I can do anything at all," he said. The offer was his habit at the end of visits. He wouldn't cry over it if the Klimps didn't call.

Bob stood, too, but Patsy remained seated. She still hadn't taken her gaze from the portrait of the mass murderer she had birthed.

"You could find out why Maesie Mattsen's hasn't been arrested," Patsy said. "She's the reason all this happened."

10

The underside of the Mattsen house provided lodging to a legion of granddaddy longlegs and cellar spiders, but the one human and all other creatures had learned to accommodate each other. A mama cottontail had a warren farther from the porch, back near the southwest corner. She was none too happy with Maesie's presence, but the rabbit had thus far chosen to tolerate the human interloper. Her brood was more complacent about it.

Maesie would stay under the house until someone came to knock it down. Because she wasn't a sound sleeper, she did not have to fret about being caught by surprise. Still, she wondered what would happen if the house was knocked down with her still under it. Who would notice? She was small enough it might be several days before someone detected the smell of rotting flesh. Worse, the demolition crew might dig a hole somewhere on the property and push the debris in it. Then no one would ever know what happened to poor Maesie Mattsen. She guessed they wouldn't care much either.

A car pulled into the short dirt driveway on the east side of the house. Maesie could see nothing but the tires, but she knew by the smooth sound of the engine it wasn't Cahill's machine.

The car door slammed and Maesie saw feet, a woman's, approaching at a near tiptoe pace. First, the porch, and then the front door. Rotting footboards and cross supports separated the woman on the porch from the woman below. Maesie listened as the interloper knocked lightly, followed by silence, and another series of knocks, a little harder this time.

"Hello?" said the disaffected voice.

What is she doing here?

Maesie smelled a lighted cigarette. Diane Olstad had paused to take a drag. Maesie now followed the sound of the footsteps as the woman walked from one end of the porch to the other. Diane stopped to knock on the door again. Getting no response, she tried the door, which was unlocked, as always, and stepped inside.

Maesie heard the steps grow fainter as the woman went through the kitchen, opened the back door, and called Maesie's name again. After walking slowly through the house, Diane returned to the front porch.

Maesie kept still as the woman stopped. "Maesie? Are you down there?"

Maesie tried to hold her breath, hoping the interloper would leave before her lungs began to burn.

"Maesie?" Diane repeated, stepping off the porch into the grass. She did not yet kneel to look under the porch.

Maesie let out the air. "What do you want?" she asked.

A cigarette butt landed on the dried grass. A wisp of smoke curled upward, but a black shoe quickly snubbed the butt.

"I remember you used to practically live under there," Diane said. "Like you were part mole."

Maesie said nothing.

"It's going to be another hot one," Diane said.

"You just came by to give the weather report?" Maesie asked.

"Not particularly," Diane said.

Maesie studied the woman's ankles and feet. Diane wore navy slacks—Maesie could see that much—with pumps. The slacks were on the high-water side, revealing thick hose the color of caramel. Diane used to dress a lot prettier, Maesie remembered.

"If you're here for an apology, I'll give it to you from in here," Maesie said.

She heard the crackle of cigarette pack cellophane and the click of a lighter. A silence that began as a brief pause extended until it became uncomfortable for both women. Each wished the other would cut through the amorphous thickness between them. The longer the silence grew, however, the more reticent to break it each woman became.

Maesie did not know Diane well, though her father and Diane's husband were always *somewhere* together. As much as the two men orchestrated in communion the rise and fall of their families' welfare, the families had never been close.

Maesie and Diane both felt abandoned by men who loved the road and the liberty it brought more than they loved their kin. Both women now experienced the deep sting of sorrow brought on by the deaths of those who loved them most: Charmin for Maesie and Luke for Diane. But Maesie refused to see that. Instead, she focused on the notion that Diane Olstad used to be the prettiest and most popular woman in Smackdab. Though Diane now looked like a scarecrow and drank enough vodka to keep every potato farmer in Idaho digging spuds year-round, Maesie still saw her as she once was. She saw a woman who always looked the other way any time she encountered Maesie walking down the road. Just like everyone else in Smackdab.

Diane broke the silence. "I brought you some food," she said.

This unexpected news interested Maesie. "Yeah? What kind?"

"The kind that's edible, as far as I can tell," Diane said. "But I haven't examined it too close. People've been bringing dishes by ever since the news. These are folks who hadn't said word one to me in ten years. All of a sudden I'm pitiful Diane Olstad. I don't know what it is about people that makes them prepare a casserole as soon as they hear someone's parted their earthly confines."

"Nobody brought me a thing," Maesie said.

"Of course not," Diane said. Maesie could tell the way Diane's ankles trembled that she was shaking her head. "It's easier to extend kindnesses once someone's died. A lot easier than when they're alive."

"I think it's more than likely because I am who I am, and they think I got everyone killed."

"Yeah, well…" Diane paused as though she had forgotten her point. Maesie wondered how far into her daily bottle the woman had progressed.

"Anyway," Diane eventually continued. "I can't eat all this food, and I thought I'd spread the bounty."

Maesie had little appetite since the shootings and less food in the house to meet it. At the mention of food now, she felt an empty pang in her gut.

"How generous," Maesie said. She wanted Diane to sense the sarcasm, but not so much she took her food and went home.

"All right," Diane said, taking a step away from the porch. "Come on out and help me with it."

"Can't you just slide something in here?"

"It's got to be awful dirty in there. Not exactly sanitary."

"I've eaten everything from bananas to apple pie and ice cream in here," Maesie said. "I can do just fine with whatever you got."

"All right then."

Diane returned from her car and got down on her knees. She slid two containers toward Maesie, one a covered Tupperware bowl and the other a round baking dish. "One's cold fried chicken and other's ham," she said. "That's the only finger food I brought. Unless you've got a set of china under there, this might have to do."

Maesie opened the Tupperware container and grabbed a chicken thigh. She attacked it like a ravenous wolf. The chicken was a little salty, but otherwise tasted good.

Maesie was now positioned where Diane could see her face better. The older woman, down on all fours like a dog on point, watched her eat. Maesie motioned to the food with the half-eaten thigh. "Help yourself."

"I don't have much appetite these days," Diane said. "I'm taking my sustenance in liquid form. As a matter of fact, I got sustained at Snoots this morning. I'm hoping that gets me through the big show at the school. I wasn't going to go, but I figured…"

Diane rose up on her haunches and lighted another cigarette. She held it on her knee with her bony fingers, which looked like the legs of a dead spider.

Maesie took a bite of ham. "I appreciate the food," she said between chews. "I still don't guess that's the main reason you came here."

"I reckon it's as good as any," Diane said.

More silence followed as Maesie gnawed a chicken bone and Diane drew down her cigarette.

"I wish I had gotten to know Luke better," Maesie said, taking a breath. "He was always nice to me, and everyone liked him."

"Yeah," Diane said. "I don't know how he turned out like he did. He didn't have the finest upbringing, and his genes were nothing to brag about either." She went silent for a moment. "He was smart as a whip, too. He was taking some of those online college courses and doing quite well. I thought he might someday become a teacher or something like that."

With the other woman lost in thought again, Maesie scooted forward to study her face. There were only traces of Diane's former beauty. Her face was so dry and tight around her small mouth that she looked like a dried potato. Women of a certain age in Smackdab once held up a younger version of Diane as the epitome of beauty. Some admired her as they also despised her for her genetic good fortune. But genetics could not hold back time, the ravages of alcoholic abuse or a bad marriage.

"I guess if you've got no ride, you could catch one with me," Diane asked.

Maesie froze with a piece of ham half way to her mouth. "Ride to what?"

"To the big farce at the school. I figure it ought to be quite a performance."

"I'm staying put," Maesie said, wondering why Diane Olstad would want to bring *her* to the service. "Besides, I don't need all those widows and everyone staring at me."

"Apply whatever guilt to yourself that feels right," Diane said, standing to leave.

"What's that supposed to mean?"

"Some people wear guilt like an expensive necklace they want everyone to see. I catch myself doing it sometimes."

"You're saying that's what I'm doing?"

Diane didn't answer.

"All right then," Maesie said. "Thanks for the food. Now don't let the door hit you in the ass."

"I guess there was one more thing I needed to tell you," Diane said. "I imagine Skunk will be coming back around real soon. You might not make yourself so easy to find."

11

Most of the town has turned out for the memorial service at the high school. There's a cousin from out of town on Skunk's side of the family I haven't seen since we were little kids. She looks the same, just plumper. That must be her husband with her. He's frowning like it wasn't his idea to come to this. All my grandparents are dead, but I have a great aunt who just walked in and took a seat on the bleacher side of the gym. She and Mom don't talk much, but it was nice of her to come.

All the widows have arrived. The only family member missing now is Mom. Bob Klimp is nowhere to be seen, of course, but the other janitors set up folding chairs in neat rows on the gym floor, with a center aisle, just as they do each year for graduation. The first and second rows are reserved for our immediate families. The folding chairs filled up fast, and latecomers have started to sit on the east bleachers.

Sharon Sandstrum, her face so ashen she looks like an apparition, is sitting on the left side of the front row in the chair closest to the center aisle. Sharon always looks like she's one gasp away from a collapsed lung. She has her oxygen tank sitting at her feet just like always. I can't remember the last time I saw her out and about. Her emphysema, or whatever she has, keeps her indoors most of the time. She's not talking to or looking at anyone, including her children and grandchildren who sit by her.

On the west side of the gym, next to the stacked telescoping bleachers, there's a large area roped off for media, but only a couple TV cameras are positioned there. Memorials for mass shooting victims don't make interesting news like they used to.

The third row of folding chairs on the gym floor have been reserved for all the big wheels—the ones who believe they're essential to the occasion. A tall man in a gray suit and an expensive haircut looks familiar. I think he's our congressman.

Five minutes before the start of the service in the high school gym, Coach and the town's part-time mayor and full-time real estate agent, Darvia Melgaard, took their seats on either side of the podium. Since high school, Darvia had her hair styled like vintage Farrah Fawcett. Darvia was in her early forties, and Coach guessed she now had a little help from L'Oreal.

The American flag hung limp from a pole on one side of the podium, and the state flag matched it on the other side. A drone of voices and a few shushed laughs filled the large space. Such was the nature of most funerals Coach officiated. Though solemn events, they provided an opportunity for those who didn't frequently cross paths to catch up with each other. Even the murders of six men couldn't deny what was a large social event.

Darvia leaned back in her chair so she could see Coach on the other side of the podium.

"Too bad it takes something this horrendous to get everyone to school," she said.

Coach nodded.

"I envy you today," the mayor said.

"Oh?"

"Everyone here is going to listen to you like they never have before," Darvia said. "And you get to comfort them and give them hope."

Coach grunted. If the town expected comfort from him at the service, they were barking up the wrong ecclesiastical tree. He was a so-so preacher, and made worse by nervousness.

Harp Denbo, garbed in a light gray summer weight two-piece suit, sat with his wife high in the east bleachers. Coach wondered why Lesley Denbo, who wore a sleeveless though conservative black dress, attended the funeral. As far as he knew, she was not acquainted with any of the dead men or their families. Judging by her sour expression, she also wondered why she was present.

Coach leaned back in his seat. "Harp Denbo may be after your job," he said, smiling at the mayor. "He's sitting up in the bleachers like he's lord of the realm."

Darvia laughed. "Why would he want my position? Is it because there's no salary, or because I have to go to the Kiwanis lunch every month and force down the rubber chicken?" She scanned the bleachers until she spotted the Denbos. "I'd be tempted to hand the mayor's job over to him if he actually lived in town. Especially if he wanted to give this speech for me."

This surprised Coach. He assumed Darvia was much more eager than he was to speak to the entire town. She may have been an unpaid politician in a tiny community, but she was still a politician. Darvia seemed to read his mind.

"There's no words I can say to make any of this better," she said, studying the mourners in the front row. "Nothing to say, nothing to do. It's all meaningless, isn't it?"

Coach shrugged. He agreed, but he couldn't say so.

He again swept his eyes over the crowd, this time to see if he could spot Maesie Mattsen. He hoped he would not. Coach had left teaching by the time she reached high school. He often saw her walking through town, her hair wild and her face serious with deep thoughts of whatever, but he could not remember ever speaking to her. Until the machine shop murders, he had known two facts about her: She was a dwarf, and she was Rolf's Mattsen's kid. Not a great résumé for success. Now, there was a third item on the list: She had become Smackdab's version of a femme fatale.

Three minutes past two o'clock, Coach looked at Darvia, raising his eyebrows to ask the silent question of when he should start. Diane was the only immediate family member missing, not counting Skunk. Coach had always had a thing about starting on time. Every church service he preached, every practice he led, and every class he taught had started on the dot. It was rude to the other families to delay now.

Just as he was about to stand for the opening prayer, the hum of the gym quieted as Diane entered from the back. She still wore the same rumpled navy pantsuit, which was the clothing she had worn since the day of the killings. Rather than wither from the focus of everyone in the building, Diane walked with certainty to the front, as though no one else were present. She sat in the empty chair at the west end of the first row.

With all key family members present, Coach stepped to the podium. He had written nothing, because he could think of nothing equal to the enormity of the occasion. He hoped God would put the appropriate words in his mouth, but he didn't count on it. He stumbled through the prayer quickly, but he did not know if it had made sense. A young woman from *The Weekly Standard*, the only fulltime reporter on staff at the West Fork paper, had arrived early to get a seat in the second row. Coach noticed her taking notes as he intoned *Amen*. Perhaps Coach would read what he had prayed when the paper came out on Friday.

The funeral home had arranged for Mike Cuddy, the high school vocal teacher, to sing a few hymns. Coach had asked him to sing four of them, but Mike, who did not care for religious songs, offered to do two. He only knew a handful, he said. Coach negotiated three, agreeing that Mike didn't have to sing *The Old Rugged Cross*, which the teacher despised.

Following the vocal teacher, seven elderly men, the remaining members of the American Legion post's brass band, played *Taps* on their cornets and trombones. They would repeat their performance several more times at the cemetery.

Then came the mayor's turn. Coach hoped Darvia would say something encouraging and inspirational to take some of the pressure off him. However, she had only one piece of paper, which she unfolded as she stepped to the podium. Coach could tell the mayor's message would be brief.

For a realtor, Coach thought, Darvia was not a half-bad public speaker. The mayor knew how to hold an audience's attention. Her voice rose and fell with perfect rhythm, exhibiting sorrow, sympathy and hope at the right moments.

"Our community's loss is first a profound personal loss to the family and the friends and loved ones of our fellow citizens," she said. "To those they have left behind—the mothers, the fathers, the wives, brothers, sisters, and yes, especially the children—all of Smackdab, and indeed the world, stands beside you in your time of sorrow.

"What we say today is only an inadequate expression of what we carry in our hearts. Words pale in the shadow of grief; they seem insufficient even to measure the brave sacrifice of those you loved and we so admired. Their truest testimony will not be in the words we speak, but in the way they led their lives and in the way they lost those lives—with dedication, honor and an unquenchable desire to be hard workers. Thank you."

Coach allowed himself a thin smile, because Darvia had nailed it. She refolded the paper and sat down. Coach heard several sniffles among the crowd. A few family members dabbed tears. Except for changing a few words, the mayor had read verbatim part of Ronald Reagan's speech following the *Challenger* shuttle disaster. Coach knew the speech because he had taught it to his senior Twentieth Century History classes for many years. Darvia had been a student in one of those classes. He felt a jolt of pride that she had remembered its importance, and he wondered if any other former students in the crowd that day recognized it. Coach wished he had thought to plagiarize something as good.

After Mike Cuddy finished singing *Abide with Me*, it was Coach's turn. First, he read from the third chapter of Ecclesiastes about there being a time to be born and a time to die and all the rest of it. Grievers of a certain age would have *Turn! Turn! Turn!* by The Byrds stuck in their heads the rest of the day.

When Coach finished with the text, he looked slowly at each person in the front row, starting at the left and moving to the right. He wanted to make eye contact with each person. In some cases, he might give a warm smile, something comforting as if to say:

God is with you and it will be all right.

However, some of the bereaved did not return his look, instead staring at the gym floor as though still stupefied by the events that brought them together. Leon Wesbecker's widow had to be sedated with Xanax to make it through the day. When Coach came to Diane, she held his gaze. Rather than a pathetic, beaten woman who was self-medicated, he saw a woman who looked at peace. He could not reconcile this image with the most recent one of Diane at the tavern.

Coach reset himself. This was the most important event in his life, bigger than any football game or any service he had led in church. But he could summon nothing to inspire or to comfort. He had been foolish to expect the spirit to wash over him and give him the right words to say. Such a thing had never happened to him before, and it would not occur now.

Coach had written on a slip of notepaper a few points he wanted to make, but nothing else. Therefore, he resorted to the same bland words he used at every funeral he had ever conducted. In short, his message was:

God knows our pain. He will be with us always.

Some people in town had heard the same message four or five times over the years. His sermon, which was no more than a homily, lasted at most five minutes. It provided nothing to address anyone's sorrow.

The bereaved families had agreed that one friend or family member representing each victim would come to the podium to say a few words. Some of the representatives did not understand the meaning of "brief." Roger Sandstrum's oldest child, Dustin, was the first to speak. Before a family member of another victim could approach the podium, a middle-aged man, a Sandstrum cousin, came up front to say more. He did not introduce himself, assuming that everyone should know him. But Coach could see several grievers in the bleachers looking at each other with bewilderment. The cousin spoke for ten minutes. This precedent gave the other families permission to send up additional speakers. Each took advantage of the opportunity.

Nearly two hours after the sharing/eulogy portion of the service began, Diane's turn came, the last to go. But she initially stayed seated. After a half-minute that seemed much longer, she stood and approached the front like a slow-moving pack mule. As she faced the crowded gym, she cleared her throat and looked down. Then she looked up again at hundreds of faces looking her way.

In a low voice that would have been impossible to hear for even those in the front row without a sound system, she said: "That didn't turn out quite the way we expected, did it?"

Coach wasn't sure if she if she meant the murders or the lengthy service.

"I don't know about you, but I could use a drink," Diane said. Instead of returning to her seat, she walked out the way she had come in.

12

While most everyone in town was at the high school, Bob and Patsy Klimp left their house for the first time since the crime. The medical examiner completed the autopsy that morning. Authorities were ready to release the body. Bob had called the funeral home to ask what the procedure was for getting Tommy ready for cremation, but he got the answering machine. No one had called back. Bob understood it was the busiest day in the history of the Smackdab funeral home.

The drive of more than twenty minutes to West Fork, which they usually made once or twice a week, seemed much longer than usual.

"Maybe we ought to stop by Wal-Mart and get some new clothes," Patsy said.

"For?"

"For Tommy. I don't want him in one of those Rage Against the Machine T-shirts he's always wearing."

"He's going to be cremated," Bob said.

"He's not going that way naked."

Bob's mouth twitched as he thought about what he wanted to say and what he should say. Best not to annoy Patsy, he decided.

"If that's what you want," he said.

As he drove, Bob remembered when Tommy was eleven. He had tried out for the town baseball team. Again. The better players Tommy's age had made Smackdab's only Little League team the year before. Most, like Tommy, had been relegated once again to the Pee Wee team with the younger kids. This year, though, all but the worst of the lot in Tommy's grade would make the Little League squad.

Tommy surprised Bob one evening by asking him to hit and pitch to him.

"I read where if you practice long enough, you can get good at anything," Tommy said.

Bob was tired and sore from work, but he didn't mind. Tommy had never asked him to play sports. Tommy had never seemed interested in improving himself athletically. He had played baseball and a little basketball as a child, but he always appeared more content to sit on the bench during the games, seldom interacting with the other boys.

Bob had never been much of an athlete, and he had regretted it. He had hoped there was still a chance for Tommy.

"I'll play as long as you want," Bob said. "Any night you want."

They did. Bob hit and pitched to Tommy every night it didn't rain the two weeks before the tryout. Bob had fun, and he thought Tommy did, too. He was no Derek Jeter, but Tommy had improved, especially as a hitter.

Because he was genetically slow, Tommy had learned the farther he hit the ball, the better his chances of getting on base. With the equipment shed behind him to block most hits, Bob pitched to his son, who began to hit the baseball so hard that he put a few dings in the shed's aluminum siding.

The evening of the tryout arrived. The Little League coach was Leon Wesbecker, who had just come in from the field and still wore his overalls. Wesbecker had coached Little League so long it was rumored he taught Ty Cobb the hook slide. Bob watched as the coach divided the boys into two parallel lines to play catch. Tommy wasn't that good at throwing and catching, but he caught most of the balls thrown to him from the player across from him. Tommy's partner only had to chase a couple errant throws. That was okay, Bob thought, because Tommy would show his skill in the batter's box.

After five minutes of catch and toss, Wesbecker stopped everyone and called out four or five names, including Tommy's. "You boys can go on home now," the coach said. "You'll be hearing from the Pee Wee coach." Tommy was two years older than the other boys named.

As they drove home, Tommy pouted. Bob was so angry he imagined hooking Leon Wesbecker's overalls to the end of a wrecking ball chain, with the shitheel still in them, and slamming him up against a brick wall until he became mush. It was not like Bob to have such feelings, but he was infuriated that Tommy did not get a fair chance. Bob could not figure what Wesbecker was trying to compensate for by dashing the hopes of little kids who just wanted to play baseball with their peers.

"You're as good as half those boys out there," Bob said to his son. "If you want, I could give Mister Wesbecker a call and see if you can't get a chance to hit for him," Bob said.

"I don't care," Tommy said. He did not sound enthused. He seemed okay with what had occurred.

"You should care," Bob said, keeping his eyes on the road and his voice calmer than he felt. "You can't let people walk all over you."

"I don't even like baseball," Tommy said, looking out the window so that Bob could not see his face.

Bob thought he still might give Wesbecker a call. Perhaps it would not get Tommy on the team, particularly if Bob said what he really thought, but it would make him feel better.

By the time they arrived home, Bob decided to be the adult. He had to let Tommy figure out for himself that the world was filled with assholes, like men who were more worried about the win-loss record of a team of eleven-year-olds than giving all boys that age an equal chance to be part of the team.

The Pee Wee team could have acquired the best hitter they had seen in years, but Tommy quit baseball. He never picked up a glove or bat again. Bob hoped he would try sports when he reached high school, but Tommy had already become reclusive. It had nothing to do with the baseball tryout, Bob knew, but he still wished he had made the boy play with the little kids that year. Perhaps Tommy would have learned something from it. Even now, though, Bob could not imagine what that would have been.

"You're awful quiet," Patsy said as they entered West Fork on the way to the hospital. "What are you thinking about?"

"I was just now trying to remember the last thing I said to Tommy. I can't recall if I said good night to him through his door. I hope I did."

Patsy said nothing.

Bob changed the subject. "I tried to call Emmalynn last night, but I got voice mail. I didn't leave a message. She says she hates voice mail. I should have texted her."

"She ought to be here to say goodbye to her brother," Patsy said.

"I thought we agreed she should stay at school to avoid this mess."

"She's being selfish," Patsy said. "All she cares about is her friends at college. About her life away from us."

"That's pretty typical of a twenty-year-old, Patsy. Don't go saying your daughter's selfish simply because I told her to stay away until the dust settles."

"Fall classes will start soon," Patsy said. "Then we won't see her until Christmas, if then. I bet she'll get invited on a ski trip by one of her rich friends."

"I think you're getting ahead of yourself," Bob said. He parked in the visitor's area at the hospital and stared at the main entrance. "Where do you think we ought to go?" he asked his wife.

"It's in the basement, the place where they keep the bodies," Patsy said. "I did some wandering around when Mom was here."

They sat a few minutes longer before Bob opened his door. "Better get it done," he said.

The volunteer at the main desk, a peach-haired elderly woman in a beige frock, did not look up from her magazine when they entered. That was a small blessing to the Klimps, who did not want to draw attention. A handful of tired-looking persons occupied the short-backed chairs in the main waiting area. After a quick glance at the Klimps, all went back to their phones and other distractions.

Patsy led the way to the public elevators around the corner. She had come to know the hospital well when her mother had been brought there to die four years earlier. Bob was less familiar with it.

At the end of a dimly lighted hallway in the basement were double metal swing doors, each with a round cruise ship window. On the wall next to the door, a black plastic sign with white lettering verified they had found the morgue.

"You think we ought to knock?" Bob asked. "They never show this part in TV shows."

"I don't guess it matters," his wife said, pushing through the doors.

They entered a small, chilly room with barely enough space for a gray metal desk and a matching shelf that was crammed with documents and stuffed manila folders. On the far side of the desk was another door. A buzzer next to the door read "Buzz for Attendant." Bob pushed the buzzer, which wasn't a buzz, but more like an old telephone ring.

A minute later, a chubby man in sea foam green hospital scrubs came to the door. He opened it just enough to stick the upper part of his body through. The name badge on his scrubs identified him as H. Copasz.

"Help you?" he asked.

"We're here to see our son," Patsy said, adding, "Thomas Klimp."

The man nodded. "Usually, the funeral home takes care of this so you don't have to see him until he's fixed up."

"They're tied up right now," Patsy said. "Can I see him?"

Copasz hesitated. Bob noticed that he hadn't shaved in a few days. Tommy used to be that way. The man wasn't much older than Tommy.

"The M.E.'s not here right now." he said. "He's pretty worn out from all the autopsies. We just finished with the killer last night."

Bob blanched, but Patsy's resolute expression held.

"We'll just take a moment," Patsy said. "I need to see him."

Copasz came the rest of the way into the office and riffled through a stack of folders on the desk. When he found the one tabbed *Klim*, he took out a small stack of papers. "You'll need to sign a couple of things first," he said. "I'll fill in the rest later. We're a little behind on paperwork. We're not used to dealing with so many bodies at one time."

"You got his name spelled wrong," Patsy said. "It's 'Klimp' with a 'p.'"

"I'll fix it later," Copasz said, though he would forget. "Wait here while I get the body ready."

When Copasz summoned the Klimps into the autopsy room, it wasn't like the ones they had seen in TV shows. There was no partition with a window through which to view the body. Their son lay on a gurney in the middle of the cramped, cluttered room, a sheet covering his body and another white cloth across his forehead. Any signs of trauma, from the gunshot wound or the autopsy, were covered. Copasz stood a few feet back with his hands clasped behind him.

"What's it doing out there?" Copasz asked. "I heard we might get some rain."

He got no answer.

Bob could not look at his son, focusing instead on the pale green walls where hung from a row of hooks an array of horrible-looking instruments that were likely used to cut on Tommy. One looked similar to a saw he had at home in the garage. Several instruments lay arranged on a metal table against the far wall.

To Patsy, Tommy looked more peaceful than she had imagined he could. She didn't want to touch his face, because she knew it would be cold, unreal. Not her Tommy. "What did we do to you, my sweet boy?" she whispered. "Did we make you this way? Was it me? Was it my fault?"

Bob took his wife's elbow. "Maybe we ought to be going," he said.

She pulled away from him. "Not yet."

"I'll be outside then," he said.

When they were back in the car and returning to Smackdab, Patsy said, "I want to have him buried in our plot at the Masonic."

"I thought we'd agreed to the cremation," Bob said. "Out of respect for the other families."

"I can change my mind. I can't bear the idea anymore of him being burned to a crisp. I just can't think of it. I thought I could, but I was kidding myself."

"You know it's not him anymore," Bob said. "Let's think on it some before we make a decision."

"We're going to bury him," Patsy said with finality. "We don't have to let anyone know we're doing it. We won't mark the grave until later. And no one knows where our plot is except one or two on the cemetery board."

"They'll talk," Bob said.

"I want to bury him. That's final."

When Patsy's voice took on a harder edge, like a guard dog making a low gurgle at the approach of a stranger, Bob knew any further argument was pointless. "All right then," he said. "But we should at least have the preacher say a few words over him."

"Guess it won't hurt if you're set on doing it, but words won't do any good at this point."

Burial would cost more than cremation, which worried Bob. He would talk to the funeral home about keeping things economical. Bob was ashamed that insurance was one of the first things that went through his mind when he heard Tommy died. They had taken out a policy for ten thousand dollars on each of the kids when they were children, enough to cover funeral costs if something terrible were to happen. If they had gone with cremation, Bob and Patsy would still have most of the payout after Tommy's body was a taken care of.

They could have used the extra money, too. The superintendent called Bob following the killings to tell him to stay home for a while, with pay. Bob appreciated that, but he knew the arrangement could not go on long. He doubted the school would ever want him back. It had taken him a long time to get the head custodian's job at the school. It was only when Donnie Renfrew, Cahill's daddy, got fired that he got the lead position. Bob had been the one to discover the camera in the girls' locker room when he was repairing a drop ceiling the next room over. Donnie Renfrew should have been arrested, but the school promised to keep the whole thing quiet as long as Renfrew never worked in another school again. The last Bob heard, Renfrew was somewhere in North Dakota, working at a Lutheran church.

Bob would have been at school this day, making sure everything was taken care of for the big memorial service. He suspected school administrators would decide that if they could get by without him, when whole the town would be present, they could do without him entirely. The district always had to look for ways to get by with less.

Bob and Patsy hadn't talked about any of that. They didn't need to, because the situation was obvious. There wouldn't be any other job opportunities in Smackdab for the father of a mass murderer. Because Bob had built their dream home, they wouldn't leave Smackdab. They were stuck. Bob had often thought about starting a small carpentry business, but who would hire him now? It all seemed pointless to think about. The loss of his son in such a way felt like having an arm ripped off. The unrelenting pain overwhelmed all other thoughts.

13

  I was never close to Cahill Renfrew, but I remember when he had a pet coyote. We were in fourth grade. Cahill found the three-legged thing disoriented and hobbling along Route 4 in the center of town. Most people would have avoided the skeletal animal for fear of getting bitten and being turned in to a werewolf, or whatever you call someone possessed by a coyote. If the coyote had not been sick with the mange or something worse, Cahill wouldn't have been able to get near it. The animal put up no fight, and Cahill carried it home. He came to school the next day bragging about how he had captured a wild coyote, and how it really liked Spam. He named it Spider. I don't know why.

  He set about trying to nurse the coyote back to reasonable health, but his dad threatened to put the coyote in a gunnysack and drown it in a pond. Instead, the coyote died two days after Cahill found it. Before Cahill could bury his "pet," Donnie Renfrew drove south of town and slung the carcass in a ditch.

  The next morning, Cahill came to school ready to pick a fight with anyone who looked at him funny. No one did, but our fourth grade teacher, Mrs. Mellwood, who was standing at the dry erase board, asked Cahill why he was late again. Cahill started kicking her in the shins. Mrs. Mellwood, who was about one-hundred-and-twenty years old, stood her ground as she received kick after kick.

  "Stop it, Cahill," she kept saying. "Stop it now."

  Her voice became more pained and wobbly with each kick, but she made no effort to move away from Cahill or forcibly restrain him. All of us kids stayed at our desks and watched with our mouths wide open. Then I came to my senses and ran out to find Bob Klimp. Bob picked up Cahill and carried him from the room. Cahill's toothpick legs were still flailing at air the whole way down the hall.

  Cahill was suspended for five days. When he came back, it was like nothing had happened. Mrs. Mellwood, who before had dressed only in skirts and dresses, wore trousers for a few weeks until her purpled, swollen legs healed. When she began wearing dresses again, we could still see large pale yellow spots on her shins.

COME UP A CLOUD

On the same two-lane ribbon of asphalt twenty miles west of where the Klimps were returning home from the morgue, Cahill Renfrew tried to outrace his rage. He pushed his car near ninety, motoring west on a straight stretch of Route 4. Heat vapors shimmered above its scalding surface.

Cahill had skipped the memorial service at the school. He had attended his grandmother's funeral when he was eight, which had satisfied any need to go to another one. The thing in the casket did not look like his grandma. In the last few weeks of her life, her face had ballooned to twice its normal size because of copious injections. In death, her face was no longer puffy, but there was all that baggy skin with no place to be tucked. She looked like a Shar Pei. Cahill feared the dog-woman in the casket would re-animate, stirred awake by the noise of the mourners who clucked and chuckled in their small groups. Finding his grandmother's face unbearable to see, Cahill had looked at her hands, gloved in something similar to women's sheer hosiery. He thought he saw the thumb of the right hand twitch, but neither his mother nor anyone else standing with him seemed to notice. He had nightmares for weeks afterward.

Now, as his mother wailed over Denver Moss at the Smackdab cemetery, the last shovel of clayed soil tamped on his grave, Cahill pushed the accelerator to the floor. Although relieved that the six men were finally being buried, he could feel Tommy's presence above ground, his spirit elusive.

Cahill couldn't figure out why he let Maesie bother him. The time she had dated Tommy Klimp was a good case in point. It had infuriated him, and for no good reason that he could see. Letting it get to him only irked him more.

Cahill had known Maesie practically his entire life, since first grade anyway. That didn't make her anything special. He had known a lot people nearly his whole life and he could easily go weeks without thinking about them. But Maesie? Something about her stuck to him like bubble gum on the sole of his boot.

Cahill tried to focus on the road in front of him. It proved difficult on account of his fury and the half bottle of Jim Beam he had gone through so far. He had found the nearly full bottle of bourbon among items Denver had left at the house. It was some kind of miracle his mother hadn't found and downed the Beam first. Cahill seldom drank, but it now felt like an appropriate use of his time.

Cahill's car, a used and abused Crown Vic he had picked up at a police auction in West Fork, pulled significantly to the left. Keeping it off the centerline required effort. Still, Cahill loved the car, the most expensive item he owned. He had spray-painted over the original white with a dull charcoal gray. It had taken him twenty cans of Krylon. Even then, he'd missed a few spots.

The auctioned cruiser still had its spotlight, which Cahill used to light up gophers after dusk. He kept a .22 rifle in the trunk to ping the vermin when the mood struck, but he saw something better, a bicyclist a few hundred yards ahead. That section of road, about five miles west of town, was the widest and best-maintained two-lane highway in the county. Delivery trucks and a handful of commuters used the road weekdays, but traffic quieted in the evening. However, traffic on Route 4 had picked up noticeably since the shootings. People who had no business near Smackdab came through to see if there was blood spattered on the exterior of the machine shop. Those people would always associate Smackdab with the murders, the thought of which burrowed itself under Cahill's skin and ate at him. The cyclist had to be one of those ghouls, Cahill guessed. Someone who had never heard of Smackdab until a few days earlier, and who decided he would pedal through town on his way to some latte-drinking froufrou city in the Northwest.

Cahill pushed the accelerator to ninety-five mph. He edged the car to the right so the passenger-side wheels gripped the shoulder. The man on the bike, who had heard thousands of vehicles speeding from behind him, knew what was coming and how fast. He had nowhere to go but into the ditch. Just before the Vic passed, the cyclist negotiated the ledge of the ditch and somehow managed to keep going without falling. Cahill looked over his shoulder expecting to see the bike upended in the ditch and lycra-clad limbs flailing in every direction. Instead the rider, still upright and back on the road, flipped him the finger.

Cahill hit the brakes and slotted the Vic in reverse. The tires burned tread as the sedan screamed back toward the cyclist. Cahill parked the car straddling the white center line and left the engine running. He hurried around the Vic, moving like a speed walker, his cowboy boots clacking on the asphalt.

The other man straddled his bike with his arms folded like he was waiting at a traffic light. Cahill didn't know anything about bicycles, but he guessed this was an expensive one weighing less than a pinky. It wouldn't take much effort from Cahill to bust it into tiny pieces. Cahill was barely five-six and one-thirty if he ate a large meal. He had been called a peewee a few times, but he thought of himself as wiry. He did not fear the cyclist, who outsized him by sixty pounds and half a foot.

"You almost killed me, you asshole," the cyclist said, though his tone was flat.

"You got no business being here," Cahill said, doubling the other man's decibel level.

"What? You mean on this public road? Read the law, asshole. I have just as much right to the road as your gas-sucking tank."

"Maybe you don't get the news where you're from," Cahill said, now ten feet from the cyclist. "We tend to get pretty violent with people we don't like around here."

"Oh yeah, I heard all right. I'm not surprised. You rednecks know only one way to solve your problems."

"I'm really going to enjoy kicking your ass," Cahill said.

"There are talkers and there are doers," the cyclist said. "Which one are you?"

It enraged Cahill more that the man still seemed calm. His voice did not rise above a conversational pitch.

"Oh, I'm a doer all right," Cahill said. He pounded a clinched fist into the palm of the other. He felt angry enough to eat the cyclist for supper, stretchy shorts and all. "After I get through with you, I'll take your pretty little bicycle and turn it into fiberglass mulch," he said.

The man took off his leather gloves and reached back to unzip a pouch in his saddlebag. He pulled out a phone.

"You're wasting your time," Cahill said. "You'll be bleeding from every part of your pussy body before the cops get here."

"I want to take a picture of you and your car before we start this little tussle," the man said, taking a photo of Cahill with the Vic in the background. "I'm sending it to someone just in case you try to pull a fast one on me. I don't mind fighting, if you have your heart set on it. But if you try to pull a gun or a knife when you see how bad I'm kicking your tail, you'll be in jail before you can spell *whoop-ass*. In your case, I guess that would be about two days."

The man laid his bike on its side in the grass and hooked his sunglasses on the handlebar. Instead of waiting to see if Cahill was serious about fighting, he made two swift strides forward and kicked Cahill in the nuts. Cahill bent over, already screaming as though his testicles were hanging from the thinnest sinew. While Cahill's head was down, the cyclist grabbed a shock of his wispy hair in each hand and yanked downward into his raised knee. Blood spurted from Cahill's nose, down his shirt and onto his jeans. He fell to the pavement like a rag doll.

"You fucking asshole," Cahill groaned, supporting himself on one elbow. "You jumped me."

"I was in front of you the whole time," the cyclist said.

With nose blood dripping steadily down his cheeks, Cahill lay on his back.

Satisfied he had made his point, the man, who had kept on his helmet should Cahill get in a lucky swing, shook free strands of blond hair from his hands and slipped on his gloves. He righted his bicycle. Cahill remained prone, groaning and clutching his groin like he suffered a severe urinary tract infection. The cyclist pedaled past him but stopped just beyond the Vic.

"Should you get any ideas about coming after me," the man said. "I carry a lethal weapon for close encounters of the cracker kind."

Back in the Vic, Cahill tried to stanch his nosebleed with a dirty paper towel he had used to check the car's oil. Rust-colored streaks of drying blood made an interesting design on the front of his shirt. He considered getting the rifle from the trunk and chasing down the cyclist. Instead, he took a long draw of bourbon. He then checked the angle of his nose in the rearview mirror. It was likely broken.

An ancient Chrysler Fury, the first vehicle he had seen on the road since stopping, approached from the east. Cahill put the Vic in Drive and made a U-turn in the direction of Smackdab without waiting for the Chrysler to pass. The Fury skidded to a stop about twenty feet away, close enough for Cahill to read the mix of fear and anger on the old man's face.

Cahill took a right on Monks Hill Road about a mile from town. Plans he had wavered on earlier now felt like something he had to do. Most houses in that area of the county were old and unoccupied. Smackdab's small growth occurred on the other side of town. Cahill took a left on a gravel road that ran parallel to Route 4 and would eventually lead back to Smackdab. The Klimp place sat on a knoll up the road. Two vehicles were parked on the shoulder.

The Klimp's mailbox, held up by a white-painted four-by-four post on the left side of the road, was the first to get it. Cahill swerved and caught it solidly with the left corner of the car's front bumper. With a crack, the post gave way, sending the metal mailbox and its junk mail contents sailing into the ditch, barely missing a pickup parked halfway in the road. Cahill hit the brakes in the middle of the road and backed into the driveway, which led up to the two-car garage on the left side of the Klimp's house. He maneuvered the car so it straddled the sidewalk leading to the house's front door.

A pair of idiots, Jordy Wakefield and a miscreant from West Fork Cahill knew only as Dirty Dave, leaned against the burr oak that arbored the Klimp's front yard.

"What the hell you standing around for?" Cahill yelled to them as he strutted to the trunk of his car.

"Waiting for a fucktard to show up," Dirty Dave said. "Looks like the wait's over." Wakefield cackled.

Cahill ignored the remark primarily because he couldn't think of a good retort, but he would show who the fucktard was not. He was a man of action.

From the Vic's trunk, he took out an eighteen-gallon plastic storage tub with a cover on top. The weight of the contents, a mix of putrid animal entrails and manure Cahill had acquired from a local farmer, caused the container to shift its shape and the cover to pop off. The contents sloshed on Cahill's shirt and jeans.

"Mary mother of Christ," he yelled. He peered over the roof of the car to see if the men under the tree could see what had occurred. They laughed and shook their heads. Wakefield said something, but Cahill only caught the end of it, which was something about "the sense of a jackass."

Cahill dragged the container and its remaining contents to the front steps of the house and tipped it over. He then took a red gas can from the trunk and dumped its contents on top of the muck.

After returning the emptied gas can and bin to the trunk, Cahill reached through the driver's side window and held down the car horn in a long wail. The Crown Vic had a muscled horn that even his dead grandma could hear.

"You're wasting your time, you dipshit," Dirty Dave yelled. "They ain't home."

Disappointed, but loathe to show it, Cahill pulled a green lighter from his shirt pocket, flicked it, held it high so his audience could see, and tossed it on the ooze. It immediately poofed into a fireball of charbroiled entrails and manure.

In the same motion of tossing the lighter, Cahill hopped in the car, which he had left running, spun out and spewed dirt and grass before he had his door shut. He flipped off the spectators and peeled out when he reached the gravel road.

The odor was so bad inside the car that Cahill had to vomit, but he didn't want to pull over until he was out of sight of Wakefield and Dirty Dave. He didn't make it, spewing a mix of bourbon and breakfast bits down his front. The puke atop the manure atop the blood from his nose created a blended odor that would necessitate multiple showers to remove from his skin. No sense trying, he decided. Once his stomach settled, he would dedicate himself instead to finishing off the Jim Beam.

14

After their short ride in the Explorer, Skunk and Rolf caught a lift in an early-eighties Pontiac Bonneville, yet another vehicle without air conditioning. The grizzled driver also appeared to be in his early eighties. The man wore Wranglers and a blowsy snap-button short sleeve shirt the color of mustard. The man looked clean, but something reeked about him. It was not the odor of sweat or outdoor work, but something that seeped from his innards. Skunk had smelled the odor on others. It indicated diseased lungs that were surrendering to a lifetime of smoking.

The old man was not aware of his own smell. He took off his seed cap and waved it dramatically as though someone had unleashed a soupy fart.

"Lord Almighty. Ain't you fellas seen a shower lately?"

"Good day to you, as well, sir," Skunk said, situating himself and his gear in the front passenger seat.

"What the hell's that smell?" Rolf asked from the back seat.

"That'd be your own self," the old man said. He began to cough as though a chunk of mud were stuck in his lungs and wouldn't come out. After three violent hacks, he spat a stream of odorous phlegm out his window. "Roll down them back windows before we all get ass-fixated," he said.

The driver inspected Skunk from top to bottom. He saw a gaunt man with three days' growth of grayish beard who wore the same jeans and faded red western shirt he had worn five straight days. The man shook his head slightly and made a clucking sound, which caused him to cough violently. When he finished, he said: "There was a time when even hitchhikers took pride in their appearance."

Skunk leaned into the man's gaze and held it, but he said nothing.

"My name's Henry," the driver said, turning his attention to the highway. He put the Pontiac in gear and pulled on to the road. He hadn't bothered to look in his mirror; a Toyota sped past him in the left lane, its driver holding down the horn.

Neither passenger introduced himself. "All right then," Henry said, shaking his head again. He hocked up another lump of ooze. "Coupla friendly types, huh?"

Skunk had looked behind him and saw that Rolf was already settling into a nap. "We're just beat is all," Skunk said.

"I wouldn't know how come," Henry said. "If you're hitching, you must not be working."

Skunk felt with his right hand for the outline of the file in his jacket, which lay on his lap. The old fart was about to set a record for getting on his last nerve the quickest, even faster than the kid in the Explorer. The geezer was headed for the graveyard as it was. Skunk wouldn't mind helping Henry along, but he figured that was his insomnia messing with him.

"How far you headed?" Henry asked.

"As long as you've got the front bumper headed east, we'll ride along."

Skunk removed his hand from the jacket and tilted his head back and closed his eyes to signal he preferred to ride in silence. He wanted to think some about Luke, which he had not done since he heard the news. He had little to think about. They never had a relationship worth noting. When Luke was small, the kid became so excited when Skunk returned from the road that the child jumped around until he came close to hyperventilating. A couple of times, Luke wet his pants. When that occurred, Luke, embarrassed, ran away to hide. Diane chased after the little wetter, ordering him to come back to see his daddy. Before Diane could corral the kid, however, Skunk headed to Snoots. He didn't want to be around a seven-year-old who couldn't hold his bladder. Skunk had once owned an English Pointer that acted similarly. He kept the dog caged behind the house with the idea of training it to pheasant hunt. He never got around to it, and the dog spent its days howling for attention. Every time the dog saw Skunk, it wagged its tail so hard it upended its food and water pans. Like Luke, it couldn't control its bladder, peeing on its spilt food. When Skunk concluded he would never make the dog into a decent pointer, he took it out to Dead Lake. The dog was so excited when Skunk took hold of its neck that it put its front paws on his chest and peed on his shirt. Skunk cut its throat and tossed the carcass in the water.

Skunk did his best to avoid Luke and Diane when he came off the road. Unlike the worthless pointer, Luke got the message quickly. He did his best to avoid Skunk, too.

Henry took Skunk and Rolf nearly fifty miles, all the way to Edwinville, Kansas, a once-thriving grain town that had ceded most of its population to larger towns and cities. It had half dried up three decades earlier. The other half was on its way to the same result whether or not locals chose to accept it. Land was too expensive, fuel prices too high, and grain prices unable to keep up.

Edwinville was small, which meant two strangers carrying guitar cases and duffel bags stood out from the locals. They would particularly stand out to Edwinville's two local police officers, who patrolled the town's streets in reconditioned Ford Tauruses for twelve dollars an hour.

It was early Saturday evening, and what passed for weekend busyness had reached its apex as Saturday shoppers were on their way out of town and cruising teenagers were on their way in, occupying reconditioned Mustangs, hand-me-down Impalas, and half-ton trucks.

The highway widened to four lanes at the city limits. A quarter mile into town, Henry maneuvered into the parking lot of a car wash just short of a traffic light.

"I turn north here," Henry said as they approached a traffic light in the middle of town. He interrupted himself to hock a stream of phlegm out his window. "Unless you want to go that way, I'm letting you off here."

"I don't suppose they got any honky tonks close by?" Skunk asked, as he prepared to slide out. "I'm talking the kind of place where a couple fellas could earn a little pickin' money?"

Skunk didn't mind stealing his daily bread if needed, but Rolf's condition made it increasingly difficult to do that. He could not easily acquire traveling money and babysit Rolf both.

"I'm a tea totaler myself," Henry said. "But there's a bar out east of town. Maybe a mile from here. It changes hands every whipstitch, but I believe it's got a Frenchy name these days. You'll know you're there when you see a bunch of beat-up trucks parked out front and big-bellied customers who could use a good shower and shave. And the fellas ain't so good looking either."

Henry laughed at his own joke.

"Much obliged," Rolf said. "I don't suppose you'd drop us out that way?"

"No, I don't suppose I would," Henry said, putting the old transmission into Drive. "Unless north and east are the same direction on Saturdays. I'm about certain to catch hell from my wife as it is for being late for supper."

After depositing the hitchhikers, the Bonneville pulled back on the road and veered immediately into the left turn lane at the traffic light. Rolf and Skunk stood for a moment with their guitars and bags laying on the pea-graveled lot of the car wash. On top of being beat-tired, Skunk was hungry, thirsty, and anxious to make his way to the honky tonk. Even if they wouldn't be allowed to play a few songs, he had enough money for the duo to get a couple of cold drafts and maybe some fries. Honky tonk fries were usually pretty decent. Those types of places didn't use healthy cooking oil like a lot of places used. And the cook rarely changed the oil, which only added to the flavor.

Rolf watched the Bonneville head north out of sight.

"Who was that old boy?" he asked.

"That was Henry, remember? The old buzzard who gave us a lift into town," Skunk said.

Rolf looked east down the road before doing the same westward. "This don't look like Smackdab," he said.

"That's because it ain't. We're still a good day's travel from home. At the rate we're going, more like two. We need to see if we can find somewhere to play so we can rustle up some traveling money. There's a place on the edge of town Henry says might be worth checking out."

"Who's Henry?"

Skunk looked in his partner's eyes to see if anything was left in there. "Your short-term memory ain't for shit, you know that?"

Rolf cocked his head like a puppy hearing an unfamiliar sound.

"Ah, it don't matter," Skunk said. "But we've got a chance to bang on these six strings."

Rolf smiled and picked up his Taylor case. "Now you're singing a tune I like," he said.

Skunk pulled his hat lower over his brow and glanced up at the clear blue sky that held nothing but the brutal sun still hours away from setting in the west. He studied his traveling mate. Rolf still smiled, but Skunk wondered if he remembered what had pleased him.

They had toured the West as far as New Mexico off and on for the past thirty years. They spent far more time together than with their families. Yet, Skunk had never thought of Rolf as his friend. They made a pretty good duo, however. Their life on the road had seldom been easy, but they never had to get their hands dirty, not with real work. That was worth something. But this was it. The last go-round for Olstad & Mattsen. Skunk couldn't babysit Rolf any longer. Whatever it was, a stroke or some other brain illness that enfeebled Rolf, it steadily worsened. Rolf did all right for now, but how long before he forgot the words to songs he had sung half his life? Or simple chords on his precious Taylor?

It might be most humane to tie a gunnysack around Rolf's head and throw him in a pond when the time came. Or do him like Skunk's old bird dog. That would be better than him being put in some nursing home that smelled like piss and old-people rot. Rolf wouldn't want to go on living with his brain baked like a Sunday meat loaf. Skunk had been with the man long enough to know that. It wouldn't be so bad when the end came, Skunk thought, if he decided to go that direction. He would be doing Rolf a favor.

The men dripped with sweat by the time they reached the roadhouse with the incongruous name of Chez Belle just past the Edwinville city limits. A large man with hands so big they looked like fleshy shovels worked the bar.

"Good evening, sir," Skunk said, doffing his hat while Rolf, keeping his hat on, stood back a few paces. "I've got two questions for you."

"Fire away," the bartender said. His eyes showed no intrigue, as though there was no question he hadn't heard before.

"First," Skunk said. "Could you point me in the direction of the owner or manager of this fine place?"

"You're looking at him," the man said, offering his hand. "Scott Harker."

Skunk shook the man's hand, which made his look like a plastic spoon by comparison.

"Skunk Olstad. Nice to meet you," Skunk said. He thumbed behind him at Rolf. "We're a country duo by the name of Olstad & Mattsen. Had a hit or two back in the day. You may have heard of us. *Get Outta My Dodge* was our biggest hit."

Scott's face showed no sign of recognizing the name.

"Second question," Skunk said. "I don't believe I've ever been in a honky tonk before that had a French name."

Scott wiped a wet spot on the counter with a white hand towel, the towel barely seen as his large hand engulfed it.

"That didn't come across as a question," he said, a small smile beginning to show itself. "But it was my wife's idea. She thought it would be funny to give the place a fancy name. To be ironic, I guess."

"Hmm," Skunk said, nodding like he could see the sense of it. "Mission accomplished, I'd say. I guess her name is Belle."

Scott shook his head. "Nope. It's Krista."

Skunk considered that for a moment. "Well, since you so accurately pointed out that it wasn't a question I asked, let me ask you this: Any chance a couple old troubadours like my buddy and me could play a few songs for your crowd? All we're asking is tip money."

Scott said the bar didn't usually have music, not since the jukebox quit working. After thinking about it a moment, he said, "I guess I don't care one way or another if you play, so long as it ain't rap."

Skunk wiped a hand across his milk-white forehead before putting back on his hat.

"Do we look to you like the kind of fellows who would play rap on our six-strings?"

"I've seen stranger things," the bar owner said.

Scott lent the musicians two bar stools and a pilsner glass for tips, and he let them set up in the corner between the end of the bar and the jukebox. It was still early evening. The sparse crowd was quiet, like early arrivals at a church service.

Skunk considered taking requests, but decided to run through a couple of easy Willie Nelson numbers to make sure Rolf could follow along. That would also help him determine the mood of the audience before deciding where to go from there. Rolf had been better than Skunk at memorizing songs, and more likely to know the words to any requested number. Skunk knew that was about to change.

"Whiskey River, take my mind," Skunk began to sing. It took a measure for Rolf to join in, but he caught up quickly. His voice sounded as good as ever. Skunk's singing voice elicited images of sorrow, as though he had had his heart broken many times. It had an edge to it, but the listener still heard hope in it. Rolf's voice, even after decades of Newports and Beam, carried a lilt of sweetness, like he had not been beaten down by the vagaries of love. Together, the men created a soulful sound that made listeners lonesome for their younger days.

About nine o'clock, the duo took a break. They hadn't made much money. The crowd wasn't well greased enough yet to offer up much cash for requests. Scott had two drafts waiting for them at the bar.

"These are on me," he said. "You guys ain't half bad."

"Then I guess that makes us at least half good," Skunk said.

The bartender laughed as he nodded at the full tables of customers. "I don't usually get this many people this early. Word got around real fast about you fellas, and people were amped up to hear we had live music for a change. Tells me I ought to do it more oftener."

Rolf sat next to Skunk and stared at his beer, but he didn't touch it. Rolf was fine as long as they performed, but he seemed to lose track of where he was as soon as the music stopped. Scott nodded at Rolf.

"He doesn't say much, does he?" the bartender said, as though Rolf weren't present.

"He does most of his talking with his six-string," Skunk said.

"He's not a bad singer neither. I was noticing some of the women giving him the eye."

"It's always been that way," Skunk said, swirling the foam in his quickly downed draft. "He attracts the pretty ones, and I get the dogs." He paused. "But the dogs're a lot more appreciative."

"This might just be your night, then," Scott said. "This bar attracts homely women like Target attracts soccer moms. There'll be more ugly in here than you can poke with a stick before the night's through."

He put another draft in front of Skunk. "I don't know what your plans are, but you could stick around a few more nights as far as I'm concerned. Free beer and all the tips you can make. I got an old couch in the back you could flip for if you want to sleep there. Or you could probably get one of these females to take you home for the night. What do you say?"

"We ain't made much in the way of tips, yet," Skunk said. "This group's tight with their paychecks."

"Just wait awhile. The liquor'll loosen them up awful good before much longer."

Skunk considered the offer. If they could stay put a few days, they might make enough bus money to get to Kansas City. When tips were less than generous, Skunk would occasionally extract funds from clientele by more direct means, provided the target had become sufficiently inebriated. But Skunk was so fatigued he wasn't sure he had the wits necessary to be sly. One of these days, if he didn't get some sleep and he was too busy looking out for Rolf, it would catch up to him. Someone would gut him with a knife or stick a pistol under his chin.

15

Jean Pankin sat on her front porch in the twilight of the day. Other than lightning bugs, which had begun to flicker their whereabouts in the yard, Jean was alone for the first time since the killings. Chelsea had wanted to stay longer following the memorial service and burial, but Jean insisted her daughter return to Council Bluffs. They both had to get on with their respective lives, as hard as that might be for a while.

Soon, Jean would have to turn on the light to see her work. In her lap lay a section of newspaper with a bottle of super glue and seven pieces of a small porcelain rooster. She had knocked the rooster onto the floor while dusting a bookshelf in the living room. Until this day, the memento from the 1968 state fair had lasted nearly fifty years of Jean's clumsiness without a scratch. If it had been any other rooster in the house, Jean would have thrown it away with little remorse. This one was special, however.

When she was a teenager, Jean had collected a few roosters for no reason other than they struck her as something to decorate her room. Family, including her parents, soon noticed her growing rooster inventory and began to give her more of them.

What to give Jean for her birthday?
Let's see if we can find her another rooster.

Jean had nothing against her collection of roosters. She still caught herself noticing old ones in antique shops and consignment stores. She had bought one or two in recent years. And she thought the lawn roosters added a certain love-of-life ambience to the yard. They brightened up the place, even now, in dark times. However, she had never intended them to be a lifelong hobby. It had taken Pink several years to catch on to this. He never said anything to her about it. One day, though, she realized he no longer gave her roosters as surprise gifts.

But it was still early in their courtship when he bought her the rooster that now lay in shards on her lap. Jean and Pink had driven one-hundred-thirty-five miles to the state fair, because Eddie Arnold was in concert there. Neither of them was a fan, but he was a decent compromise. Pink thought Merle Haggard was close to God, although Conway Twitty came close, too. Jean preferred pop and soul to country and western. She had just bought the *Stone Soul Picnic* album by The Fifth Dimension, and it was already wearing out from constant play on the Zenith phonograph at home.

John Davidson was also scheduled to perform at the fair, and Jean would have enjoyed staring at that fine specimen of a man for an hour or more. But Pink said Hell would have to "freeze fifty times over before he'd be caught dead at that kind of concert." Jean was unsure what kind of concert Pink meant. It was a good thing they had trusty Eddie to fall back on.

Before the concert, Jean and Pink strolled the midway. It was humid – just the opposite of Pink's fifty-times frozen-over Hell – and Pink had grabbed a cardboard fan from the Farm Bureau booth so Jean could generate a little breeze on her face as they walked.

People didn't seem to mind the heat so much back then, as Jean remembered it. Few homes had air conditioning. If they had A/C at all, it was the window kind. Jean's family had an attic fan, which provided sufficient cooling most of the summer.

Pink's sixty-three Chevy Bel Air didn't have air either. They had made the trip to the fair with all four windows rolled down and the cabin-turned-wind-tunnel so loud they couldn't hear the AM radio. They were sopped with sweat by the time they parked the car in the grass lot at the fair.

"Would you like a pop?" Pink asked as they passed a concession station.

Jean was still petite in those days, and she consumed without worry.

"Let's wait till we see a snow cone place," she said. "But if the first one we come to doesn't have cherry, we'll keep looking."

The first snow cone cart they came across had cherry. Pink bought one for Jean and a grape for himself. The cone cups quickly became soggy. Syrupy water dripped through the bottom. Jean held hers away from her so the liquid wouldn't drip on her dress, but Pink attacked his like it was the only thing that could keep him cool. A purple stain already formed around his mouth. Jean was about to ask if he needed a napkin when she realized something had caught his eye.

"That booth's got some roosters for sale," he said.

An angular old man in unwashed olive work pants and an equally grimy western-style snap shirt manned the booth. Every snow globe, magnet, plastic fly swatter, and cheap whistle was imprinted with "1968 State Fair" in black all-cap lettering.

The porcelain roosters that caught Pink's attention looked most like Golden Laced Wyandottes. They were about three inches tall and (poorly) painted black and orange. They had googly eyes like they had choked on a worm. Pink picked up one and held it up in the sun like he was examining a valuable object. Jean hoped Pink would not offer to buy it for her, and she was about to tell him so. Then she realized the rooster reminded her of him. His cheeks became rosy, and he got wide-eyed any time he became embarrassed, like when Jean would casually note she was on her period, or, for that matter, mentioning anything to do with human plumbing.

Back then, Pink still held her hand when they crossed a busy street in West Fork. He still opened the car door for her when he remembered to. When he came to court her, he always stood at the threshold to her parent's house, his hands behind his back like he was still in the army, waiting for her mother to welcome him inside.

While Pink continued to study the ugly rooster, the evening sun backlighting it and making it less unattractive, Jean said what was on her mind before she could consider if it was prudent.

"Do you think we'll get married someday?" she asked.

Pink turned his attention to her. Eyes wide, cheeks rosy. "That'd be all right by me," he said with no hesitation. In that brief moment, Jean pictured their long life together: Three or four kids, bunches of grandchildren eventually, a nice house in the country with five or six acres, and the two of them growing old and plump together.

"Then buy me the rooster," she said.

Their life together had its dark moments, the worst being when their younger daughter, Lila, died in a school bus accident. But every family had dark times. Jean believed most of her life with Pink had been good. Perhaps wonderful was not too hyperbolic, she thought.

She wrapped up the newspaper holding the rooster shards and glue. She would try again tomorrow when her eyes and her mind could focus better on the task. She wished the days were shorter. Each one now felt infinite.

16

Tommy is finally being buried, and he's only a touchdown throw away from where my corpse is waiting out the end of time. You are welcome here, Tommy's earthly vessel. No one here bears you ill will. But don't get too comfortable. You won't be here long.

"This is not good, not good at all," said Mark Lathrop, shaking his head as they stood over the open grave at the Masonic Cemetery.

"That's why we're doing this so early," Coach said. "It cuts down on the potential for attention."

The morning teased a weak mist from a nimbus blanket moving through. It was barely enough to dampen the grass in the cemetery, but Lathrop, who had been shaving his head since his early thirties, wore a bone-colored Panama to keep the wet off his bald pate.

Lathrop, a third generation funeral director, had recently taken over full time from his father, who had moved to Montana with his wife to "get away from it all," though there wasn't much in Smackdab to get away from.

The younger undertaker looked haggard. With six—now seven—burials, this had been the busiest week of his life.

"As soon as anyone finds out he's buried here, all heck will break loose," Lathrop said.

Some people avoided cursing around Coach when he became a pastor. That included Lathrop, who was one of Coach's former students and a fullback on the school's 1997 team. Coach had liberally used profanity at practices, so Lathrop had often heard Coach get creative with modern English. When he became a minister, however, many in Smackdab presumed he had become so transformed that he found such talk abhorrent to his sensitive ears.

Coach felt good this morning. Relieved. This would be his last official act as Pastor of Community Church. He would give his notice at the end of Sunday's service. He would quit immediately. None of this two-week notice business. Until they found a permanent replacement, the church board would have to find someone to fill in at the pulpit. There would be plenty of volunteers who would like to preach their version of The Word to the faithful.

It was a few minutes before seven, and Tommy Klimp's casket hovered on a burial-lowering device above the hole. Coach's Volvo and a silver hearse were parked behind them. Before sunrise, Lathrop and four part-time funeral home workers had set the casket in place. By now, all the assistants had told someone else where Tommy was being buried. If not them, Jerry Debs, who sat on his backhoe twenty yards on the other side of the hole, would disseminate the information. Jerry had pulled his greasy Chicago Cubs cap over his eyes, like he was trying to catch a quick nap. More than likely, Coach guessed, the digger nursed a powerful headache he acquired after a long night at Snoots. Coach had seen the man plenty of times at the tavern, and the minister knew him to be a chatty drunk. Coach predicted the whole town would know the location of Tommy's grave by Jerry's third beer of the evening.

When Patsy Klimp made it clear she wanted Tommy buried rather than cremated, Lathrop and Coach double-teamed her in a failed effort to change her mind. Bob had given up trying. When Patsy stood firm, the two men suggested burying Tommy somewhere outside the county. No, Patsy said. She would need to visit the grave frequently. Having lost those arguments, the two men got her to agree to the early-morning burial.

Hearing the crunch of pea gravel beneath tires, Coach and Lathrop watched the Klimps pull up behind the Volvo in their Ford sedan.

Lathrop again shook his head. "This is not going to be good at all," he said.

Patsy wore a sky blue shift dress that dropped to her knees. Bob wore a too-small white dress shirt and cranberry tie. Lathrop said, "Let's get this done, folks. Before everyone finds out." He was already moving into position beside the casket.

Coach looked north where twelve ancient oaks lined the cemetery along Pitchfork Road, just inside a six-foot-high weatherboard fencing that was peeling of its white paint. The Klimp plot was situated in the far southwest corner of the cemetery at the bottom of a gently sloping hill. The geography, plus the trees and fence, made it impossible to see all but the tip of the grave-digging backhoe from the road. Coach hoped that would slow the spread of the burial news.

Nearer the entrance and far off the gravel drive that wound through the graveyard were six freshly covered graves. Five were victims of the shooting. The sixth murdered man, Willie Percival, was taken to Oklahoma for burial. The sixth fresh plot in the Masonic was for Lois Marque, who was ninety-seven when she died five days earlier at a nursing home in West Fork. Some of the gravestones in the Masonic dated to the late 1880s, and those earliest ones were carved with Norwegian names.

Coach read a few verses from the eighth chapter of Romans and said a short prayer. He didn't know what else to say, and the Klimps had low expectations. The service lasted less than five minutes. After the prayer, Coach again attempted to prepare the Klimps for what might happen.

"People will find out soon enough he's buried here," he said. "There are no secrets in this town." He glanced at Jerry Debs, who watched them from the backhoe.

"We're not trying to be secretive," Patsy said. "We're just doing what needs to be done. We can't very well keep Tommy in our living room."

"And we've got this plot here already," Bob added, loosening his tie.

Lathrop added: "You'd be smart to leave the grave unmarked. No stone."

"It might have been a better idea to bury in him in the old Spanish graveyard," Coach said. "No one hardly goes there, but it's still close."

"It's done," Patsy said, turning to go to the car.

"Emmalynn should have been here," Patsy said on the ride home. "I heard you talking on the phone last night. You always let her off easy."

"She's got a lot going on," Bob said.

"I'd like to know what. Summer school's out, and she doesn't have a job there. Other college kids come back to Smackdab for the summer."

"Their brother didn't kill six men," Bob said.

"You sound so cruel."

"Cruel? I'm stating the facts. The plain truth is, Emmalynn's the sister of the notorious killer, and it would only be the best for her future to stay away from here."

"She'll be one of those kids who never visits family," Patsy said. "What am I saying? She already is."

Emmalynn had called home the night before to speak to Bob. As usual, she called her father on his cell phone rather than the landline, should her mother answer. Her dad was more empathetic to the challenges of college life, though he had gone only one semester before deciding that life wasn't for him.

"Should I come back for the funeral?" Emmalynn had asked.

Bob knew she had waited to call until it would be impractical for her to come. He didn't blame her.

"You stay put," he said. He could feel her relief.

"It won't be a real service," he said. "We'll bury him and be done with it. We need to keep the fuss to a minimum. No need to offend the town."

"Well, if you're sure…"

"I am," Bob said. "You've got enough going on as it is, getting ready for the new semester and all."

"I have loads to do," Emmalynn said. "It's going to be a tough semester, and I'd like to recharge a little before it starts. Some of us are talking about driving up to Chicago this weekend, maybe go to some clubs."

"Be careful."

"Dad?"

"Yes, honey."

"There have already been whispers on campus. It's just that… I'm afraid it could hurt me getting a job out of college. The Klimp name."

Bob took a deep breath. The family name was in its death throes. He had never been sure of its origin, because he had never cared enough about genealogy to look into it. With Tommy dead, he was the last of the Klimp men. And now, he realized, Emmalynn wanted no connection to it.

"Dad? Did you hear me?"

"I did, yes. It was never a very pleasing name."

Emmalynn laughed nervously. "Kind of weird, yeah," she said.

"You could always go by your mother's maiden name," Bob said.

"Fuglestad? That's worse than Klimp."

"Yes, but there is no notoriety associated with it," Bob said.

"I don't know, Dad. I have to think about it."

"You need to do what's best for you."

"I will," she said.

Bob felt the tension between him and Patsy smoldering like subterranean lava. Everything they talked about now had a rawness to it. No pleasant topics existed. The most mundane matters were now out of bounds. The prospects of rain, getting up a grocery list, or what they might have for supper that night were too supercilious to discuss. The idea that they still had basic needs like food and sex and hope seemed selfish in light of what had happened. Bob believed they did not deserve anything good in their lives, no matter how banal their needs might be.

"What would you think about donating a park bench for the croquet court?" Patsy asked.

"A bench? Those old boys bring their own chairs."

"I meant as a memorial. You've seen benches like that. Where there's a little plaque on them."

"You can't be thinking about a memorial for Tommy. We'd be run out of town, if we won't be already. It was just a few days ago you were talking about how we needed to keep his grave unmarked. And now you want to put a bench at the park? It would be chopped into kindling before the first sunset."

"Those men liked Tommy. He liked them."

"Those men are related nine different ways to the ones Tommy killed. No, Patsy. They will not want us putting a memorial bench at the park."

"Well, maybe the plaque would be too much, but we could donate the bench."

When Tommy was younger, he spent many afternoons after school watching croquet. The croquet court had been a part of Smackdab longer than anyone alive. It occupied the southern edge of the city park at the opposite side from the playground. Retirees played there every day in good weather. It seemed they had been the same small group of men the past many decades. But the makeup changed as some players died and slightly younger ones took their place. If the weather allowed it, four or five showed up each day. Never the same men, though, as dictated by medical appointments and other obligations. Each man brought his own equipment. Some mallets were cylindrical; others were rectangular. Some were old, made of ash or maple, the painted stripes faded. Others were newer, made of composites. Some players preferred their mallet handles cut short. Others kept their mallets long so they wouldn't have to bend their ancient torsos.

The court's hard surface was dusted with sand, just enough to provide a light crackling sound as the balls traversed it. The players were determined to keep the hobby going, to keep the court from being replaced by a swing set. They were determined to do anything but play golf, to do anything but sit at home. They did not recruit new players. They were too proud for that. But they would willingly hand their mallet, mid-game, to anyone who stopped to watch. Some predecessors had bequeathed their antique mallets to younger men in town, who had given no thought of playing until the deceased man's widow or child showed up with the mallet.

"You could make it," Patsy said, still thinking about the bench.

Bob had difficulty seeing the road, his eyes blurred with anger. "I've got to replace the mailbox post first, don't I? I mean, what part of this situation do you not get?" he asked. "First you changed your mind about cremation, and I held my tongue, despite common sense telling me the whole town's going to be pissed off. And now you want to memorialize

Tommy with a park bench? We used to be respectable people in the town, but now we're nothing. Nobody wants any memory of Tommy. Don't you see that? They want everything about him wiped off the face of the earth. For some of them, that includes you and me."

"Fine, then," Patsy said with no trace of annoyance. "I'll look up benches online."

17

What little rain that passed through earlier had fizzled; the day warmed quickly. An out-of-town rig hauling a Caterpillar pulled up in front of the Mattsen place, better known as the old Sandstrum place, at two minutes past eight. The dozer's operator looked at his watch and cursed under his breath. He liked to start early, and he liked to start on time. Still, he knew he could make it to his second site by eleven. From the looks of the house, the pitiful garage beside it, and the shabby cedars, the bulldozer could quickly take it all down and mash it into nothing. That could take all of an hour.

As the man stepped down from the truck cab, he glimpsed the creature crawling out from under the house.

You see something new every day.

The troll, or whatever she was, was covered in dirt. Her hair, entangled with dried leaves and cobwebs, was matted from her scalp to her shoulders.

Smackdab's just full of strangeness.

He watched as the little person dusted off her clothes, which did little good, but he could read the printing on her T-shirt: *Haters Gonna Hate* in Old English script.

"Good morning," she said, like it was no big deal. She raked her fingers through her stack of hair, removing only a few bits of detritus.

He pointed at the little woman with his thick pinkie. "You missed a spot or two," he said.

"I'll let my team of stylists deal with it later," she said, though she made a half-hearted stab at whacking dirt from her T.-shirt.

"Did you lose something under there?" the dozer man asked.

She shook her head. "That's where I sleep," she said.

Again like it was no big deal.

"I'm here to take her down," he said, nodding toward the house.

"I guessed as much."

"You got anything inside you need to retrieve? I've only guesstimated an hour for this job, so…"

Maesie hurried into the house to collect a few things. The Caterpillar's arrival hadn't surprised her. A power company worker had come the day before to disconnect the power line that ran from the road to the house. A water company guy had dropped by, too. Cahill had never returned, but she heard the Vic pass by twice.

Maesie had a plan, though she knew it was not a great one. Dead Lake, four miles west of town, provided the centerpiece of a fifteen-hundred-acre swatch of prairie land that a non-profit environmental group had bought decades earlier. The organization planned to re-introduce native species of plants and wildlife to the area. What they got instead was blessedly hot in the summer and inhumanly cold in the winter. The wind, whether cold or hot, rarely took a breather. Few things grew, and fewer animals wanted to stake a claim. The largest wildlife to take hold there was mosquitoes.

The lake was the baneful centerpiece of the protected land. The closest stand of trees was more than one hundred yards east of the lake up a slope of tallgrass. With nothing to block it, the sun shimmered off the glassy surface of the water throughout the day and made it appear like a brilliant diamond in a bed of green emeralds. But Dead Lake was best admired from afar. No fish survived there because of a sulfur upwelling at the lake's bottom. It had been that way for many years. Nobody swam in Dead Lake, unless they wanted to smell like rotten eggs for a week.

Still, the lake offered a satisfactory spot for Maesie to set up an open-air camp. It was remote enough that no one would stumble across her, yet close enough to Smackdab that she wouldn't feel too isolated. She could sneak into town at night when she needed, staying out of sight of anyone who might do her harm.

Maesie packed belongings and loaded them on a rusted Radio Flyer wagon that had belonged to her mother when she was a child. Most recently, Charmin Mattsen had used the wagon as a planter for geraniums, parking it near the mailbox by the road. Since Charmin's death, the wagon had accommodated nothing but dirt and dandelions. When Maesie flipped over the wagon, the brick of dirt came out easily and thudded on the ground. Maesie tested the wagon's mobility. The left rear wheel wobbled. Otherwise, the conveyance seemed good enough to make the lake trip.

Maesie did not care about much in the house. Most of her wardrobe came from yard sales or, when she could get a ride, the West

Fork Goodwill. Most of what she left behind—photo albums and keepsakes—had mattered only to her mother.

    The only photo she wanted was a Polaroid of her parents outside the West Fork courthouse when they got married. In the picture, her father, shy of one-hundred-fifty pounds and most of that bone, looked cornered. His powder blue polyester sport coat, two sizes too big and obviously borrowed, draped him like a tablecloth.

    Maesie's mother was the reason Maesie kept the Polaroid. The young woman in the picture, garbed in a cream-colored dress that quit about six inches above her knees, looked happier and prettier than she was in real life. Maesie believed Charmin would have kept her looks if she hadn't married an unrepentant wanderer and given birth to a dwarf.

    Maesie put the photo in the side pocket of a Beauty and the Beast vinyl suitcase, which her mother gave her on her eighth birthday. In addition to the suitcase, Maesie loaded the wagon with a tattered Winnie the Pooh sleeping bag and camp cooking equipment. She also packed her fiddle; two Wal-Mart bags stuffed with a nearly-full bag of potato chips; a half-used jar of peanut butter; four cans of fruit cocktail with pop-top lids; two boxes of cinnamon Pop-Tarts; an opened package of Oreos; a Ziploc bag crammed with cold fried chicken; one box of matches; three kitchen knives wrapped in old newspaper; one garbage bag; two-and-a-half rolls of toilet paper; and *Great Expectations* in paperback, which she read once a year since she was fifteen.

    In the center of the rolled-up sleeping bag, Maesie stuffed her father's long barrel .22 revolver, also wrapped in a Wal-Mart bag, and a box of cartridges. She wasn't much of a shot, but she might get lucky and wing a rabbit if she got hungry enough. More important, the gun would be good to have while she was out in the open and vulnerable.

    Maesie considered taking one last look at each room. Unlike Rolf, Charmin took pride in the home she had made of the place. She kept it clean. Maesie could still hear pans clanging against each other in the kitchen as her mother put them away in the cabinets. She could hear Charmin snapping wet sheets as she hung them on the clothesline out back. She could hear her mother humming a song, always out of tune and unrecognizable, as she folded laundry on the foot of her bed.

    Maesie decided not to take one more look. She covered the wagonload with a folded eight-by-eight blue plastic tarp, which she cinched with kitchen string. As she left, towing the wagon down the road behind her, the dozer man nodded and throttled up the machine. Maesie did not look back as she heard the cracking of dried lumber, which surrendered easily to the force of the Cat.

A half-mile into her trek, Maesie's feet began to hurt. She guessed blisters would begin to form by the second mile. She wore two-dollar orange flip-flops, the only footwear she possessed. She had meant to buy a cheap pair of sneakers with her first machine shop paycheck, which would have come the day after the shootings. Her previous pair of sneakers had blown a sole earlier that summer. She would have to dig up a used pair someplace. The sawgrass at Dead Lake would easily slice her feet.

Maesie stopped to rest. She sat atop the loaded wagon and took a swig from the water jug. It now occurred to her, when she reached Dead Lake, it would be hard to walk back to town any time she pleased. The way her feet throbbed, they might look like chunks of raw roast beef before much more walking. She pondered some, took another swig of water, and pondered further.

Few vehicles had come down the road since she had left for the lake. She had considered that to her benefit. Now, though, she wished for the unlikely event that someone would take pity and offer a ride.

She untied the string that bound her belongings and, one-by-one, starting with the suitcase, carried each item across the roadside ditch up to a fence line infested with thistle and knapweed. Except for the fiddle, revolver, a half-roll of toilet paper, and two sanitary pads, she dropped everything into a high clump of weeds. No one could easily spot the belongings unless they were looking for them. So what if they did? She thought. The bags contained nothing of value to anyone. After tossing the wagon over the fence, she picked up the fiddle and stuck the revolver, toilet paper, and pads in her backpack, and headed back to town.

Half an hour later, Maesie stood in front of the small one-story house with beige vinyl siding and white trim. A vertical piece of trim on the northwest corner of the house had come loose at the top. It leaned toward the road. A mix of toys—a baby carriage, plastic lawn mower, large plastic ball and various small cars and toy soldiers—were strewn throughout the dirt yard. The only item that wasn't a toy: a child-sized wheelchair with a ripped vinyl seat. A smallish yellow dog of indeterminate parentage sunned near a half-deflated wading pool. The mutt raised its head slightly to spy Maesie, but it saw nothing worth stirring for and returned to its lazing.

When Maesie knocked on the door, a gray-eyed, towheaded boy of eight or nine years answered. He wore a gray T-shirt a few sizes too big and black nylon gym shorts. Maesie thought the kid's name was Jason or Justin, but everyone called him Junie. He was the oldest Percival child. His father, Willie, was the first to be gunned down at the machine shop.

"Is your mom home?" Maesie asked.

Junie nodded. He squinted from the harsh sunlight and looked at the fiddle.

"That yours?"

"Every bit of it."

"Do you play it?"

"Nah, I just like to haul it around in case I come across a fiddle player in need of one."

The gaunt child studied Maesie for a moment, looking for some indication she was joking. He saw none.

"Well?" Maesie said. "Do you mind telling your mom I'm here?"

"I don't mind at all, but you can do it yourself. She's in the garage," Junie said, scratching his butt. "In the car."

"Going someplace or just getting back?"

The boy shook his head. "Neither," he said. "She sits out there and cries. I've been taking care of my sisters. I don't suppose you know how to work a plunger?"

"Not on your sisters, I don't," Maesie said. "Maybe I'll go take a peak in the garage. See how your mom's doing. If I leave my fiddle sitting out here, your mutt won't want to gnaw on it, will it? This fiddle's the most important thing I own."

Squinting, Junie looked at the dog. "I don't know how she feels about your music," he said.

Maesie found Delia Percival sitting behind the wheel of her car in the darkened garage. The interior temperature topped ninety degrees; Maesie began to sweat profusely, more than from her walk back to town. She had to climb around and over boxes, plastic storage bins, toys and lawn equipment, which occupied every bit of floor space not taken by the car. She squeezed into the passenger side. Delia laid her head on the headrest, her eyes closed.

"Delia? You awake?"

"Maesie Mattsen, as I live and breathe," Delia said without opening her eyes.

"The one and only."

Delia had been three years ahead of Maesie in school. A shade under five feet tall, Delia would yell "Hey, Twin!" any time she saw Maesie. Otherwise, they had never said much to each other.

Delia and Willie Percival had married when she was seventeen and he was a year older. He was already in Job Corps by then, learning to weld. Delia gave birth to Junie a few months later. Delia worked off and on at a restaurant in West Fork until the third baby came along, born prematurely. Soon after that, the baby girl was diagnosed with cerebral palsy. From that point, Delia stayed home full time.

Good times all around.

"Want some corn casserole?" Delia asked. "People've brought over three different kinds of it. We got two dishes of cheesy potatoes, too. We'll either be clogged up or shitting corn for weeks."

"Thanks for the visual and all, but I'll pass," Maesie said. "Diane Olstad brought by some of the goodies she'd been given."

"How's Diane doing anyway?"

"About like Diane does, I guess. All things considered."

"Yeah. All things considered," Delia said. Maesie analyzed the other woman's face. In the gloom, she thought she could see Delia's chin begin to pucker as though she was about to cry.

"Life's a bitch and then you die, right?" Delia said. "Or as Willie liked to say at least once a day, 'Life's a bitch, then you marry one, then you die.'"

Both women attempted laughs.

"When's the first time you realized life wasn't all you thought it'd be?" Delia asked, not waiting for an answer. "For me, it was before me and Willie even got married. Before I knew I was pregnant with Junie. I loved Willie with all my heart. At least, I thought I did at the time. But who really knows when they're sixteen, right? Hell, who knows at any age? But anyways, me and Willie were in love. And I knew deep in my soul that I wanted to spend the rest of our lives together. And it felt good, you know? There for a while. But even then something told me that my life had already peaked. It would never get any better."

Delia raised her head and looked at Maesie.

"I don't mean nothing against the kids. God, no. They're the best things that ever happened to me."

Maesie nodded.

Delia rested her head again.

"Willie wasn't so bad either. Course, just about every day I fantasized what it would be like to divorce him. Just normal daydreaming, you know? Start fresh. He could take the kids and I could move away. Start over. Maybe even go to community college or something. Then when the kids got a little older, say Cammie was Junie's age now, they could come live with me. Shit, now… Getting married and having kids, and busting my ass waiting tables. What a life, huh? But that was the pinnacle of success for me."

"That's not a bad life," Maesie said. "Sounds pretty good all things considered in some ways."

"You mean because I'm not a dwarf."

"No. I just mean having a family to love isn't the worst thing."

"Yeah, and I'd have given someone's left nut for just one day without all of it," Delia said.

She gripped the steering wheel, which was damp with her sweat. "I've been sitting out here for two hours, roasting my ass off, trying to think if I should end myself. But I can't decide if the kids would be better off or worse off. My parents would keep them, but mom's got enough health problems of her own. And with Willie's parents moved back to Oklahoma, I don't know. It was hard enough making ends meet before, and now... Maybe the kids would do fine in foster care. It could happen they'd end up with some nice folks who could afford to buy them more than I can. Or maybe not. It'd be a real crapshoot, for sure. Maybe I should strap them in here, too, and fire up the Corolla."

"Don't say that, not even as a joke."

"I will say it. We don't have two dimes to rub together. Can't even pay for the funeral. They've got a collection jar down at the drug store for us and a couple of the other families, but that won't amount to much. Smackdab's not exactly home to a lot of rich types. And you know Sharon Sandstrum's not going to help out."

"I heard you widows were going to sue her," Maesie said.

Delia closed her eyes again and smiled. She wasn't listening. "Junie's a good little man," she said. "I swear he's better than me at taking care of his little sisters. He's a survivor."

It became so quiet in the car Maesie thought she could hear the sweat streaming down her chest between her breasts.

"Why did you come over here anyhow?" Delia asked, as though she had just remembered Maesie was in the car, too.

"I guess to say I'm sorry," Maesie said.

"You couldn't just send a card like everyone else?"

"I mean I'm sorry for my part in things. I'd like to make it up somehow. I know that's impossible, but you know... I want to do something."

Delia looked at Maesie. "What exactly was your part in things?"

That stopped Maesie cold. She hadn't meant to get into *that*. "I, uh," she began, knowing she was stammering and sounding like a guilty fool. She tried to control herself. "I just mean he was mad at me. And if I hadn't been working at the shop, Willie would still be here. That's all."

Delia laughed like she had just heard a joke with a punch line she never would have guessed. "Poor Maesie Mattsen," she said. "Trying to take the blame for the murder of my dearly beloved."

"Like I said, Willie would be alive right now if I didn't work at the shop."

"Do yourself a favor," Delia said. "Get over your self-pity. It's not very attractive."

Both women sat silently for a minute until Maesie surmised Delia had nothing else to say to her. Maesie left without saying anything more.

COME UP A CLOUD

18

My mom could sing. She still can, but her voice is huskier these days. She now sounds like an older version of Janis Joplin, minus the lung power. Anyway, when I was young and Mom still had some happiness in her, she sang when she did housework. She didn't know all the words to songs, but she would sing the parts she knew over and over. That's how I was introduced to I Wonder as I Wander. *It's a churchy Christmas song, but Mom didn't care. She belted it out as she ran the vacuum, and I soon found myself singing along with her.*

I wonder as I wander out under the sky
How Jesus the Saviour did come for to die
For poor on'ry people like you and like I;
I wonder as I wander out under the sky.

That should be Maesie Mattsen's theme song now. On'ry people wandering under the sky. It sounds a tiny bit romantic, but there's nothing pretty about tramping across the countryside shouldering a boulder of guilt. It makes no difference in the end.

Maesie was in her third day of homelessness. After visiting Delia Percival, she tried to keep out of sight the rest of the day. Smackdab had several abandoned buildings and houses, but none that Maesie could enter without breaking in. Breaking and entering seemed a minor offense compared to what she had already abetted at the machine shop, but she couldn't do it. It was one of the rare instances when she wished her mother's genes hadn't so forcefully overpowered her father's. Instead, she hovered in the cloaked shadows of tall trees and sheds at the backs of houses, changing her location often until the sun sat and enabled her to move more freely.

The first night, she attempted to sleep in the park behind a large boxwood that obscured her from cars passing by. But the spot was popular for trysts, and Bennie Duroque spotted her on his two a.m. round. At first, he thought he had caught a couple of teenagers *in flagrante delicto*. When he shined his Strion LED flashlight, the most expensive equipment he owned (he was not allowed to carry a firearm after a number of cats began dying), Duroque saw that it was poor Maesie Mattsen.

"Get on home," Duroque said, as he did to the occasional teenage couple he found in the unisex bathroom. He would normally follow that with the threat to call the miscreants' parents, but that did not work with Maesie.

Momentarily discombobulated, Maesie forgot for a half second where she was. "I haven't got a home anymore," she said.

"Heard about that," Duroque said. "But you can't sleep here. City ordinance."

Duroque kept the light shined on her while she brushed off sticks and leaves that had stuck to her clothes. She picked up her fiddle, and walked down the road. If someone like Bennie Duroque could find her so easily, she knew someone like Skunk Olstad with more evil intentions would have no trouble.

She decided to walk to the GasGo, the only Smackdab business open twenty-four hours. Brenda Sue Wakefield leaned against the counter with both elbows resting on it. She read a dog-eared Louis L'Amour novel, one of several worn paperbacks kept behind the counter for slow periods. Her head jerked slightly when she saw Maesie, but she quickly re-focused on her book.

Maesie selected a twenty-ounce Mr. Pibb from the cold case and grabbed a bag of Cheetos on the way to the front.

"How come you're working the overnight shift?" she asked, setting the two items on the counter.

Brenda Sue didn't look up from her book while she scanned the pop and snack. "Patsy," she said.

"Oh yeah. Right."

That meant Brenda Sue hadn't found a capable replacement for her late shift employee.

"Three-twenty-nine," Brenda Sue said.

Maesie pulled a crumpled five-dollar bill from her pocket. It was the largest bill she had left.

"Who's watching the kids?" Maesie asked.

"Jordy, supposedly," Brenda Sue said, ringing up the sale and setting the change on the counter. "Dollar-seventy-one back at you."

Maesie reached up, sliding the change with one hand into the other one waiting at the counter's edge. "Nobody's applied for the shift, yet?"

Brenda Sue turned a page. "A few," she said. "But none of them with enough sense to find their own rear with a GPS and an ass-detector."

She looked at Maesie for the first time since she had entered.

"You look like you been in a tornado," she said.

"Kind of feels like it," Maesie said. Her head was the only part of her visible over the counter. "I don't suppose I could apply for Patsy's shift."

"No law prevents it," Brenda Sue said.

"I know where my ass is."

Brenda Sue acted as though she was reading the paperback again. "Because it's so close to the ground and easy to find?" she asked.

"I can do anything a taller person can do."

Brenda Sue set down the book and studied Maesie for a moment. Maesie could understand Brenda Sue's reluctance to hire someone mixed up in a bloodbath the week before, but the woman did not shrivel from a challenge. She put in enough hours to equal two jobs, had three little ones at home, and a husband who was too focused on avoiding effort to be of any help.

"I know one thing," Brenda Sue said. "You'd have to give more frequent bathing a shot. Probably wear some clothes that didn't smell like a hog lot, too. If you come back tomorrow night cleaned up, we'll talk further."

Buoyed by the possibility of employment, Maesie wandered the streets without thinking much about the blisters on her feet. She swigged and snacked, the fiddle tucked under an arm, until the night sky in the east began to lighten to the color of dirty lavender.

Soon, though, she began to feel conflicted about the opportunity at GasGo. She needed money, but she did not want to be stuck there permanently like Brenda Sue. What if she were still working there a year later, because she still needed money? What if she could never get ahead?

And there was Skunk to think about. When Skunk and Rolf returned to town, the GasGo would be the first place they stopped. Rolf would crave an extra-large cup of Mountain Dew, as he did every time the duo hit the town limits. Skunk would oblige him. Working at the GasGo would be making it easy for Skunk to find her. Perhaps she was overreacting. Maybe Diane had only been trying to rattle her as payback.

While the day was still slightly cool, Maesie returned to the park and washed the orange Cheetos gunk off her hands in the restroom. She lay on a picnic table and slept a short time until she was awakened by the clack of croquet balls. She rose again, feeling none refreshed, and returned to the restroom to splash water on her face.

Time to get this show on the road.

Maesie hiked to Jean Pankin's house, who lived two-and-half blocks southeast of the park. The heat of the day was already getting into full swing. Maesie began to sweat again, adding another layer to the dried perspiration from the day before.

Jean appeared surprised, but pleased to see her.

"Maesie Mattsen, get on in here," she said when she opened the door. "You'll melt down to nothing if you stay out in this heat any longer."

Jean invited Maesie to take a seat. She went to the kitchen to fix pour a glass of iced lemonade without asking if Maesie wanted it. Bringing Maesie the glass, Jean sat down next to her on the couch. Maesie knew she smelled bad enough to make paint on the kitchen walls curdle, but Jean didn't seem to notice.

"How have you been, Maesie?" she asked. For a woman who had just lost her husband of forty-plus years, Jean appeared cheerful.

"Tolerable," Maesie said.

"Tolerable? You don't care to elaborate?"

Maesie took a gulp of her drink. It was slightly sour, but Jean had made it with actual lemons, which was supposed to be better than the powder stuff Maesie was used to.

"When someone asks how someone else is doing, I don't expect the asker truly wants to know," Maesie said.

"I would have to disagree. I asked you how you are, because I'd like to know. What you experienced..." Jeans clicked her tongue and shook her head.

Maesie took a deep breath and nearly coughed at her own stink. "I learned early in life that if you share your true feelings on anything, you'll only have them wadded up like a big mud ball and slung back at you, making you feel like a big pile of horse turds for saying what you were really feeling." Maesie paused, embarrassed. "I apologize for my language."

Jean took no notice, but her tone was sharp. "I cannot believe Charmin raised you to feel that way."

"I guess I'm an independent thinker," Maesie said.

Jean's eyes softened. "I heard about your house," she said.

"A big pile of toothpicks now," Maesie said. She made an explosion sound. "Those old cedars, too. Gone with the wind."

Jean clicked her tongue again. "I don't know why Sharon is in such a hurry to tear down something that stood all those years. When people give directions out that way, they still say 'past the old Sandstrum place.' Now what will they say?"

She leaned into Maesie and whispered as though others were in the house. "Sharon's as rich as an Arab sheik, you know." She pronounced it *A-rab*. "Especially with Roger's life insurance money. She doesn't need to make any more by selling off the acreage."

Maesie took a long swallow from her glass.

"Cahill says you and the rest are getting ready to sue her," Maesie said. "And he says Sharon's going to stash her money in the Caymans or someplace."

Jean laughed, somewhat forlornly. But she neither confirmed nor denied the rumor of a lawsuit.

"Where are you staying now?" Jean asked.

"I'm temporarily in between living arrangements."

Jean frowned, taking Maesie's hand in hers. "Where did you spend last night?" she asked.

"The park and a few other places, but it's no big deal."

"I'd say that's a very big deal," Jean said. "We can't have that." She reached under the table and patted Maesie on the knee. "You're welcome to stay here with me as long as you need."

Maesie wiped condensation from the lemonade glass. With her wet finger, she wiped a clean streak through the dirt on her forearm. She could not believe Jean's offer to be sincere. Jean was as nice as anyone in Smackdab, but there had to be limits, such as when a certain someone gets your husband killed.

"Your offer means a lot to me," Maesie said. "But I couldn't do that on account of my role in things. The reason I came here was to tell you I'm sorry for what happened at the machine shop."

"I'm sure sorry, too, but what happened out there is not your burden to carry. That sick young man was set on doing something mean, and he did it." Jean looked down at her hands, allowing her sadness to show on her face. "I don't want to feel sorry for myself. Pink and I had many wonderful years together, filled with much more happiness than heartache. Most of the others could say the same. But I suspect it's hardest for Delia Percival. She and Willie didn't have that long together. And what they had wasn't a bed of roses."

Jean looked at the sun coming through the front window.

"That last night, before Pink died, was just like thousands of others," she said. "Supper. Watch a little TV. Pink fell asleep in that chair," she said, nodding toward a recliner with the best view of the television in the corner. "Every night at ten, I'd wake him up so he could go to bed. I'd start by calling his name once or twice, and then I'd have to shake his foot. He'd snort awake because he'd be snoring so loud I couldn't focus on what I was reading. Every night since, I'll be sitting right here in this spot and think I need to be waking him up soon. Then I start to cry, and that embarrasses me. I don't know why I let it."

"And you wonder what you have to be embarrassed about," Maesie said.

"You know, don't you?" Jean said, giving Maesie's knee another pat. "Your Mom was a sweet woman. She was always so nice to me when I'd see her at Poulsen's."

"I wasn't referring to myself," Maesie said. "Mom died and I got over it. There wasn't anything more to it," Maesie said. "Mourning the dead is a luxury I can't afford."

Jean held Maesie with a quizzical look. "Mourning is not a bad thing. Pink and I never got over the loss of our daughter," she said. "And I won't ever get over the loss of him. I don't see that I could do differently if I wanted."

Jean looked out the window again. "I hoped I'd go first, but it wasn't meant to be."

The women sat silently, uneasiness between them, when Jean nodded at the fiddle. "I didn't know you were a musician," she said.

Maesie's absently scratched her arm. Bits of dirt slid off in a fine powder. "I'm not so sure I am," she said.

"Perhaps you're selling yourself short. Why don't you play for me?"

"I don't normally play for other people. In fact, I never played for anybody except Mom."

"I bet you're good."

"Nah. I just make noise to keep myself company."

Jean showed a mischievous smile. "I insist you play for me in exchange for the lemonade."

Maesie hesitated and then propped the fiddle between her legs on the couch. She felt self-conscious, embarrassed. But she began tentatively to play something in a minor key, something she had made up on the spot.

A few measures into the piece, Jean began to cry.

Maesie stopped. "I'm sorry," she said. "I should've played something happier, except I don't know how. Everything I bow comes out sad and lonesome. Mom said I could've played with Hank Williams if I'd been born back then."

Jean took a tissue from a box on the coffee table. "It's a beautiful piece, and I enjoyed it," she said, blowing her nose. "You know, Pink was a lot like you. We'd sit out back of an early evening, if it was cool enough, and he'd sing to me once in a while if I nagged him enough. He said he was no good, but I loved his singing voice. It was sorrowful like your fiddle." She nodded at the instrument. "You've got a real talent. Just remember, any song you play is a unique gift to God."

"I don't know about that."

Another pat on the knee. "Why don't you stay with me tonight? I could use the company," Jean said.

"Thank you, but I've got others places I need to be."

"Forgive me for saying so, but I'm sure a shower would make you feel better."

"That sounds real tempting, and I'd like to take you up on that, but I don't have any clean clothes with me. It'd be a waste of time to get all cleaned up."

Jean studied her visitor as though she were inspecting a fresh recruit. "We could probably find something around here that we could make work."

"Thank you, Mrs. Pankin, but I'll get out of your hair now."

As she stood, Maesie extended her hand to Jean, who took it and squeezed hard. Maesie failed to sense the woman's deep need. "You're not in my hair," Jean said. "In fact, you've made my day."

Before Maesie left, Jean made her take a thermos of lemonade and a small plastic container of chocolate chip cookies. "They're not real fresh anymore," Jean said about the cookies, "but I think they're still edible."

She took Maesie's hand again. "You go out there and try to focus on the good, all right? Don't be so hard on yourself. I know you think everybody's against you, but it's just not so."

19

Skunk and Rolf did not stay overnight in the little Kansas farm town; they did not remain to see if they could generate the kind of tips the bar's owner promised. Instead, they borrowed a GMC diesel from the tavern parking lot. It was a good find. Its fat tires whined so loudly they rattled Skunk's eardrums, but he had gotten used to it by the time they reached the next county. Better, the truck was just a couple years old and had two-thirds of a tank of gas. Its owner was so smashed that Skunk had no problem removing the keys from the table where they lay next to the drunk's head. However, another bar patron, perhaps two-and-a-half sheets to the wind rather than three, spotted Skunk taking the keys and roused the truck's owner.

With Rolf and their gear in tow, Skunk had walked through the quiet parking lot, clicking the GMC's remote until he saw its lights flash. Whatever Scott had invested in Chez Belle, he had put nothing into security lighting. Other than the lighted sign over the building's entrance, the exterior was as dark as a coalmine.

Just as the pair tossed their belongings in the truck's bed, its owner, alerted by the other patron, showed up.

"Zat's my truck," the man slurred.

"Hop in the truck," Skunk ordered Rolf under his breath.

Getting his first glimpse of the owner in an upright position, Skunk could now see he stood six-one or better, with two hundred fifty pounds of what could either be fat or muscle. It was hard to tell in the dark, and Skunk had no desire to find out. The guy was young, though, maybe thirty at most, and showed off a full Grizzly Adams beard.

Skunk slowly pulled the customized chainsaw file from its hiding spot in his jacket.

"This ain't your truck," Skunk said. He held up the keys. "The guy who owns it said I could take it for a spin."

The big man teetered momentarily as he tried to get his synapses to fire more quickly. "Nah, you little pissant. It's mine, and I don't loan it to nobody."

The man, ten feet away from Skunk, took two more steps. Skunk edged to the rear of the truck and let down the gate. He had to move quickly before the man's buddies came to look for him.

"I'm sorry," Skunk said. "I won't take your truck. But first come over here at look at the bed. Some drunk asshole puked in it."

The notion that someone soiled his precious vehicle angered its owner more than the thought someone might drive off with it.

"Let me see, goddamnit," he said, approaching the back of the GMC.

As he did, Skunk stepped aside and made a quick thrust to the man's lower back. The man was too drunk to feel much, but he went limp. The upper half of his body slumped onto the truck's gate. Before he slid off, Skunk grabbed him from behind. Maneuvering the large man onto the truck's bed was like wrestling a tranquilized black bear. Adrenaline, along with the fear of being seen, gave Skunk the strength to get it done. When the truck's owner was fully in the bed, Skunk slammed the gate shut and hopped in the driver's seat.

While Rolf slept, Skunk drove the purloined truck due north for an hour before turning east about fifty miles south of the Nebraska line. Skunk embraced the all-night drive. He still couldn't sleep, so he was happy to have something to do. Keeping to rural blacktops, Skunk worried little about encountering cops. Before turning east, Skunk had pulled off into a cattle pasture to examine the condition of the truck's owner. The man was unconscious, but still alive. The knife had drawn some blood, which had coated a small portion of the bed. It was impossible to tell if the guy was passed out from inebriation or getting stuck. While Rolf remained asleep in the cab, Skunk dumped the driver in a little draw where the body couldn't be seen from the road. Skunk was getting back in the truck when he reconsidered. He dug the man's phone from his jeans pocket and called 911. He left the phone on and sending a signal. It was up to a cop or an EMT to take it from there.

Shortly before sunup, near the Missouri River, the truck's gas gauge slid past *E*. Skunk did not want to dump the car too close to any town, but he did not want to walk far either. Before much traffic began to pick up on the blacktop, Skunk pulled into a cornfield and left the GMC half way down an irrigation path.

"Where're we going?" Rolf asked, awakening to see nothing but tall cornstalks all around him. "Are we lost?"

"We're going to walk," Skunk said. He wasn't sure how far they were from the river.

Rolf scowled. He did not move from his seat.

"I know we've been doing a helluva lot of it lately," Skunk said, giving his voice a soothing tone. "But we got no choice. I promise you we'll get a ride soon."

"Well, shit," Rolf said, sinking further into his seat. He sat that way for a moment, his head bent forward as though he were praying. When he looked up, he asked: "Could we eat something first? I feel like I ain't ate nothing good in weeks."

"We'll find a McDonalds or something like it in the next town. I'll make sure you get yourself a couple of Egg McMuffins if I have to make 'em myself."

After an hour of walking, with several rest breaks for Rolf, they reached a small town on the Kansas side of the river. The first place they found that sold food was a convenience store. Farm trucks occupied the store's four fuel pumps.

"We'll get those Egg McMuffins when we get across the river, but how about a Hostess Cupcake or something first?" Skunk asked his band mate.

"I'll live with that," Rolf said. "So long as you toss in some sunflower seeds, too."

Skunk smiled. Whatever had toasted Rolf's brain, Skunk thought it had made him more agreeable than he used to be.

After they bought a few things at the store, they hitched a ride in the bed of a farm truck, an old Dodge Ram whose driver was headed over the river. The truck was in good shape, looked garage-kept, and likely not used for farm work. A going-to-town truck, Skunk surmised.

"Better keep your heads down," the old man behind the wheel said. "The cops don't like seeing folks riding in the back of a truck no more."

Skunk and Rolf obliged. The bed was cleaner than many motel rooms they had stayed in. Rolf lay on his back and spat sunflower seed shells in the air. He watched the crosswind whip them around.

Just over the bridge, the truck exited onto a parkway parallel to the river and eased to a stop on the shoulder. The driver waved through the back window to signal the end of the ride. Skunk and Rolf again obliged.

"Where are we now?" Rolf asked, looking at his surroundings.

"Across the river in St. Joe, Missouri," Skunk said. They were a couple hundred feet east of the river in an industrial area with mountains of construction sand, oil storage tanks, and disarrayed aluminum culvert pipe.

"It's not the prettiest place I've ever seen," Rolf said.

"Can't argue," Skunk said, "but it's a helluva lot closer to Smackdab than where we were a day ago."

"Maybe we'll be in Smackdab tonight then?"

"I'm about whipped," Skunk said. "First thing we need to do is find that McDonalds. Then we'll see if we can't locate a decent hotel room. I've also got a little business to conduct. After all of that, we'll see about finding a way to Smackdab."

An hour of walking through the city in a northeast direction did not produce a McDonalds. They did, however, come across a pawnshop. Skunk had hoped to see one since they had left Colorado.

"I need to borrow your Taylor," Skunk said to Rolf.

Rolf looked at the guitar bag he clutched and then at his partner. "You got your own strings. What do you need mine for?"

"We need money for a motel. So I'll leave your guitar here at this store. Just for the time being."

Rolf never parted with his guitar. He had played a middling Takamine for years until he finally found the Taylor, used, for a price he could live with. Every time he pulled it out of his bag at a gig, a few people in the crowd, the ones who respected fine instruments, buzzed their admiration.

"I don't know, Skunk," he said. "Why don't you hock your Martin?"

"You know it's not as good as yours. They won't give me next to nothing." The Martin, a 1969 Brazilian Rosewood that had been given to Skunk by his father, didn't sound anything special when Skunk played it, but it was worth more than the Taylor. Like Rolf, Skunk rarely let his guitar out of his sight.

"This ol' thing wouldn't give us enough for one motel night," Skunk said. "Nah, it's got to be the Taylor, unless you want me to have a look at what you got in those pillows."

Rolf handed over his guitar.

The pawn shop paid Skunk two-hundred-fifty dollars for the Taylor, a fraction of its value. When Rolf asked how much he received, Skunk said, "Enough."

They walked north now, toward the center of the city. A block from the pawnshop, they came across an old Dairy Queen on the edge of a grocery store parking lot. The DQ looked like one of the originals, with no drive-through.

"You want a chicken sandwich? Maybe a dipped cone or something?" Skunk asked.

By evening, Rolf would forget why he no longer had a guitar. For now, though, he sulked.

"I don't give a good goddamn," he said.

Still hungry, they walked further east. Forty minutes later, their shirts soaked with sweat, the two men had crossed a residential part of the city populated by neat bungalows and churches to arrive at a four-lane highway, which was lined with retail outlets. They had reached a suburban business district, home of fast food eateries and cell phone outlets.

In an effort to lighten Rolf's mood, Skunk carried Rolf's bag in addition to his own duffel and guitar. Skunk had taken in no liquids since the night before. With the extra load, he had begun to feel ragged. He needed to consume a swimming pool's worth of water. They also needed to get out of sight. Assuming the GMC's owner had survived and remembered any details from the night before, and if the Kansas cops got a boner about tracking them down, it wouldn't be too hard to find two sorry-looking hitchhikers dressed like shabby cowboys. When the cops located the abandoned truck, even the dumbest Barney Fife could guess Skunk and Rolf had crossed the river.

"The first cheap hotel we come across, we're checking in," Skunk said. He looked north and south. It was the kind of road that would have two or three fast food restaurants every half-mile. It should also have motels. Without a charged phone, he couldn't check which direction was the shortest walk to one of them.

"Which way you wanna try?" he asked Rolf.

The other man said nothing.

"All right then. South it is."

Ten minutes later, Skunk spotted an old motor lodge on the opposite side of the road. It was an old one-story building set back fifty yards from the road with front-facing rooms. The facades of the rooms alternated between red brick and sandstone. The place was an anachronism among its motel chain neighbors, but it was the kind of place Skunk and Rolf liked best. Such motels were cheaper than the chains, and they were locally owned. The duo had stayed at one in Utah that served homemade pie, free, every evening. They only had to walk into the office and take their pick of fresh chocolate or lemon meringue.

Rolf fell asleep on his bed five minutes after they checked in. Skunk bought three bottles of water from the clerk, thinking a little hydration would calm him down. He had surrendered to trying to sleep and took a shower instead. After five minutes of waiting, the shower water never warmed beyond tepid.

Rolf awoke just past eight in the evening to see Skunk sprawled on the other bed watching a *Law & Order* re-run. Rolf didn't know where he was, but it didn't matter. He awakened in nearly identical rooms half his life.

"We got a gig tonight?" he asked.

Skunk shook his head. He didn't want to take his attention away from the show. The first half of each hour-long procedural was his favorite. After Lenny Briscoe and his partner of the season arrested the suspect, Skunk lost interest. The courtroom stuff bored him.

Rolf patted his belly. "I'm getting awful hungry. Ain't we going out?"

"I'll go out here in about thirty or so," Skunk said. "I'll bring something back for you." He pointed a finger at Rolf. "And I don't want you wandering off while I'm gone."

"Where would I wander off to?"

Skunk shushed him. "Be quiet until a commercial, will ya?"

As soon as Lenny Briscoe cuffed the suspect, Skunk pulled himself up from the bed and retrieved something in a sandwich-sized cellophane packet from his duffel bag. He donned the only jacket he owned, wrinkled from being stuffed in the bag, and left the room without a word to Rolf.

They had walked by a CVS pharmacy not far from the motel. Before looking for a place to eat, Rolf bought a bottle of Tylenol PM. When the cashier put the purchase in a small bag, Skunk asked for a larger one. He stuffed the bag and its contents in the breast pocket of his jacket and went in search of a place to eat.

Skunk sought a particular type of restaurant. He would know it when he saw it. He passed a Burger King and a KFC before he spotted the place he was looking for. By the end of the night, he hoped to be flush with enough cash to make it to Smackdab without having to stick another drunk.

20

Leon Wesbecker's widow lived a mile northwest of town. It would normally be an easy walk for Maesie, but exhaustion coupled with blistered feet turned the walk into a slog. It took her nearly an hour of traipsing to reach the old white two-story farmhouse, the sole interruption in an eighty-acre run of ten-foot high seed corn. The driveway alone was nearly a quarter mile from the road.

The house and lawn were bounded on the north and west side by a windbreak of poplars. A large hay barn with a cupola had once occupied a spot northeast of the house. Leon Wesbecker had farmed some, but, like many others around Smackdab, the business had not been profitable for small-timers for a generation or more. The Wesbeckers rented their cropland to a large farming outfit. The Wesbeckers' daughter lived in West Fork. The two sons lived downstate.

Ten years earlier, the Wesbeckers tore down all their outbuildings except for a machine shed used as a car garage. They burned down the hay barn, which had begun to sag in on itself. That had been a sad occasion for old timers around the area. Other than the Smackdab water tower, the barn's cupola had been the most visible structure on the surrounding landscape. The dried lumber burned so well when torched that it turned the indigo night sky the color of an overripe peach. Maesie and her mom had sat on their front porch a mile south and watched sparks dot the void. To Maesie, the conflagration was as beautiful as the Kiwanis Fourth of July fireworks in West Fork.

Three cats—a calico and two yellows—basked in the shade of the Wesbeckers' front porch. Two scattered when Maesie hit the first step, but one of the yellows sidled up to her and rubbed against her leg. The porch floor, its gray paint peeling, creaked beneath Maesie's feet as she shifted from one sore foot to the other. The cat mewed for her attention.

Maesie knocked once, waited, and was about to knock a second time when the door opened. Alice Wesbecker was in her early seventies, but she looked ten to fifteen years older. Though her skin was rubbery and sallow, her blank expression seemed frozen to her skull. She showed no signs she recognized Maesie.

"I'm Maesie Mattsen."

Nothing in the older woman's eyes changed.

"I worked at the machine shop with Leon. I did clerical work."

"Um hmm." The woman's eyes seemed to see beyond Maesie.

"Uh, I just came by to speak to you for a moment."

The widow said nothing.

"I'm sorry about Leon."

No response.

Maesie had originally planned to ask to use the bathroom—the lemonade had swiftly worked its way through her system—but she decided she could hold it.

"Well, okay then," Maesie said, taking a step back. "I'll see you around."

When she reached the gravel road, Maesie looked back to see Alice Wesbecker still looking at the same spot where Maesie had stood. Before she reached the gravel road, Maesie hopped into the weeds and peed.

From the Wesbecker place, it was three-quarters of a mile back to Route 4 west of Smackdab, a short hike west on the two-lane, then south another quarter mile on a gravel road to where Maesie left the Radio Flyer in the weeds. Three vehicles passed going her way, but no one stopped to offer a ride.

No human or beast seemed to have bothered the belongings she had left near the fencerow. She righted the wagon and conducted a full inventory check. Bugs had found a way into the bag of potato chips, but the rest, including the Oreos, appeared unspoiled. She packed the container of Jean's cookies and the thermos, which Jean had put in a plastic grocery bag, with the other items in the wagon. She sat a few moments in the weeds and took off her flip-flops. On her right foot the thong had rubbed raw the area between her toes. On both feet, water blisters had formed on the balls of her heels. The pain was less noticeable when she walked, but her feet throbbed like bass drums when she rested. While she considered what to do next, she munched a few chips after blowing off the remaining insects. Following a few more minutes of rest, she walked toward town, pulling her possessions behind her.

A vehicle approached slowly from that direction. It was too far away to identify any occupants, but the truck was royal blue and looked new. It was nothing Skunk Olstad or her father would drive unless they stole it. The truck slowed to a stop beside her, and Harp Denbo powered down his window. Maesie had never spoken to him before.

"Do you know who I am?" he asked from above her.

Maesie nodded.

"I'd like to speak with you for a moment," he said. He did not look down at her from the high cab. Instead, he kept his gaze on the road ahead of him.

"Free country," Maesie said. She had never heard Denbo speak before. His accent reminded her of characters from *The Sopranos*. She wanted to hear him speak more.

"I heard you were wandering around like the Hebrews in the wilderness," Denbo said. "I hope you don't spend forty years doing it like they did."

"Me, too."

"Oh?" He looked down at her now. "And where do you intend to be when you finish this wandering?"

Maesie now wished he would look somewhere other than at her. His cold eyes shot through her.

"I'll probably start work at the GasGo in a night or two." *Not that it's any of your business.* "Then it won't take long to find a cheap place I can afford."

"No," Denbo said.

"Excuse me?" Maesie asked.

Denbo peered forward again, as though there was something much more interesting further up the road than Maesie. "You're not going to take a job in town, or get a place in town, or doing anything else in town," he said. "You see, there's a disease…" He paused before starting again. "You've made quite a mess, and it's time to head in the other direction so the town can fully recover."

"I'll go where I want," Maesie said. She no longer found his voice interesting, and she decided she would be just fine if she never heard it again. She resumed walking toward town, faster now. Denbo reversed the truck to keep pace with her. As Maesie tried to hurry, the wagon hit a rock hard enough to knock off the violin. It bounced under the rear wheel of the pickup. The fat left rear tire crunched the instrument like it was an empty peanut shell.

When he heard the noise, Denbo braked and looked in his rearview mirror. He pulled forward ten yards, and then back again further in the middle of the road. He stopped when he got to the fiddle.

"Was that yours?" he asked, peering at mangled maple and strings.

Maesie stared at the fiddle. Denbo could have run over anything else she owned, and she would not have shed a tear. But the instrument was too much. Her nose stung, and it took all her strength to keep from crying.

"Well," Denbo said, a thin smile breaking out. "It doesn't look like it was a very good one."

He looked at Maesie. "It's one less thing you have to carry out of town."

After the truck left, Maesie leaned against the loaded wagon and took time to collect herself. Tears trailed down her face for the first time since her mother's death. She took a swig of flat, hot Orange Crush from a two-liter bottle. She spit out most of it, deciding the bugs could have that, too. She dumped out the remaining liquid and tossed the bottle in the ditch. It was early evening by then. She decided she should give no more time to mourning the fiddle. She kicked the pieces, still connected by the strings, into the ditch alongside the discarded bottle.

Her feet couldn't take the hike to town. She needed to think of someplace else to bed for the night where no one would harass her. Dead Lake was the other direction, but farther than the distance to town. Lightning flashed on the southwest horizon.

One Mississippi.
Two Mississippi.
Three Mississippi.
Thunder.
Shit.

Wind began to pick up from the southwest.

Maesie could see the top of a small copse of willow and birch in the middle of the cornfield. It was two hundred yards or so from the road on the other side of the fencerow. She again crossed the ditch and threw her belongings piece by piece over the fence and into the cornfield. She squeezed between the second and third rows of barbed wire, catching the back of her T-shirt on a barb. She heard the material rip, but she kept going.

Maesie made slow progress pulling the loaded wagon down the rows of tall corn. The soil was brick-hard and cloddy. Fifty feet down the first row, Maesie scared up a corpulent raccoon. The varmint squeaked at her like a loose wheel on the Radio Flyer before scampering across her row.

The stand of trees was not directly in front of her, so Maesie cut east across several rows before continuing south. That meant knocking down several stalks in each new row to get the overloaded wagon through. One of the Wal-Mart bags filled with snacks fell off. Maesie left it.

The corn tassels were now bending further toward the northeast.
Lighting.

One Mississippi.
Two Mississippi.
Three…
Thunder.

The air felt electrified; the sky to the southwest had turned the color of new denim and was moving Maesie's way. She was not the first to take shelter in the small stand of trees. In addition to the raccoon, which had climbed up a birch and was cursing Maesie for coming uninvited, a half dozen squirrels chattered among the trees. The copse was in a small depression. At its center was a pool of stagnant water rimmed on two sides by a sandstone shelf. A bullfrog lazed on a rock and stared at her.

The place was relatively cool, and though it wouldn't protect her completely from the approaching storm without adjustments, it was better than nothing.

"Sorry fellas," she said. "I'm moving in for a while."

Hearing no objections from anything other than the raccoon, she began to set up housekeeping.

The first fat drops of rain disturbed the limpid bullfrog pool as Maesie finished tying the blue tarp at its four corners to overhead branches. The raccoon and squirrels had quieted. The only sound was the approaching storm. Maesie decided the copse was a decent place to stay the night. She felt hungry, but she had tired of junk food. She thought about the squirrels, thought some more about them, and then pulled out the revolver. After loading six rounds, she tracked a squirrel on a limb twenty feet above her, waited for it to pause, and shot with no expectation of hitting it. The squirrel fell to the ground with a thump, a few feet from the pool. The bullfrog jumped in the water at the sound of the gun and disappeared.

Maesie watched the squirrel squirm through its final death throes. The copse was now quiet except for the wind swishing the leaves. No animals scurried.

Shit.

Maesie had not intended to prepare a fire. She had not intended to skin and gut the squirrel. Had not intended to eat it, because she had not expected to kill it. She picked up the squirrel by its tail and flung it out into the cornrows. She wondered if the other animals understood the squirrel was dead, and that she had murdered it.

The surviving squirrels began to move around the branches again, chittering as though accusing her.

Murderer.

Feeling ashamed but too tired to think about it, Maesie leaned against her rolled-up sleeping bag and slept.

She woke just before dawn, feeling stiff, sore, and out of sorts. The thunderstorm had never materialized. It had swept east of town leaving Smackdab dry. The air temperature remained hot and sticky.

Denver Moss' elderly mother lived east of Smackdab, about half way to West Fork. Maesie felt her feet would be bloody stumps by the time she reached the house. If she ever got over her anger at Cahill, she would ask him for a ride out there. That would be later.

Sharon Sandstrum lived in town, but Maesie wasn't up for that visit. Not yet. She would visit Diane Olstad. Maesie would take her time, though. Diane wouldn't be up for hours if she had spent the previous night at Snoots. Maesie stuffed the pistol in her backpack and headed to town.

21

As Maesie made her bed in the copse, Cahill sat by himself at the tavern and nursed a beer. He seldom went to Snoots, because he rarely had any spare change. He had a few dollars this night, however, after giving the rest Sharon Sandstrum had paid him to his mother.

Prior to the carnage at the machine shop, Cahill had usually dealt with Roger when the Sandstrums needed a chore performed. They contracted a lawn service from West Fork to tend to their three-quarter acre lawn, but other work came Cahill's way. Unskilled jobs were nearly impossible to come by in Smackdab, particularly given Cahill's reputation for a hair trigger temper. But Roger had given him occasional work, such as a monthly run to West Fork to fill Sharon's prescriptions. She did not trust the pharmacist at Poulsen's, a young woman a few years out of the Iowa College of Pharmacy. Instead, Sharon got medication for her emphysema and myriad other ailments from the CVS in West Fork. Roger would summon Cahill to the machine shop, give him sixty dollars for less than forty dollars in prescriptions and tell him to keep the change.

Cahill had gone to the Sandstrum home that morning to collect his one hundred dollars for kicking out Maesie. He had never liked visiting her at home. She always looked at Cahill with a scrunched-up face as though he smelled like a wet sheep. Indeed, she saw him as town riff-raff, and Cahill knew it galled Sharon to depend on someone like him to help her.

Cahill was not fond of Sharon either. Sick people made him uncomfortable, and Sharon, with her perpetual wheezing like an asthmatic hound dog, was as feeble as anyone Cahill knew. He preferred to deal with her via phone, but he needed the money. It wasn't going to appear on his doorstep via carrier pigeon.

COME UP A CLOUD

He had expected one of the Sandstrum adult children, who had come back to town for the funeral, to answer the door. But it was Sharon. She looked as frail as usual in a faded housecoat with a periwinkle pattern. She rasped like she had just run a sprint. Wads of Kleenex were stuffed in each side pocket of the coat. Cahill wondered if the used tissues were from mourning or from the usual Sharon maladies.

He would never understand rich people. If he had the money, he would dress the part. Even if he were chronically ill, he would make sure he had a nice bathrobe, like the thick terry cloth ones they supposedly had in fancy hotels. If he won the lottery or otherwise came into a wad, he would right away buy a pair of alligator square-toed boots and toss his Durangos in a ditch. A few weeks earlier, he had seen an old boy in West Fork with a pair of Luccheses. He had salivated about them ever since. The fancy boots looked out of place on the end of the man's chubby legs, but they would look awfully good on Cahill. Too bad money and style were wasted on the wrong people.

"Come in," Sharon said, smiling as she stood aside to allow Cahill to enter.

He hesitated, because she was acting nicer than usual. Before, she always wanted to complete business with Cahill on the doorstep.

"I hope it's not too early," Cahill said. "And I don't want to interrupt your company." He assumed Sharon's children were still in town. One of them, he thought, had a kid or two.

"They've all gone," Sharon said. "They headed out the morning after the funeral. Couldn't stand to be here with their mother any longer." She motioned Cahill inside.

Cahill stepped into the front foyer. He took off his cap, which was rare for him when he went indoors. He wanted to watch his manners to avoid giving Sharon any reason to withhold the money.

"What happened to your face?" Sharon asked.

Cahill gingerly touched his nose. "Got in a disagreement with a door," he said. He no longer thought his nose was broken, but it might just as well have been. It was red and swollen; two purple streaks spread under his eyes from the bridge.

"Must have been quite a door," she said.

Cahill liked the smell of the house, which was different from his home. It wasn't just the absence of stale cigarette smoke or cat litter. Sharon had her house cleaned regularly, and Cahill detected a mix of lemon furniture polish and clean leather.

Cahill followed Sharon into the great room, which was trimmed in mahogany and filled with leather furniture the color of oxblood. For such a large room, Cahill wondered why there was no television to watch. He took a seat on the edge of a love seat, and Sharon sat in a club chair facing him.

Between them was a craftsman coffee table with thin vertical slats on each end. Nothing but a chess set with jade pieces occupied the table. Cahill's fifth grade teacher had taught him how to play chess, and Cahill discovered he had a knack for seeing several moves ahead. He got into it so much that he and some of the other kids, including Tommy Klimp, stayed inside at recess to play. Cahill had not played since.

An ever-present black bag, similar to a case for a laptop computer, sat on the floor next to Sharon's feet. It held the circuitry that kept oxygen flowing to her lungs. A clear breathing tube straddled Sharon's face, and she was hunched over like a woman thirty years older. Cahill guessed this was not a good day physically for her. But she was lonely, and she wanted to talk.

"What's going on out there in the world?" she asked.

Cahill wiped his hand across his swollen nose and sniffed. Something about the air in the room had begun to aggravate his sinuses. "I don't watch the news much," he said.

"I mean the world of Smackdab. Is everything getting back to business as usual?"

Cahill thought about his encounter with the asswipe on the bicycle. There had been a decided uptick in gawker traffic in recent days, but he would not mention that.

"I think maybe everyone's still in shock," he said.

Sharon nodded. "Perhaps so," she said. "I wonder how long it will take people to forget all that Roger did for them."

She stared at the Oriental rug beneath her feet. "He really believed in bettering the community, fixing up the city park and other things. But he'll be forgotten soon enough."

Cahill blinked.

Sharon wrung her hands, which were slender and frail. Cahill imagined how easily the tiny bones in them could snap.

"When you lose someone who's very dear to you, you're in shock at first," Sharon said, staring at the chess set. "You don't have much capacity to reason through it. Before you can, everyone shows up, and they feel terrible, too, and they want to make you feel better so they can feel better. You're hardly ever alone the first few days. There's this buzz of activity that keeps you from having to focus too much on the depth of your loss, and then there's always things you can take to help numb the pain. Then, just as quickly as everyone arrives, they're gone again. And you're all alone, more alone that you've ever been. And you start to get it: The only one who ever loved you completely is gone for good. The force of reality starts to crush you, and you wonder if it will ever let off."

Sharon paused. She hadn't been looking at Cahill then. "What do you think? Will the hurt ever let off?"

Cahill did not believe he was the right one to ask. "I've never lost someone close to me, except my Grandma," he said.

"I guess you're here for your money," Sharon said, her voice hardening.

"If that's all right with you," Cahill said. He began fiddling with his cap, which he held with two hands in his lap.

"She's gone then?" Sharon asked. "Where to?"

"Don't know."

"She didn't say?"

Cahill hesitated. He wasn't sure how truthful he wanted to be with one hundred dollars in the balance. "I didn't know that was important to you," he said.

"I have an anxious buyer for the land already. There should be no snags to prevent the sale from moving quickly."

Cahill put his cap back on his head. It made him feel less vulnerable.

"And all her things are gone?" Sharon asked.

Cahill hesitated again. "She don't have much worth taking. I figure she left town because of what people think of her."

"Good. The dozer should be there now."

She parted her gray lips as if to say something further, but she stopped.

"So, anyway," Cahill said. "Who's the buyer?"

"Is that any of your business?"

"Just wondering. Thought maybe it's someone I know."

"No one you know," Sharon said. She rose as quickly as her lungs would allow, indicating the visit was over and Cahill should leave. She dug in one of the pockets stuffed with tissue and pulled out a fold of five twenty-dollar bills.

"I've heard the rumors," she said, handing the money to Cahill. "I don't need to explain this to you, but if you must know, Roger and I had been talking about dozing the house and selling the land for years. Someone inquired about the property, so Roger was about to give Maesie Mattsen her notice. The Caterpillar man was already arranged."

Cahill stuffed the cash in his jeans pocket. It didn't feel as good to take it as he had hoped. He knew he should keep his mouth shut so Sharon would give him more work.

"If you're supposed to give thirty days' notice, how come the cat guy was already scheduled?" he asked.

Sharon held the front door open for him, her wheezing steadily increasing.

"I won't need your services any longer," she said, in between breaths.

22

Bryttni Morgan checked her watch again. Her bartender shift at Smokin' Hot BBQ ended in three hours. Thirty minutes following that, she would crawl into bed alone, warmed by a shot of Maker's she'd take before leaving the rib joint, and sink into a deep sleep. She wasn't on the schedule the following day, but she had to study for a psych test. She would will herself to open her books by eleven, noon at the latest. The way the evening was going, she would be another one hundred or so dollars closer to paying for the following semester's tuition. It would be the first time in two years she would be able to afford two semesters in a row.

Business at the restaurant that night was decent. All seats at the bar were taken except for one, and Bryttni stayed busy. She still had time to entertain herself by observing the couple seated near the middle. They were on their first date, she guessed. First daters often sat at the bar, if they had a choice. As they made small talk, it was easier at the bar to look at other things rather than each other. The man mostly looked at the big screen TV over the bar. The Cardinals were losing five-three to the Mets. The woman looked at her drink, rotating it on its napkin.

They were a little older than Bryttni. She imagined this would be the second go-round at dating for both of them, because each would have gone through their first divorce. The woman would have paid for a sitter for her two rugrats that night, because her ex would have his own plans. Her firstborn might be as old as twelve, so perhaps the woman didn't pay for a sitter. Maybe she decided to trust the children to stay alone for a few hours. That would save a chunk of change, considering how much babysitters charged these days. The man didn't have that issue. His brood would be with their mother and her boyfriend, the roofer. Bryttni guessed this was a blind date, and the only time they would be together. She was out of his league. He wasn't much to look at with his Roman nose and big ears, but the woman looked close to pretty in the dim light of the bar. She hadn't lost all her looks from starting a family in her youth.

Bryttni was distracted when an old man in a grimy cowboy hat took the remaining seat at the bar, next to the man on the date. As Bryttni set a menu in front of the new arrival, she realized he was younger than she first thought. He smelled like he hadn't had intimate contact with soap and water for a few days. His fingernails were jammed with grime.

A teal-colored short jacket with embroidered red roses on each sleeve hung off him. He either was not the original owner of the coat, or he had lost fifty pounds since he acquired it. The jacket would need more than one dry cleaning to get all the stains off it. Her grandmother used to watch reruns of *The Porter Waggoner Show*. And this patron looked like he could have been on that show, maybe with the backup band, and definitely in better days. Bryttni suspected the man would not be supplementing her tuition fund with a large tip.

The man on the blind date had been looking for an excuse to inch his stool closer to his date. He frowned and said something to the woman as he nodded toward the cowboy. He scooted a tad closer.

"What can I get you to drink?" Bryttni asked the new arrival.

"The cheapest bourbon you got," the cowboy said, digging a small wad of crinkled dollar bills from the jacket's inside pocket. "And a separate glass of water."

Bryttni set the tumblers of bourbon and water in front of the man, along with a menu. "In case you want to order something to eat," she said. She guessed he wouldn't, judging from what little money he lay on the bar.

He dipped his index finger in the water glass, and then held it over the glass of bourbon, letting a few drops mix with the alcohol.

"What's good here?" he asked, ignoring the menu.

"A lot of people who sit at the bar order the pork sandwich. I don't know if it's any good, because I'm a vegetarian."

The cowboy studied her like she just said she was a Martian. "What the hell you working here for then?"

"The tips are pretty good," she said. "Some nights anyway."

"Must be," he said, twirling the menu on the bar's surface like it was a top. "I'll just enjoy my drink for a moment before deciding how hungry I am."

Bryttni checked on the progress of the blind date. Their food had arrived. The man had ordered ribs, and the woman settled for a salad with grilled chicken pieces, a typical first-date order for a woman. Bryttni wondered if the guy would get laid after all. Otherwise, the woman would have ordered something heartier.

"Did you hear about the shootings in that little town the other day?" the man asked his date as he pulled a rib bone from the slab.

"You mean the town with the silly name?" the woman asked. "Tadpole or something like that?"

"Smackdab," the man said. "I think," he added, like he didn't want to appear too interested in the story. "Another nutjob shot up a whole mess of people."

Bryttni noticed the cowboy lean slightly toward the man. Like her, he was interested in the couple's conversation, but he didn't mind showing it.

"What'd you expect from inbred white trash?" the woman said. "The only way they know how to solve their problems is by shooting somebody."

"Here's the funny part though," the man said. "The shooter was upset over a breakup with his girlfriend. She was a midget. I'm talking a real munchkin."

The woman twirled her beer glass in the water ring on the bar top. "Like I said, inbred white trash." She laughed to herself and shook her head. "A midget. Amazing."

Bryttni returned to the cowboy to ask if he was ready to order. He motioned her to lean in, close enough that she could smell his stale breath.

"Tell the fellow in the pretty yellow shirt I'd like to talk to him," the man said. "Tell him to come over here."

Bryttni glanced at the far end of the bar though she didn't have to. Troy—she didn't know his last name—was parked there like he was several nights a week, in a yellow Ralph Lauren button-down.

Troy always wore pressed shirts, which he tucked into belted khakis or occasionally a nice pair of factory-faded jeans. He looked like a typical just-out-of-college office worker having a drink after work, which was what he wanted everyone to think. His real job was selling ecstasy and whatever else he had available from time to time.

Occasionally, Troy came into Smokin' Hot with his sidekick, a creepy little dude named Lamar. Lamar did not wear the Troy uniform. He tended toward less formal wear, such as graphic tees and baggy canvas shorts that ended below his knees. Tonight, Troy soloed.

Troy did not do all his business at Smokin' Hot. But three or four times a night, a frat boy in a Vineyard polo shirt would walk up to Troy like they were buddies. Something would happen under the bar, and the frat rat would leave a few seconds later.

Bryttni guessed the night manager was taking a small percentage. She minded little as long as narcs didn't show up some night and put her out of work.

Bryttni studied the grim sequel to Porter Waggoner. He couldn't be an undercover cop, unless the police had a budget for a Hollywood-quality makeup artist.

"Troy? He doesn't come to people," Bryttni said. "They go to him."

"Time he turned over a new leaf," the cowboy said, taking another sip of bourbon.

"He'll want to know why you want to talk to him," Bryttni said, wondering why she had to be in the middle of it. This grimy old fart wouldn't even leave her a decent tip.

"Let's not insult each other's intelligence," the cowboy said. He smiled, but Bryttni saw no mirth in the man's eyes. She didn't believe she scared easily, but the man's eyes were off. Dark and mean like a cur's.

She went to the other end of the bar.

"See the odd ball with the cowboy hat behind me?" she asked Troy.

He looked around her at the small man sipping his drink.

"Let me guess," Troy said. "That's your grampy."

"He wants to talk to you."

Troy spread his hands like a priest and looked on either side of him. "I'm right here," he said.

"He wants you to come over there, and I get the feeling he's not used to being turned down."

"What's the matter? Did he forget his walker in the car?"

"I'm just passing along his request," Bryttni said. "I've got drinks to make. So if you two want to pass notes, keep me out of it. The sooner he leaves, the better I'll feel."

Troy sighed heavily, looking up at the ceiling like an adult who was tired of dealing with an infantile child.

Skunk left the rib joint after a quick and cryptic conversation with Troy. They agreed to meet later that night in an office parking lot Skunk hoped he could find without asking directions. He had ordered no food at the overpriced eatery, and, remembering that Rolf would be starving by now, he made a quick stop at the KFC to order a three-piece.

Rolf was sprawled on his bed. Another episode of *Law & Order* was on, with the volume turned up much louder than necessary. It didn't appear Rolf was watching. He seemed to stare at the wall behind the set.

Skunk remembered this episode. A lady abortion doctor was murdered. Briscoe and Logan would soon suspect a wacko minister.

"Where you been?" Rolf asked Skunk.

"Elsewhere," Skunk said. He tossed the box of chicken on Rolf's bed. "Have at it."

Rolf swung his legs over the bed. He immediately tore open the box and pulled out a leg.

"We got a gig to go to?" he asked, while chewing.

"No show tonight," Skunk said. "We're going to hang here for a while."

"Fine by me," Rolf said, chewing. "As long as I got some chicken."

Skunk crawled on his empty bed and leaned against the headboard. He wished he could sleep a few minutes before he went out again. He took four of the Tylenol PMs and, with admiration, watched Rolf eat. A border of grease rimmed the man's mouth.

"I heard some people talking about Smackdab," Skunk said. "It seems your kid was involved in the shooting."

Rolf paused no more than a second before tossing a bone in the box and grabbing another piece. "What shooting?"

"Ah, nothing," Skunk said, feeling it was more trouble than necessary to recount what he knew. That was good enough for the other man, who proceeded to rip meat from bone like a Rottweiler.

Skunk had plugged in his cell phone before his foray, and he now tried to give Diane another call. It went immediately to voice mail. He dialed Snoots.

"Who you calling?" Rolf asked, now working his way through a glob of mashed potatoes.

"The bar," Skunk said. Even his addled roommate would know which bar.

Billie picked up after ten rings.

"Guess who."

"What do you want?" Billie sounded cold. Skunk could hear George Strait on the jukebox in the background. Skunk had tried to sweet talk her into paying Olstad & Mattsen to be the house band for a while, but Billie was one of the few people in Smackdab who was never intimidated by him.

"I've been trying to get a hold of Diane," Skunk said. "But like usual, the bitch won't answer her phone."

"Maybe it's because you call her names like that. And who am I? Her secretary?"

"Just wondering if you'd seen her tonight."

"You missed your son's funeral."

"What's this about Rolf's kid being involved?"

Even with noise on Billie's end, Skunk could hear the hesitation in her voice. "Nothing. She worked at the machine shop, but she didn't get shot."

"Are you sure there's not more to it than that?"

Skunk could hear nothing but Strait and the hum of customer voices.

"You still there?" he asked.

"I've got thirsty customers and no time to chew the fat with you," Billie said. She hung up before Skunk could say more.

After disconnecting, Skunk scooped all the coins he had thrown on the dresser and went to use the pay phone he had seen earlier in the parking lot of a convenience store. Diane, not recognizing the number, answered.

Skunk knew he had to be cool to keep her from hanging up. "How you holding up?" he said.

Silence on the other end.

"Don't hang up on me," Skunk said. "I just called to check on you."

"What do you want?" Diane asked. She sounded tired, beaten.

"I just told you. I wanted to see if you're holding up all right."

"I'm holding," she said.

"I'll be back soon. Maybe a couple of days."

"Leave it alone."

"I need to take care of my familial responsibilities."

"You don't have a family anymore, Skunk. You haven't had a family in years."

"I got wind that Rolf's kid's mixed up in this. I think I'm getting the picture. The Klimp kid came to kill Maesie, and our boy got killed instead."

"Just stay away from her," Diane said. "You can't just show up and cause trouble when you've never been much to show up in the first place."

"Who said I was going to cause trouble?"

Diane said nothing. She disconnected.

23

Coach underestimated Jerry Debs. The foam hadn't settled in his first beer at Snoots before he mentioned, as a matter of fact, that it was he who put the dirt on the infamous, murderous Tommy Klimp that morning at the Masonic. Jerry was never a soft talker, so everyone at Snoots could hear him. He said the sparkplugs were so dirty on the backhoe, he feared half of us buried there woke up from all the noise. Jerry has some interesting theories about what we dead people do with our time. (Sleeping is not among them.) Jerry said he would have to do something about those plugs before the next dig. I predict he will not do so in time.

As Debs pontificated about Tommy's burial, Jordy Wakefield blew the foam from a fresh beer at the same table where he had met with Denbo a few days earlier. Wakefield did not know why Denbo had chosen to consult him, if consulting it was. Wakefield had never spoken to the man until he showed up at Snoots that morning. Denbo said Smackdab was about to undergo some changes, and he asked if Wakefield wanted to be on the right or wrong side of those changes. Wakefield did not know what Denbo was talking about, but he did not want to be on the wrong side of Denbo, no matter what was involved. Wakefield had heard the rumors that Denbo had been an assassin for the mob. Wakefield wasn't sure that was true, but a guy like Denbo wouldn't need to use a gun to murder anyone. His maws were so big he could choke a regular-sized man in seconds. Besides, Denbo had money. Some of it might come Wakefield's way if he helped out Denbo a little. He had nothing else pressing to do.

Dirty Dave Hart took the chair opposite Wakefield.

"Did you put a shovel in your truck before you came?" Wakefield asked.

Dirty Dave nodded. "How about you?"

"You know I got a bad back," Wakefield said. "What good would a shovel do me?"

"First, you could shovel that shit about you having a bad back. And then you could use it to help dig up that bastard. I ain't doing it all by my lonesome."

Dirty Dave had yet to realize he and Wakefield were not equals. Wakefield was Denbo's second in command. He would have to educate Dirty Dave on the pecking order. First, Dirty Dave needed to understand the seriousness of Wakefield's back problem.

"I got the medical papers to prove my back's messed up," Wakefield said. He made like he was going to stand up to go fetch the affirming documentation. "I can run out to the house to get them and be back in thirty."

Dirty Dave waved him off. "Whatever. But it better be more than just me doing the digging. Where's your new butt buddy Denbo? Ain't he coming on this adventure?"

"He trusts me to take care of things, and I've had me a thought. All we got to do is get the keys to Jerry's backhoe. He drove the damned thing here again tonight."

Dirty Dave saw the beauty of Wakefield's idea and smiled. Once the gravedigger had a few more beers, he would gladly hand over the keys. After they used the backhoe to dig up the casket, they could also use it to haul the casket away from the cemetery.

"And where does Denbo want the thing delivered?"

Wakefield glared at him. "He don't have to think of everything, you know. I thought of the backhoe, and I've got in mind where to take the casket."

While they waited for Jerry Debs to get another drink or two in him, the conspirators discussed where they could find another hand. Dirty Dave motioned to Cahill, who sat by himself at a corner table looking like he'd cut anyone who tried to share the table with him.

"How about the Renfrew boy," Dirty Dave said.

Wakefield scowled at Cahill, who returned the favor.

"Did you already forget that stunt he pulled the other day at the Klimps?" Wakefield asked. "And from the way his snout's all swelled up, I'd say someone recently beat the tar out of the runt. If he ever had sex, he'd have to take the bottom, because he's always fucking up."

"Yeah, but we need *someone* to help," Dirty Dave said.

"Not him. He couldn't even kick the midget out of her house," Wakefield said. "Letting a midget push you around don't make you much of a man."

Cahill noticed the two men looking his direction. He put one leg up on the empty chair in front of him, and, gazing at Wakefield, grabbed his nuts and tugged.

It didn't take long to get the keys from Debs, who was told he needed to give them up so he wouldn't be tempted to go on another drunken heavy equipment drive until he sobered some. Debs had lost his truck to the bank, and he drove the backhoe everywhere in the area, occasionally even as far as West Fork. People were used to hearing the machine running down the road at night because Jerry went to Snoots every evening. Depending on how much he'd had to drink, he would roam Smackdab's streets sometimes until one or two in the morning. Like periodic thunderstorms, those in Smackdab who kept regular sleeping hours had gotten used to the rumble of the Kubota.

After buying Debs another draught, Wakefield hopped on the backhoe and drove it to the cemetery. Dirty Dave argued that he had just as much right to run the backhoe as Wakefield, but Wakefield had the keys in hand.

The conspirators had recruited a third, Rodney Jensen, a second cousin of Jean Pankin. Jensen worked at the hog operation and had come into Snoots that night looking for entertainment because there was nothing good on TV. Jensen and Dirty Dave followed the backhoe in Jensen's truck. Even with the backhoe's help, it took nearly two hours to lift Tommy Klimp's casket from the hole. Dirty Dave and Jensen had sweated through their clothes, while Wakefield kept cool atop the Kubota.

When they reached the casket, the bunch hooped and hollered like they were out for Halloween pranking. But no one was eager to jump down in the hole and situate a chain around the casket. Wakefield, who never left his seat on the machine, threatened the others that if they didn't, by God, get down in there and get the chain put in place, he would tell Denbo. They got to work.

It required some digging with shovels to snake the chain around the casket. When that was finished, plus a six-pack of beer, and the chain was attached to the backhoe's bucket, Wakefield lifted the casket out and began the slow trip to the machine shop, which was half a mile from the cemetery on the eastern edge of town. The chain was wrapped around the backhoe's bucket in a way that caused the heavy casket to droop to the right side of the backhoe. That side nearly scraped the road's surface. Wakefield took his time, however, trying to avoid potholes and other bumps that might cause him to lose his cargo in the middle of town.

With dirty sparkplugs, the backhoe popped noisily along the route. A few vehicles passed the improvised cortege, but anyone out that late would say nothing. Those leaving Snoots had a good idea what Wakefield was doing. If not exactly in favor of the activity, they did not oppose it. Bennie Duroque's cruiser was spotted a block away at one point. The constable could have easily seen and heard the backhoe, but he and the car turned the other way.

When the macabre motorcade had arrived at the machine shop, Wakefield lowered his cargo next to the front of the building and waited for his half-drunk companions to stumble from the truck that followed him to the machine shop.

"Lean it up there against the building, top to bottom," he instructed them after Jensen had unhooked the chain.

Dirty Dave looked at the casket and knew the three of them, assuming Wakefield got off his lazy ass, could not pick up the casket. "Use the goddamn backhoe. That's what it's for."

"It's probably easier to do it by hand," Wakefield said.

"Well, it ain't going to be easy with just the three of us," said Dirty Dave, who was sobering and becoming unsettled by what they were doing.

"Have I got to do everything?" Wakefield said. "Hook that chain back up. I'll try to get it started, but you worthless sacks of sheep crap better be able to guide it into place. You think you can handle at least that little job?"

The men on the ground studied the casket, which looked like a slab of slick granite in the poor lighting. They weren't sure they *could* handle it.

With the chain reconnected, Wakefield maneuvered the casket as close to the building as possible. He lifted it so Dirty Dave and Jensen could stand under it. They tentatively grabbed hold like they believed they could somehow help position it. If the chain broke, however, or if Wakefield suddenly dropped the bucket, they knew they would be crushed.

"I'm going to lower it slow," Wakefield said. "As I do, you numbnuts position it so the top part leans against the building. I want it to look like those old timey pictures of dead outlaws where they prop them up against a building for everyone to see."

Any confidence Dirty Dave had in Wakefield's ability to accurately maneuver the six-hundred-pound casket evaporated as he sobered. "Are you shitting me?" he asked. "You'll smash us like ants with this thing."

"I not going to smash nobody, you fool. Why don't you give me just an ounce of credit here? Now get a hold of it and guide it into position."

The men on the ground put their hands on the casket, but neither did much to help maneuver it. They were poised to jump away at the slightest jerk of the backhoe's bucket.

As they expected, Wakefield failed to finesse the casket and dropped it with a bang against the building, putting a sizable dent in the shop's aluminum façade. The casket sat at a one-hundred-twenty-degree angle against the building, but leaned left-to-right at a sixty-degree angle so that only its upper right corner made contact with the building. It teetered as though a decent breeze would push it to the ground.

Dirty Dave stood on the left side with both hands on the casket, afraid to let go. Jensen, who realized he would have been better off staying home and watching *Shawshank Redemption* for the fifth time, had a similar grip on the right side. If the casket fell, it would fall toward Dirty Dave, possibly bursting open and spilling out Tommy. That would put a neat bow on the whole affair.

The situation for the three men was precarious, though Dirty Dave used a different description.

"This is shit-fucked," he said, yelling at Wakefield. "You got to use the bucket to keep the goddamn thing from falling on us."

"Can't," Wakefield said. The lone security light outside the machine shop was too dim to reveal the look on his face, but it would have betrayed no concern. "You're in the way," he said. "Best thing you can do now is let go and run before it smashes you."

"Mother Mary of Jesus, what have we done?" Dirty Dave said with a whimper.

Rodney Jensen mumbled something under his breath.

Dirty Dave did not intend to stand there any longer. "I'll count to three," he said. "Then we both let go and hightail it. All right?"

He didn't wait for Jensen to agree before he began counting. "One, two…" Dirty Dave let loose and ran.

"You asswipe," Jensen yelled as he let go, too.

The casket fell to the ground and rolled on its side. Neither of the two men on foot was there to see it. They had run away and did not look back. Wakefield walked down Route 4 to Snoots to get his truck.

COME UP A CLOUD

24

Skunk was running late. Yellow Shirt Troy had given him directions to an office building he said was five minutes from the BBQ place. Skunk translated that to about thirty minutes on foot, but he walked forty before he eyed a three-story office building a block ahead and fronted by a large parking lot.

The lot was well lighted, empty of all but a white maintenance truck parked next to the building. Troy had told Skunk to come around the left of the building, past a row of green dumpsters. Skunk had wanted to make the exchange in the restaurant's parking lot, but Troy insisted on more privacy.

Tucked in the breast pocket of his jacket, in the CVS bag, Skunk carried the remaining meth he had taken from Sheena, who had taken it from her husband, Leo, who had intended to sell it his Navajo customers. Skunk felt uneasy about this meeting, but he had little choice. At the BBQ place, he had asked Troy if he wanted to increase his inventory at a deep discount. Skunk regretted mentioning a discount—it made him look weak and desperate—but he could do nothing about that now.

A forest green Camry with a healthy dent in the front driver's side panel idled in a four-vehicle parking area behind in the rear of the building. Skunk wondered if the four-door Toyota was a hand-me-down from Troy's parents. He looked young enough to still live at home. Perhaps he had borrowed the car from his mom. It didn't look like appropriate wheels for a big-time dealer. But Skunk wasn't up to date on what passed for acceptable drug dealer transportation.

Troy rolled down his window; a black guy occupied the front passenger's seat.

Yellow Shirt's muscle?

"Where's your transpo, Buddy?" Troy asked as Skunk stepped closer. Skunk hated to be called Buddy, Pal or anything else that connoted a superficial closeness. He wasn't anyone's buddy, and definitely not the buddy of a half-ass drug slinger.

"My car's right where I left it," Skunk said.

"We've been watching you walk this way for about a half a mile. Did you leave your car in Kansas?"

Skunk ignored the dig.

Troy nodded at the CVS bag skunk held at his side. "You got something for me in there, or have you been shopping for lipstick?"

Skunk jiggled the bag. "Depends on what you got for me, I reckon," he said. "If you ain't got five hunnert, it don't matter much what's in the bag."

"And if you don't have what you promised, it doesn't matter if I've got five hundred or a mill," Troy said.

"Well then?" Skunk said.

Troy mumbled something to the man in the passenger seat. The small guy reached down to get something on the floorboard. Skunk felt for his file, but knew it would do him no good if the situation went wrong.

The other man handed something to Troy, which was also wrapped in a CVS bag. "Got the money right here," Troy said, holding up the bag so Skunk could see it. "Now, let me get a quick peak at yours before we draw attention."

Skunk took two more steps toward the car. He could see the other man better now. Skunk realized he wasn't black, but lighter. Mexican maybe? He was older than Troy.

"You'd better do likewise and show me there ain't just your tampons in that bag," Skunk said.

Troy pealed back the bag so Skunk could see the end of a stack of bills, but it was hard to tell how much money it amounted to. If the stack added up to half a grand, it must contain fives and ones. Skunk reached in his bag and pulled out a cellophane bag of crystal, which represented half the supply. He handed it to Troy, who examined the contents.

"That's half. You get the other half when you hand over the money."

"Looks like some decent stuff here," he said. "This is going to help out a lot. I was running a little low."

"Came all the way from Utah," Skunk said. "Made by a cook named Hernan. One of the best in the Southwest. You're getting a helluva bargain."

"You got that right. See you around."

The Toyota's old belts squealed as it sped away.

Skunk hurried around the corner of the building and watched the Camry exit the parking lot headed west.

Skunk began the long walk back to the motel. Adrenaline had kept him going the past hour, but he had started to come down. The four Tylenol PM he took earlier had begun to make him lethargic. He hoped he could finally sleep. As he walked through a residential area with bungalows and arbored sidewalks on both sides, he looked for a yard where he could rest. Before he could choose a spot, he eyed someone entering through the double white doors of a small yellow brick church across the street. Though it was dark, a light above the doors illuminated the entrance. The young man who entered the church looked like Luke.

Skunk crossed the street and entered the same door as his son. The Everlasting Tabernacle of God, a small one-story affair, shared a half-acre with an empty asphalted parking lot that would accommodate thirty cars at most. Inside the church's front door, Skunk entered an unlit foyer which was little bigger than a coat closet. Rather than fumble for a light switch, Skunk paused to allow his eyes to adjust. The outside light shown through a small diamond-shaped window above the door. A coat rack occupied one side of the entryway and a rolling metal shelf stacked with worship bulletins on variously colored paper took up the other.

Skunk opened the next set of double doors and entered a small sanctuary. The room had two rows of blond oak pews with a center aisle. Instead of a pulpit, a lone microphone stood at the front end of the center aisle. In each front corner of the sanctuary was a closed wood laminate door. A triangle wall sconce above the door on the right side gave the chapel an ethereal gloom. A plain wooden cross hung on the back wall.

Just as Skunk approached the door with the light above it, a heavyset man with a graying crew cut entered through it.

"Evening, Brother," he said. "What can I do you for?"

"I'm looking for the kid that just came in here," Skunk said.

The large man looked puzzled. "Kid?"

"Not a kid really," Skunk said. "He's twenty-one now."

"I haven't seen or heard a soul," the man said. His face crinkled like he was trying to make his brain work a little harder. "There was a time, about a year ago, when some kids got in here. We think they were looking for wine, but we just use grape juice. They were real disappointed when they found out it was Ocean Spray."

"No, this was my son," Skunk said. "I saw him for sure. He walked straight in the front door, just like I did."

"Guess I forgot to lock it again," the man said. He offered Skunk his hand. "I'm Brother Dale, the pastor," he said. "Just trying to get things ready for Sunday morning."

Brother Dale had thick hands with stubby fingers, but his grip was strong and calloused. Not the hands of a full-time preacher. The way Brother Dale looked at him made Skunk uneasy, as though the man could see into him in a way others could not.

After freeing himself from the large man's grip and gaze, Skunk nodded at the other closed door. "Anyplace else he could have gone?"

"That's just a closet where we keep communion supplies," Brother Dale said. "We keep it locked since the famous grape juice caper. But then again, could be I forgot to lock it, too."

After testing the door, he pulled a large ring of keys from his pocket and unlocked it. He peaked inside before standing with the door open to let Skunk look as well.

"Unless your son can walk through walls…" he said.

Skunk peered in. "You sure nobody came through the other door?" he asked.

Brother Dale shook his head. "Not without me hearing them, they couldn't. I can hear the front doors open from way in the back. I heard them open once, I came out here, and there you were."

Skunk doffed his hat, got on his hands and knees, and peered under the pews. He stood up, and scratched his head before returning the hat to its regular spot. "Guess I'm seeing things," he said. "I coulda swore it was Luke. But I've been real tired lately and maybe my eyes are playing tricks on me."

"If you don't mind me saying so," Brother Dale said, "you do look like you've been through a rough piece."

"You could say that. Luke got himself killed last week. I thought I'd seen him, or maybe his ghost. Put a real jump in me."

"I'm real sorry for your loss," the minister said. "It's not unusual to think we see our loved ones right after they pass." Brother Dale put his large hand on Skunk's skinny shoulder. "I bet you've had your son on your mind so much you couldn't help but see him like he was in the flesh."

"That's the odd thing," Skunk said. "Because I haven't been thinking about him that much. We wasn't real close."

Brother Dale's eyebrows twitched. Skunk expected him to blurt some churchy hobble gobble about making amends with the Lord. Perhaps it was true, but Skunk didn't need to hear it from part-time clergyman who hung drywall or whatever for a living.

Instead, the preacher said, "You've had your son on your mind more than you think. And to lose one so young, and so traumatically…"

Skunk had not mentioned how his son died. Brother Dale's eyes glazed for a second as though he could envision the bloodbath in Smackdab. "Seems like some among us become upset about the littlest things these days. And they have no way to express their anger but with violence."

"You got that goddamn right," Skunk said.

He looked around the sanctuary again, slowly, and shook his head. "He sure did look real to me. Maybe I'm losing my mind."

"Could be the Lord sending you a message."

Skunk scratched the tip of his nose and smiled. "No offense, but me and the man upstairs don't normally communicate," he said. "Now the guy down below, maybe…"

The minister looked hard into Skunk's eyes. "Don't take this thing lightly," he said. "I don't know your plans, but think about how they square up with what God has in mind. Maybe your son was sent to tell you to wake up and take notice. Take a different path."

"Take no offense, but waking up ain't a problem," Skunk said. "It's the getting to sleep part I'm having issues with. I haven't felt right since I don't know when. Right now, getting to Smackdab's the only plan I got. And I'll take whatever path gets me there the quickest and cheapest."

The pastor reached for his wallet in his back pocket.

"I know it won't get you far," he said. "But take what cash I have on me."

He took out all the paper money in his wallet. "Forty-two dollars," he said. "If I'd skipped the combo meal and the large shake tonight, I'd have a full fifty."

Skunk hesitated before taking the money and pocketing it in his jeans. He wasn't used to being offered money with no expectation. It did not occur to him to thank the minister before exiting the church.

Rolf had been sleeping a lot lately. That much he knew. Some real deep sleeps. Each time he woke up, it was like he had taken a long nap in the middle of the day, the kind where a person momentarily forgot where he was. Lately, though, his memory no longer snapped back all the way. The feeling was something like the look the sky got at dusk when clouds cast over the whole of it and turned it the color of pewter. Kind of gauzy and unnatural feeling. Everything in Rolf's brain was fuzzed up and out of focus for lack of good light. Rolf could still *see*, but not as clearly as he used to.

He knew they were on their way to Smackdab, though they were taking their sweet time about it. The reason for the trip was cloudy, too. Rolf could not remember if Skunk had explained it to him, and Rolf didn't want to ask again. He felt ashamed that he couldn't remember.

Rolf thought about Smackdab. It would be all right to see Charmin and Maesie again. Or was Charmin still around? No, he remembered. A car had got her. He remembered that for sure. The funeral costs had put him in a hole he was still trying to dig out of.

Maesie was still around, he knew. Where else would she be? Was she still in school? Rolf couldn't get a hold of that memory.

He knew Olstad & Mattsen weren't playing shows anymore. He knew, because the Taylor was gone. Out of habit, he kept reaching for it next to his bed. Skunk had done something with the guitar, but Rolf couldn't remember what or why. Something about it made Rolf angry, though. He was used to getting mad at Skunk, but any hard feelings would dissipate quickly. It usually was hard to stay mad at Skunk, who knew what was best. This time, though, the anger held tight to his temples.

Why *were* they returning to Smackdab? Something about it wasn't right. Smackdab always meant trouble. This time, Rolf had a feeling it could be worse than usual. He clutched the pillow bundle to his chest and, feeling better that way, fell asleep.

25

As a hint of light shone in the east, Cahill wheeled the Vic through town as he tried to fight off sleep. Lightning gashed the obsidian sky to the west. Cahill could smell moisture in the air, which lightened his mood. He considered going to the city park, sprawling on the dry grass and letting fat cool drops refresh him. It had been a long time since he had done that.

As Cahill passed the machine shop, he caught sight of the backhoe under the cold blue aura of the parking lot's security light. It was the first thing to amuse him in days. When Snoots closed a few hours earlier, Jerry Debs couldn't find his keys and couldn't remember where he had left his machine. Debs stood in the parking lot of the bar, staring into oblivion and trying to remember the previous hours in his sotted haze. Cahill offered him a ride.

"Nah," Debs said, slurring his words from three too many beers. "It'll come to me soon enough, what I done with the backhoe. Damned if my mind isn't a complete blank on the subject right this moment, though."

Just as Cahill drove on past the machine shop, something odd near the building caught his eye. He rammed the Vic in reverse and backed into the lot.

The brushed-silver casket lay on its side between the backhoe and the building. In the dim light, Cahill could discern dirt stuck in the crevice between the lid flange and the main frame of the box. The metal shell was scraped raw of its finish in places where the chain, laying on the ground like a sleeping snake, had been looped around the casket. The handle running along what was now the top of the casket was bent outward.

As the backhoe idled, the rain cap on its exhaust pipe kept a sorrowful beat. Cahill wanted to push the Vic's accelerator to the floor and get as far away as possible, but something kept him where he was. Something wouldn't let him leave.

Cahill knew Tommy's spirit was loose and in control.

You and me used to be all right with each other. Don't forget that.

But Cahill could not expect the spirit of Tommy to remember something Cahill himself had forgotten until then. He and Tommy had something like a friendship when they were in middle school. They, including Maesie, were inexorably linked to each other by everyone else. They were the left-out kids. They did not want to be associated with each other, but their classmates made the connection for them. They were the odd ones—the dwarf, the albino, and the weirdo. For a short while, Maesie was even further outside the orbit of normalcy when Cahill and Tommy became temporary friends.

Cahill had once spent the night at the Klimp house. Cahill's parents had had another one of their blowouts involving flying kitchenware. When the adults elevated to fists and threats of cutlery, Cahill feared his noggin might get in the way of an airborne meat tenderizer. Desperate for any place to be other than home, he called Maesie's house, but the Mattsen phone had been disconnected again. He called the Klimp home instead.

"Oh darn. Tommy goes to bed at ten on Friday nights," Patsy said when Cahill phoned. It was past eleven o'clock on a rare night off from the GasGo for Patsy. She sounded delighted that someone had called asking for her son.

"Maybe you could call back tomorrow," Patsy said. "Or I'm sure Tommy would be happy to call you."

"That's all right," Cahill said. "I just had a question about, uh, I guess it's our algebra assignment. I had a question about that."

A metal baking pan hit the kitchen wall in the Renfrew abode. Cahill was on the front porch, but the sound carried well through the house's thinly plastered walls. Patsy heard it on her end.

"Is there something going on at your house?" Patsy asked. Everyone in Smackdab knew the Renfrews liked to mix it up a little while sharing a twelve-pack.

"Nah, it's all right," Cahill said.

His mother yelled something punctuated by *worthless cocksucker* and what sounded like a piece of silverware hitting the wall. Cahill's father laughed with a meanness in his voice, which meant their foreplay was rapidly escalating.

"It doesn't sound all right to me," Patsy said.

Cahill said nothing.

"Get some clothes and a toothbrush packed and I'll be over there in ten minutes."

When she brought him back to the Klimp home, Patsy insisted Cahill drink a cup of microwaved hot chocolate. She made a pallet for him on the floor next to the bed where Tommy slept. When Tommy woke up the next morning, he stared at his visitor, giving no indication of surprise or pleasure to have had a sleepover without his knowledge. Some people weren't morning types.

Cahill followed Tommy into the living room. Tommy, who had donned a Viking helmet as he rose from his bed, plopped down on the sofa and turned on the TV.

"The Discovery Channel all right with you?" Tommy asked.

Cahill guessed it was, though he had never watched that channel. A show about a survivalist was on. Two minutes into the program, the guy was threatening to drink his piss.

Unlike Tommy, Patsy and Bob Klimp made a fuss over Cahill's presence.

"Good morning, boys," Bob said. He held a cup of coffee, its steam wafting toward his face. He acted jumpy, like an average guy who felt unworthy to host a VIP in his home. "Ready for some breakfast?" he asked.

"Let's have steak," Tommy said. He held the remote toward the screen, prepared to switch channels the moment a commercial came on.

Steak? Cahill thought. *Who has steak for breakfast?*

Bob chuckled. "Who do you think we are? The Rockefellers?"

Tommy and Cahill looked up at the man. "Who?" Tommy asked.

"Like Donald Trump. Or Jay-Z," Bob said. "Now pick something breakfast-like."

"What're the choices?" Cahill asked.

"Just about anything. Pancakes, waffles, omelets."

"I only eat cereal," Cahill said. "Do you have Lucky Charms?"

"Gosh. I'm sorry. I don't believe we have those," Bob said, patting his jeans as though he might have forgotten a box in his pocket. "Let me go in the kitchen and ask Tommy's mother. If not, I'll run out and get a box."

On the TV show, the piss-drinker was sucking yolk from a bird's egg when Patsy entered the living room to announce they had no Lucky Charms.

"Bob drove up to the GasGo to get a box," she said. "He should be back about the time your show's over."

Cahill nodded without a thank you.

"Steak," he said, shaking his head after Patsy returned to the kitchen. "That was ballsy."

Tommy giggled. "It was worth a try. Dad's acting all weird. I've never heard him say good morning like that."

"I should start calling you T-Bone," Cahill said.

For the first time, Tommy switched attention from the TV to his visitor. "Really," he asked. "You would do that?"

Cahill shrugged. It was just a thing to say. "I don't know. If you want, maybe."

"Yes," Tommy said, his face all seriousness. "Please do that. Everybody has a nickname."

"No, they don't. I don't have one."

"Yes, you do," Tommy said. "Everyone calls you Casper the Freaky Ghost."

Cahill dug into his knees with his fingernails, just below the hemline of his gym shorts. He did so when he felt his anger rising, transferring his focus to the pain. It never worked.

"I hate that fucking name," Cahill said. "If you call me that again, I'll end you."

Tommy raised a hand in surrender and returned his attention to the show. The survivor guy was now waiting for a helicopter to rescue him. Cahill wondered if the camera crew would be rescued as well.

When Bob returned, Cahill followed Tommy into the kitchen. Tommy's sister was seated at the table. It was ten-thirty, and Emmalynn Klimp had just gotten up with a bad case of bed head. The straw-colored hair on the left side of her head jutted perpendicular from her skull. Her eyes were puffy from her having slept on her stomach. Still, Emmalynn Klimp was the prettiest girl Cahill knew. Though a year younger than he, she was already out of his league in terms of looks, intelligence, and potential. Like all other girls of her ilk, she looked at Cahill like he was a weeping boil.

Cahill took the chair opposite her. He wished he were brave enough to sit next to her, but he didn't want to make her cringe. She already seemed unhappy enough at his presence.

Scowling at Cahill, she asked, "Where'd you come from?" Then to her mother: "Mom, why is he here?"

Before Cahill or Patsy could answer, Tommy said, "He's my friend."

Judging from the cockeyed smirk on her face, Cahill guessed Emmalynn was about to deliver an insulting retort. But her mother set the newly purchased box of Lucky Charms on the table along with three bowls and spoons.

Emmalynn studied the box. "You never let us have cereal like this? What gives?"

"It was Dad's idea," Patsy said. "You can ask him."

With a furrowed blond brow, Emmalynn scrutinized the back of the cereal box. Then she scrutinized Cahill and grinned.

"Oh, I get it." Her smile quickly drooped. "It's because Tommy's ittle wittle friend is here," she said in a baby voice. "Why don't we get to have sugar bombs when my friends stay over?"

She answered her own question. "Because they come over all the time. This will probably be the only time in the history of the world that Tommy will have a friend over, so we need to treat it like a national holiday." She used air quotes on "friend."

Patsy set another box of cereal and a half-gallon of one percent on the table. "You can have some of these Wheaties if the other cereal doesn't suit you," she said, holding her gaze to see if Emmalynn had more sass to offer.

The cereal selection controversy had made Cahill too uncomfortable to open the box of Lucky Charms. He sat with his hands in his lap.

"Oh, Jeez," Emmalynn said with a dramatic sigh. She grabbed the Lucky Charms box and opened it. "If we've got Lucky Charms, I'm having Lucky Charms."

"Me, too," Tommy said. Cahill had never seen the kid look so happy. At school, he kept quiet and avoided eye contact.

After Emmalynn filled her bowl, she reached across the table and filled Tommy's. Then she tilted her head toward Cahill with her eyes on him. *Well?* Her eyes asked.

Cahill slid his bowl across the table so she could reach it.

It was the largest box of Lucky Charms available. Even after each child had two bowls and felt the beginnings of a strong sugar buzz, half the box remained.

"You can take the rest of the box home with you," Patsy said to Cahill.

Cahill saw the disappointment on the faces of the other two. "Nah," he said. "We've got a full box at home."

Cahill hoped his generosity would win over Emmalynn. He was in love with her.

Cahill had never gone back to Tommy's house. Cahill was too busy being a Renfrew, skipping school and getting into general mischief. The T-Bone nickname never stuck. Taking pity on Tommy, Cahill tried it a time or two, but his heart wasn't in it. Besides, Cahill did not have the social status to bestow nicknames on anyone.

Emmalynn never acknowledged Cahill at school. He once caught her eye in the hallway. He smiled, but Emmalynn's neutral expression swiftly became one of revulsion. She looked away as though she had caught a glimpse of an abomination no respectable human should have to endure.

Cahill now willed himself to leave the Vic so he could turn off the backhoe. He risked being accosted by Tommy's hovering spirit so he could save Jerry a few dollars on gas. After he switched off the ignition, Cahill studied the casket, the first one he had seen up close since his grandmother's funeral. He had expected to be assaulted by his own fear, but he felt nothing. It was just a slab of meat in a box, he knew. All memories and experiences that were banked in a person's brain were gone the moment the synapses stopped firing. He wondered what difference it made.

Before he drove home to get some sleep, Cahill went by the Klimps' house and left a note telling them where to find their son.

26

Patsy slept with the help of Ambien, but she believed the vision was real. They sat in the backyard, in red and black folding armchairs she had acquired with her employee discount at the GasGo. The Klimps had used the chairs once, a July fourth evening when Bob and Tommy shot off bottle rockets in the pasture. Patsy and Emmalynn sat in the chairs and watched while eating rapidly melting homemade chocolate ice cream. Patsy cheered the show while Emmalynn, who was eager to go off with her friends, stewed. Since then, the chairs, dusty and cobwebbed, hung from utility hooks in the garage.

In Patsy's dream, Tommy first appeared as his death age of twenty-one years and five months. He held a lighted bottle rocket in his left hand, a black Bic lighter in his right, and he wore a black Metallica T-shirt that Patsy had ordered online for him the previous Christmas. A moment later, he was blond and twelve again, before his hair darkened and became curly at the tips. Patsy tried to yell at him to get rid of the bottle rocket before it exploded in his grasp, but she could make no sound. The firework exploded at the moment the specter became a young man again, this time wearing a white T-shirt with red splotches across the abdomen.

I have to know why, Tommy.

One corner of Tommy's mouth turned upward in a sheepish smile, but he did not answer. Just like that, he was twelve again, sitting beside her where Emmalynn had been a moment earlier. He took a sip from a strawed juice box and set it in the chair's cup holder.

The setting changed. Patsy and Tommy sat in the same folding chairs, but now at the edge of the machine shop parking lot. The chairs were positioned along the shoulder of the road close to traffic. Tommy still clasped the juice box. Smoke wisps from the bottle rocket curled upward from his free hand. Like a possessed robot, Tommy's chair inched onto the road and into the path of an old John Deere tractor driven by Leon Wesbecker. Wesbecker did not notice; Tommy did not care.

What did I do wrong? Tell me so I can make it right.

The juice box had become a carton of milk like those served at the school cafeteria.

You can't make it right.

Tommy's voice was muffled, hard to understand, as though his mouth were filled with marshmallows. A white sheet now enwrapped the top of his head; a second sheet covered his body so that his face, drained of blood, was the sole visible part of him.

This has nothing to do with you.

But it does. I'm the one left to deal with it.

Twelve-year-old Tommy giggled.

Patsy pleaded for him to stop, which made him giggle more. Patsy became angry. She tried to get out of her chair to reach for Tommy, but vinyl straps held her back. She wondered when Bob had installed seat belts on the chairs. No wonder they never used them.

When she looked up again, Tommy was gone. He had taken his chair with him. The setting once again was the back yard of the house. The grass was covered with crushed milk cartons.

Patsy awoke, sweating, and looked at Bob, who lay on his back next to her. Though asleep, Bob's face looked troubled. Was he deep in a dream like hers? More likely, his back pain made his sleep uncomfortable. Bob did not trouble his mind with thoughts the way Patsy did.

Patsy and Bob had been married eight years when Tommy was born. They had nearly given up trying to have children. When Patsy became pregnant, she knew it was a miracle. But it had been a lot harder than either parent expected to add a third human to their household after so many years as a couple.

Colicky and feeble in his first months, Tommy proved to be a difficult baby. As new parents, Bob and Patsy often made the twenty-minute trip to the hospital ER in West Branch. Except for Patsy's chronically ill mother, neither had surviving family in Smackdab. They had no one to lean on for help, and the baby's ailments, never anything serious, had exhausted them.

One desperate night, when Bob was away, Tommy wailed for an hour. Nothing Patsy did could assuage the baby. Alone and out of patience, she shook him. It was a small shake, and it happened once. But that instance was enough to terrify Patsy. When Bob came home an hour later, Patsy was still hysterical. She stood over the baby's crib in his darkened nursery.

"I shook him, Bob," she said, "like he was a carton of orange juice."

Bob reached down and touched his son's peach fuzz head.

"He seems to be all right," he said.

"But what if he's not? What if his tiny brain's a bowl of Jell-O now?"

"Let's keep an eye on him. We'll see how he is in the morning. If it seems like something's wrong, we'll take him over to West Fork to the doctor's."

"How will we know for sure?"

Bob tried to assure his wife.

"We're his mom and dad," Bob said. "We know everything about him, and we'll know if there's a problem."

Patsy stayed awake that night, standing by the crib and keeping watch over the small human snoring lightly in the crib. She could have sat in the rocking chair Bob had found at a second hand store and refinished for such a purpose. But Patsy wanted to punish herself for endangering her child. She wanted to feel the ache in her shins and hips as she stood, her legs locked, hovering over the tiny human she had endangered.

Tommy woke once to be fed, but Patsy saw no ill effects then or later that morning.

"What do you think?" Patsy asked Bob when they examined the baby. She wanted so much for him to be all right that she did not trust herself to be objective.

Bob picked up Tommy and cradled him in his arms. The baby cooed. Bob softly massaged his son's pate, looking for swelling or other signs of injury

"He seems all right," Bob said.

"So you don't think we need to make a run to the doctor?"

"I guess not," Bob said. "But let's watch him close."

For the rest of Tommy's life, Patsy feared that one small shake was responsible for the way her son turned out. He had been an odd boy who transitioned into an odd man, though Patsy and Bob could point to no one thing that foretold his last act. He was different, but so were lots of people.

When Tommy was eight months old, Bob and Patsy had decided, without needing to say it, that one child was enough. By then, though, Patsy was already three weeks pregnant with another baby. Emmalynn was a nearly perfect child. Healthy, happy, social. Her teenage years were typically challenging, but Emmalynn was *normal* in the way her parents had hoped for Tommy.

He had not been a bad child, though nothing made him particularly joyful. When he was small, he did not play with toys like his little sister did. He would be content to sit on the living room floor for lengthy periods, tracing the lines in the varnished hardwood with his chubby finger, or pressing his ear to the floor as though he heard a creature buried alive in the foundation.

When he was five, Bob and Patsy had him tested for autism in West Fork, but the pediatrician said there was no indication of a problem. Tommy was a healthy boy, he said. Just because he was quieter than the average five-year-old did not make him odd. Get over it, the doctor said in so many words.

When Tommy was eight, he began to talk more, but not about anything other boys his age had become interested in. He became obsessed with Mayan pyramids, learning everything he could about them, particularly about the burial chambers. Each morning at breakfast, Tommy would share with his mother another morbid fact he had learned online about human sacrifice.

"Did you know the Mayans used to cut out the hearts of the sacrificed people while the hearts were still beating?" he asked his mother.

"Interesting," Patsy said, by then used to her son's routine regurgitation of the previous night's reading.

"That must have been a heckuva party, huh?"

"Must have been, I guess," his mother said, trying not to dampen her son's interests, which she found macabre. When she asked a question about what he had read, Tommy took it as a cue to saturate her with details she did not want to know. She believed it best not to over-encourage him.

She looked at her son from behind. His head of hair, suffering from a severe case of bed head, reminded her a little of Johnny Depp in *Edward Scissorhands*. An innocent child who found ghastly customs fascinating. That's all it was.

"Some of the blades were made of black obsidian," Tommy said. "I wonder where I could get a knife like that."

"I doubt you could just pick one up at Wal-Mart," Patsy said, setting a bowl of microwaved Quaker Oats maple and brown sugar oatmeal in front of her son. "And for good reason."

Tommy took a bite without testing its temperature. He liked his oatmeal blistering.

"Most of the time, though," he said, "the Mayans, they didn't cut out the heart. They just disemboweled the ones they sacrificed."

Patsy wondered how old she was when she first used "disemboweled" in a sentence. Had she ever?

"You know how long the large intestine is?" Tommy asked, not waiting for an answer. "About twenty feet long. Can I have sausage?"

For Christmas, his parents indulged Tommy with a large volume on Mayan culture, much of which Tommy deemed inaccurate and poorly researched.

Patsy couldn't get back to sleep. She arose and went to Tommy's bedroom. Except for a few seconds the day of the shootings, she had not entered his room since. It was still dank with dried sweat and curing dirty laundry. Patsy did not flip on the ceiling light. In the murk, however, the room looked as though a caffeinated wild cat had been let loose in the small space. Tommy had never kept it clean, but it was worse than usual. Investigators and crime scene technicians had removed every item from Tommy's closet, shelves, drawers and under his bed. Most of it, which they judged was useless to their investigation, lay on the floor in a helter-skelter clump. The cops had taken several items, including Tommy's computer, which they had yet to return. They needed to confirm whether Tommy had acted alone before officially closing the case.

His mother abetted him from the time he was a baby.

Patsy shoved aside a pile of clothes and books on the bed to make room to sit. She had not spent this long in the room in years. She felt like an intruder in a place she was never allowed without Tommy's permission. It was like being in a stranger's room. Tommy's life had been so cloistered that his room summoned few shared memories.

The bed was piled with books by authors like David Mitchell and Robert Heinlein. In one corner, a gray fleece pullover draped over part of it, was a half-built replica of R2-D2 from *Star Wars*. Patsy remembered that. When he was thirteen, Tommy had given her a list of items he needed her to buy, including the largest metal mixing bowl she could find.

She had forgotten about it after she bought the supplies and only now realized that Tommy had never completed the project. The mixing bowl, which was intended to be the robot's head, was mounted atop a sheet of pliable stainless steel tin Tommy had fashioned into the robot's torso. Using a Sharpie, he had colored rectangles and circles to accessorize the head and body. That was as far as he went with it.

Another item Patsy had never seen in Tommy's room before the shootings: a poster of da Vinci's *The Last Supper* taped crookedly on the south wall of the bedroom. The head of Bono from U-2 had replaced the head of Jesus. The face of Judas had been taped over by a cutout photo of Tommy.

Patsy stood to exit the room when she stepped on something that dug sharply into her bare foot and snapped. Under a dirty pair of nylon shorts, she found a model of a Viking longboat. The sea serpent figurehead at the bow of the boat had broken off under Patsy's weight. She held the boat in her hands and tried to imagine Tommy building it. The model was a little more than a foot long, made of wood, with a red and white main sail. The boat must have been one of the few projects Tommy had seen through to the end. Patsy had never known about it.

She remembered another breakfast table conversation, soon after Tommy switched his attention from Mayans to Vikings. He was about twelve.

"I want to be a Viking when I grow up," he said, shoving a sausage link in his mouth.

Patsy was stacking cleaned coffee mugs in the cabinet by the sink. "I don't think they have Vikings anymore," she said. "Except the football kind."

"You said I could be anything I want when I grow up."

Patsy paused from her task to look at her son. "You're right," she said. "You can do anything you want."

Tommy wiped sausage grease from his upper lip. "They did the coolest thing when they died," he said.

Always with the death stuff.

"Sometimes they would put the dead people in their boats and bury the whole thing. But sometimes they put the dead guy on a boat on the water and set it on fire. The dead guy sails off into the afterlife. And get this: Sometimes they would kill a slave girl, one that hasn't had sex, and send her on the boat so she could serve her master in the next world. I'd sure like to see that happen."

Patsy stood over Tommy. "I wish you wouldn't read so much about death."

Tommy belched. "That's the best part."

Patsy set the pieces of the boat on the bed and left Tommy's room. She went back to bed as the outside light grayed toward dawn. She would ask Bob to clean Tommy's room at an appropriate time, because she would never go in there again.

Two miles west, Diane Olstad lay in her son's bed, as she had done since his death. The first night, the smell of Luke enveloped and comforted her. More than a feeling her son was in the room, she knew it. When the next morning came, however, her smell had replaced his. An odor of cigarette tar had erased his musk.

The second night, she had slept with an unwashed T-shirt of his on her forehead. Plenty of worn clothes were strewn across the carpeted floor of his small bedroom, but her smell was inexorably overpowering his. Just as she had been sure of his presence the first night, she was now just as sure of his withdrawal from the house. If she chose to abandon his bed to return to hers, the air in Luke's room would become stale, his smell lost forever.

She knew this, and it panicked her. She was already losing a sharp memory of her child. The precise features of his face, the angle of his shoulders, and the cadence of his gait were losing some of their clarity. In an age of selfie saturation, Luke did not like pictures of himself. The only good photo Diane had of him was his senior portrait from three years earlier. However, that was not what Luke had looked like at the end. In the past year, his face had become sharper-edged as he moved into adulthood. He had begun to look more like the son of Skunk Olstad.

As she lay in his room, Diane wondered what her son had been thinking his last night in the same bed. Had he been planning to move out? He wanted to, Diane knew, but the appropriate time was still in the future. He wanted to save money for a new truck first. That would give them more time together, but she had already begun preparing to lose him. Perhaps that was a consolation: She had already begun to let him go before he died.

27

Smackdab has been a bad-luck town all the way back to the Civil War. There's a stone obelisk at the northwest corner of the park with the engraved names of twelve men. Hell, they weren't even men. A couple were as young as fifteen. The way we learned it in history class was a bunch of locals joined a volunteer infantry outfit that got as far south as eastern Tennessee. Before they could see much battle, twelve of our guys were burned up while sleeping in a hay barn. Officially, the fire was set by a rebel sympathizer.

Skunk told a different version: Most battles were seldom sustained fighting and more like periods of waiting interrupted by occasional skirmishes. Battle lines were so unclear it was hard to tell where the Union side ended and the rebel side began. Any time a large number of men with basic needs hung around for an extended time, it would attract certain service professionals. Bands of prostitutes tagged behind the armies on both sides, ready to provide aid and comfort. The Union had theirs, and the rebels had theirs. But the whores did not always care which side they comforted as long as the price was fair.

Our soldiers, fresh as hyssop and far from home, were eager to experience true Volunteer State hospitality—the kind not easily acquired in Smackdab under the noses of their loved ones. One night, the twelve visited a temporary brothel, which was set up in a barn. While our boys were in the midst of receiving services, a handful of rebels showed up outside. When they realized their whores were boning the enemy, they set the barn on fire.

I like that version better than the one we learned in school.

Here's another bad-luck example, which was the last tragedy in Smackdab before the machine shop killings: In 1995, a school bus carrying the boys and girls basketball teams and cheerleaders collided with a grain truck on Highway 31 twenty miles south of Smackdab. The bus driver and five kids were killed. I remember Mom talking about how these were some of the best kids in Smackdab. The younger daughter of Pink and Jean Pankin was one of them.

COME UP A CLOUD

Mom said the soybean farmer who was the part-time minister at the church before Coach never recovered from dealing with the aftermath of the bus crash. The tragedy was too much for him. Mom said he eventually lost his faith and became like a shut-in for the rest of his life, leaving the Sunday sermon to anyone who felt they had something to say. Eventually, Coach took over.

Coach was making steady progress on a bottle of Gordon's sloe gin when he arrived at the gate to the Old Spanish graveyard. The silver-painted metal letters on the arched entrance gate identified the spot as the Freberg Lutheran Cemetery, but hardly anyone knew it by that name. An old farmer had donated the acreage in 1919 when the Spanish flu walloped Smackdab. Death dates from that year and the next were chiseled on more than half the tombstones.

A Bible salesman from Massachusetts brought the virus to Smackdab. A young veteran of the Great War, he was passing through town in hopes of finding a few believers with coins to spare on a leather-bound edition of the King James. The fate of the man was already sealed when he reached town. He passed out from high fever his first night while having dinner at a café, and he died three days later in the boarding house that used to stand at Twelfth and Broadway. The Bible salesman wasn't buried in the Spanish cemetery. His body had been cremated in an attempt to stem the spread of the flu. His ashes had been deposited in a large tomato can and sent back east to his family. By then, it was too late. Three of the salesman's fellow boarders became ill. Soon, townspeople were dropping like dominos. The flu claimed forty-two people in the area, including a Marine veteran who had survived the Battle of Belleau Wood less than a year earlier. All were interred at what became known as Old Spanish.

The epidemic spared much of the countryside. Many immigrant farm families believed a cut-open onion would attract the flu germs and keep them from remaining airborne. In each room, farm folks set cut-open onions in dishes. A visitor couldn't enter some farmhouses back then without being blanketed in the odor of yellow onions. Even now, a few farmhouses smelled of onion during the winter flu season.

It was supposed to be a secret this time where Tommy's grave was, but options were limited. The pastor and the mortician once again protested the location. After the city cemetery, however, Old Spanish was the most convenient choice from the Klimps' perspective. Coach knew Tommy would not last long in his current location, unless Jerry Debs had become a Trappist Monk and taken a vow of silence since morning.

Coach fumbled for the flashlight he stored in the Volvo's glove compartment, but he couldn't immediately locate it among the road maps and other junk he kept there. It didn't matter. The night was clear, and the

Little Dipper was easily visible above the northern horizon. Casting shadows on the gravestones with the light would only make the place creepier.

He walked down the gravel drive to the back end of the cemetery. The graveyard was small, an acre at most, and sat next to a country church that had been torn down in the eighties. Few families used the cemetery anymore. Coach had conducted one service there prior to the Klimp burial. That had been a ninety-five-year-old woman, whom Coach had barely known in life, who wanted to be buried next to her infant child and her parents. Her husband, dead fifty years, had been buried in town. Coach liked the lady's thinking. He wouldn't object to being buried in a spot like Old Spanish. It was peaceful and remote.

At Tommy's second burial, Coach said what he figured Patsy and Bob would want to hear without repeating himself too much from the first burial. Coach couldn't think of anything honest to say that would make the Klimps feel better. He didn't care. He had hoped to be free of the whole affair by now. That would happen the next day. Immediately after the opening prayer at church, he would tell the congregation he quit.

The Klimps had not alerted the county authorities when Tommy's casket had been dumped at the machine stop. Instead, Bob asked Mark Lathrop to pick up the scraped and dented casket in his hearse and keep it until the Klimps figured out what to do. Bob got grudging permission from the board of the Spanish graveyard to put Tommy there. The Klimps had to promise not to tell anyone, and to never put up a gravestone.

The cemetery board should have been more specific. This time, when the Klimps arrived in Bob's pickup, they hauled a cedar outdoor bench. Patsy and Bob toted it over and set it a few feet back from the foot of the hole. After making sure the bench did not wobble much on the hard sod, the couple stood back a few feet from it.

"If I'd known you wanted chairs, I would have brought a couple," Mark Lathrop said. "But I didn't think we'd be here long enough to matter."

"It's not for sitting," Bob said.

Lathrop and Coach rotated their sights between the bench and each other.

"We promised there would be no tombstone," Patsy said. "No one said anything about a bench."

Bob, his face sheepish, jammed his hands in his pants pockets. "It was either here or the city park," he said.

That night, Coach could say what he wanted over Tommy's fresh grave. He took a final swig from his bottle and picked up a dirt clod from the burial mound. It had been a dry summer, and the clod crumpled easily in his hand. He let the dirt fall from his fist like sand from an hourglass. "Dust to dust and all that shit," he said. He let loose a boozy belch.

Crickets chirping nearby went silent. Coach hadn't noticed the sound until it ceased. Now the graveyard was dead quiet. Every creature around had stopped as if they expected a sermon.

Coach obliged. "I've come to say a few words over the somewhat recently departed," he said, tottering a little from the buzz of the sloe gin. "Normally, I would say that the deceased was a good man, or woman as the case may be, even if it wasn't necessarily so. But this is a unique situation, a special situation, indeed. This man, Thomas Alan Klimp, was a coward, a sniveling, rotten-ass, murdering coward who ruined the town and the lives of everyone in it. Fuck him and the horse he rode in on."

Coach tossed the empty bottle on the grave, unzipped his fly, and began a long, slow piss on the grave.

His mind wandered to Billie Quick. Earlier than day, he had asked if she would consider going down to West Fork one evening for a bite to eat. Coach hadn't planned to ask. It had come out as he ate his eggs.

"Afterwards, we could possibly take in a movie if a tolerable one is showing," he said, diving in further. He shoveled a forkful of eggs in his mouth to make himself quit talking. He kept his head down, focused on his food.

Billie had her back to him at the griddle. She turned slowly. Coach looked up. Billie smiled, but it was a sad kind like a teacher would give a student who's trying hard but still thinks two times two equals twenty-two. She said nothing, but her eyes said a lot.

You poor, sad sap.

In all his years of being a renter, he had never thought of Billie as a woman until recently. He had begun to wonder what she thought of him. It had started to matter to him. Now he knew. He was nothing more than a has-been football coach and a half-ass preacher.

Disgusted and feeling sorry for himself as he thought about his foolish proposition to Billie, Coach tucked himself, but not before leaking on his trousers.

"Goddamnit. I can't even do that right," he said. As he zipped, he heard the thumping growl of diesel engines and whining ATVs. Teenagers, Coach suspected, come to drink a few beers among the dead.

Two pickups and three ATVs pulled up behind Coach's Volvo. Instead of kids, Coach saw Harp Denbo walking toward him through the gloom. Denbo stopped in front of the lead vehicle's high-beam headlights. Other men, equipped with digging tools, but not yet identifiable in the glare, joined their large leader.

"Come to join the party?" Denbo asked when he saw the minister.

"I wish Jerry was a quiet drunk," Coach said.

"He wouldn't let us have the keys to his machine this time," Jordy Wakefield said, stepping closer so Coach could see him. He was the only one besides Denbo without a tool. "We sure tried though. He's so drunk now he'll be sloshed for a month."

"I guess you'll have to break a sweat this time, if you dig him up," Coach said.

"You don't think I broke one the first time?" Even in the gloom, Coach could see the hurt on Wakefield's face.

"Enough with the chatting," Denbo said. He motioned to the men behind him. "Get to it. The casket won't dig itself out." He moved toward Coach, expecting him to move. Instead, Coach reached down and picked up the gin bottle, just so he would have something to occupy his hands.

"You've already proved your point," Coach said, looking behind himself at the mound of fresh dirt. "Why don't you let it go? Nobody comes out here. The dirt will settle and grass will fill in. In a year or so, you won't even know he's here."

"See that grave?" Harp asked, pointing at a gravestone two over from Tommy's plot. The stone told no story except that Wilbert Alva Bowman was buried there, and that he was born in 1904 and lived seventy-one years. "That's Jordy's great uncle on his mom's side," Denbo said. That was news to Wakefield, but he knew better than to say anything. Denbo pointed at the fresh mound. "Do you think Jordy wants this diseased trash buried so close to such a cherished member of his family?"

He made a wide sweep with his stretched-out arm. "Everybody in this place is related to somebody living. And I know they feel the same way: No mass murderers should be buried next to these good souls. I thought you understood about the cancer. I thought you understood it's our civic duty to remove it. I hope you don't disappoint me. If you don't want to help, stand aside so we can get this done. I've got other requirements of my time besides digging up caskets every night."

"Where you taking it this time?"

"Just beyond the line," Wakefield said. "Let Johnson County deal with."

Coach took inventory of the situation and knew he couldn't sway the group to change their feeble minds. He wondered why he should care. He stood aside for Denbo, motioning to the fresh grave like a maître d'.

"Help yourself then," he said.

Coach walked past the other men as they came forward with their digging tools at the ready. One of them, Ted Schroeder, attended church most Sundays with his wife and three kids.

Coach never felt so much self-revulsion. He got in the Volvo and slammed the door shut just as he heard the first sound of shovels hitting loose dirt.

28

The grave robbers were exhausted from their work at Old Spanish, and they did not want to drive twenty miles to the county line. They chose a much closer location as their drop-off point.

The Klimps heard the trucks pull into their yard in the middle of the night. The interlopers didn't bother to keep their voices down.

Take hold, Dave.
Goddamnit, not there.
You ain't doing a goddamn thing, Jordy.
Everybody lift on three.
Scraping of metal against metal.
The sound of something heavy landing on the un-giving heat-baked ground.
Cursing.
Dammit, Jordy, you mashed my finger.
The sound of wood splintering and snapping.
Laughing.
Doors slamming and trucks speeding away toward town.

At daylight, the Klimps ventured out to the front yard to confirm what they knew they would find: Tommy's casket lay on its side beneath the oak. The crumpled remains of the cedar bench lay next to it. Together with the help of an iron pry pole, Patsy and Bob pushed the box back in its upright position. One top corner at the feet end of the casket was caved in like a deflated basketball.

The Klimps exchanged feeble ideas on what to do next. Mostly though, they stared at the box. Patsy's stolid façade had begun to cleave.

"How long are we expected to keep this up?" she asked with a stammer. "How much punishment are we expected to bear?"

"Don't know," Bob said, his eyelids heavy from lack of sleep. "But we can't deal with anything else until we get the boy buried." Patsy wouldn't like some hopeful lie, he knew. "Permanently. For good. Once and for all…"

"I get the point," Patsy said, waving off her husband.

They studied the casket in silence. A silver Nissan pickup slowed as it passed on the gravel road moving east to west. When the gravel dust whipped up by the vehicle resettled, Bob said: "Let's bury him here. We could fence off a little area in the pasture. Up on the ridge next to the turbines. Put in some grass seed and flowers, if you want. We could put another cedar bench up there, and you could put any words you want on it."

Patsy shook her head.

"Mom's Aunt Flora wanted to be buried on her farm, remember? Should've been easy enough, except the government had to get involved. It took a month or better to get an easement. Where would we put him till then? On the back porch? In the garage?"

"At this point, I wasn't thinking of asking permission," Bob said. "No one would know that we buried him up there. We could post No Trespassing signs."

Patsy clucked her tongue like she was talking to a naïve five-year-old. "Oh, Bob. Everyone knows everything around here. They'd just come and dig him up again. People don't care any about trespassing. They all think we gave up our basic rights after the… the thing."

"If you've got a better idea, spit it out," Bob said. "But so far, yours haven't turned out too good."

Patsy stared up at her husband, her mouth pursed and her dark eyes steeled. He was taller than her by four inches, but she had always been able to intimidate him with the appropriate look.

"Are you putting the blame for all this on me?" she asked.

Bob retreated a step, but he would not give in. Not yet.

"Depends on what you mean by 'all this.' But if you mean the two burials and counting, then yes, I'm saying a fair bit of it's on you. If we'd cremated him like we talked about to begin with, we'd be done with it. Getting on with things."

Patsy's head snapped back.

"Getting on with things? Is it that easy for you? Just to move on past the death of our son?"

"That's not what I meant, and you know it. You're trying to put words in my mouth that I don't want in there. I'm just saying we can't do anything else until we get him buried, or, I don't know the right word…"

"Disposed of?" Patsy's chin jutted like it did when she was ready for a serious fight. "Is that what you mean? Disposed of like a used-up mattress ready to take to the ditch?"

She snapped her fingers. "There's an idea," she said, her voice dripping with sarcasm. "Let's dump Tommy in a ditch somewhere like a dead cow. Then you can get back to living your life free of worry. Order another windmill or two while you're at it."

Bob was about to say *turbines* when they heard another vehicle approaching, this time from the west. A dark gray Oldsmobile began to slow, but the driver must have seen the Klimps standing in the front yard. The tinted windows made the driver impossible to identify, but the Klimps knew the car. An old schoolmate.

Patsy gave the car the finger, tracking the car with her digit as it sped toward town. When the car was out of sight, she looked at Bob again.

"Let's leave him right where he is to show those fools that we're not going to let it get to us."

"Ah, hell, Patsy. You're not going to open it, are you?"

That would be something, Patsy thought. The whole town could get an eye-full. Just what they wanted. But she wouldn't do it at the expense of Tommy. He had been through enough. She headed to the house. "Back in a moment," she said.

Patsy threw away little, and she kept old shoeboxes until she found a suitable use for them. A dozen or so were stacked on the top shelf of the master bedroom closet, including a large one that Bob's Wolverine steel-toed boots came in. She cut the folds off the lid and wrote a terse message in large block letters with a black marker:

SHAME.

She went back outside with the crude sign and a roll of duct tape. Bob rested on his haunches at the base of the oak, fiddling with a blade of grass.

"Do you think the two of us could scoot him around so the casket is square with the road?" she asked. "I want everyone to see my sign."

She held it with pride so Bob could see it.

He sighed. "Patsy..."

"Don't you start on me," she said with a slight tremble in her voice. "It's shameful what those people are doing. The whole town is shameful."

"Dammit, Patsy," Bob said, his voice hardening. "Quit talking like you're the victim here. The victims are the ones Tommy killed."

Patsy's eyes turned glassy. She hadn't cried since Tommy's death, and she knew she was on the edge of letting go. She couldn't allow that.

"We can't leave him out here forever, you know," Bob said, his voice gentler now.

"You were right," she said. "We should have cremated him."

"And?" he asked, his eyebrows twitching.
"We need to have another funeral first."
"Well, shit, Patsy. Haven't we had enough funerals already?"
"Not the kind he wanted. And this time, they won't be able to dig him up."

29

Another Sunday. Another day Coach did not want to face. He had half-prepared a sermon, or perhaps a full sermon that was half-assed. Either way, the congregation would sit in the pews with glazed eyes, wondering what his point was. Hell if he knew.

On Sundays, the one day each week that the bar was closed, Coach skipped his usual eggs and toast breakfast. Billie always left early to visit her aging mother at a West Fork nursing home. Just as well, Coach thought. He wanted to avoid Billie for a while.

Coach had no appetite, and not only because the sloe gin from the night before left his stomach sour and his head beating like a subwoofer. He was always too stressed each Sunday morning to eat. Instead, he would usually swing by the GasGo on his way to church to get a watery coffee the color of weak tea. That would hold him until after the service when his appetite returned. Even on Sundays when he felt reasonably prepared, all his years leading classes and football teams hadn't inured him to the nervousness that swelled inside him when he stood before the small crowd of worshipers. This service would be the worst, because this time he would finally quit.

Coach headed out to his car behind the bar. Denbo was waiting for him, leaning against the rear panel of the Volvo. Denbo's blue truck, which looked like it had just been waxed, was parked on the other side of Coach's car. Denbo looked as fresh as his truck, his brown hair neat and combed back off his forehead like he had just come from the barber. If Coach had not witnessed it, he would not have believed Denbo had overseen a grave digging hours earlier.

Denbo, his arms crossed on his chest, smiled. "I was beginning to think you were sleeping in this morning," he said.

Caught off guard, Coach hesitated before reaching to open the car door. "I'm in a hurry."

"This won't take long," Denbo said. "It was interesting running into you at the graveyard last night," Denbo continued. "When we came up on you, you looked like you had seen a ghost." He laughed. "I mean, your eyes were so wide you looked like a raccoon caught in a garbage pail."

"We call it a trash can around here," Coach said.

"Whatever."

"Are you sure this isn't going to take long?" Coach asked. "Because really, I need to get to church."

Denbo held up a hand. "Just a moment now," he said. "Anyway, you seemed to have knocked back a few last night. Am I right? More than a few, I would guess."

Coach said nothing.

"Is that an appropriate way for a minister to act?"

"I didn't know you cared about the church. Any church," Coach said, this time opening the car door. "But you're right. So, it's a good thing I'm quitting the pulpit this morning, which is why I need to get to…."

"Hold on a second," Denbo said, this time moving to stand in the door opening so Coach couldn't get behind the wheel. "I have a feeling you were out there last night because you think a lot like I do. Maybe you don't want to admit it, but you know there is something foul about this town that needs to be removed."

Coach jingled his key ring impatiently.

"And you know what? We need someone like you, someone to preach the right message from the pulpit. We have a long and difficult road ahead of us, and we need a strong voice like yours. Good people want to hear from their pastor, and they need to hear the truth, whether or not they like it."

"The truth about the so-called cancer, I suppose," Coach said.

"You try to act like a doubter, but you can't deny what I say. And it's more than just words. You'll want to make sure the right kind of person is attending your church. Good, solid citizenry. Conversely, you'll need to remove your lesser element. The Klimps go to your church, don't they? You could start there. There's some other riffraff we need to work on eliminating in Smackdab, too. The dwarf, who was involved in the killings, that albino she runs with…."

"I want none of this," Coach said. "And I don't understand why it's your concern either. You don't even live in town. And you don't go to our church."

"I'm Catholic," Denbo said, opening his hands as though that explained everything. "And just so you know, I'm buying some acreage Louise Sandstrum had bulldozed. I'll have a house built on it by next spring. Much better than the one I have now. A three-story Victorian that will look like it was built more than a century ago."

Denbo's eyes became glassy, and he looked away. "I want this to be the last place I ever live. I love how Route 4 widens in the middle of town, and how the parking spots are diagonal in front of the stores. And I can picture how it must have been forty or fifty years back when those stores were occupied by clothiers and druggists and so on. Just like in the best movies from Hollywood's golden years. Clean movies about solid, small-town values." He looked at Coach. "And it could be that way again. I grew up in Philadelphia. Did you know that? But I was never meant to stay there. As soon as I got the chance, I wanted to move some place free of crime and grit. Some place nice and wholesome."

"The place you imagine doesn't exist," Coach said. "And it never did. Every town has problems."

"You're right," Denbo said. His smile held, though it now seemed to be forced. "But the biggest problems, the most harmful ones, can be corrected."

"By getting rid of people you don't like?"

"I don't dislike anyone, but there are certain kinds of people that do not belong here if Smackdab is to become all it can."

"You sound a little like you work for the Nazi Chamber of Commerce."

"Don't twist my words like that. It should be beneath you," Denbo said. "Certain persons simply need to re-locate somewhere else where they can be among people more like themselves."

"You get Jordy Wakefield and his ilk to do your dirty work," Coach said. "Therefore, your words ring hollow."

"You're right. Wakefield shouldn't get too comfortable either."

"Step aside," Coach said. "I've got to get to church."

Denbo complied. "Give serious consideration to what I said," Denbo said. "The boulder is already rolling down the hill, and you can't stop it." The man smiled, but there was nothing amiable about it. Coach felt his testicles constrict.

"I have given it serious consideration," Coach said.

As he drove away, he watched Denbo in his rearview mirror. The man still stood where he had been; his smile revealed the crooked tooth.

30

    Maesie had spent a second and third nights in the copse. She never returned to the GasGo to officially apply for a job. Denbo had scared her more than she wanted to admit. She spent the hottest part of each day in Smackdab, even climbing a large oak tree in the park where she managed a small nap hidden in its canopy. When the sun began to drop below the horizon, she returned to the copse. Another day had arrived, and Maesie walked along the gravel road toward town. She couldn't keep up the routine forever. She had no money, so she had to do *something*.
    She saw the gravel dust cloud well before she saw or heard the vehicle approaching her. Harp Denbo, she expected, or one of his sycophants. She was prepared to hop into the weedy ditch to hide, but she felt too tired and hot to care any longer.
    The Vic came into view, dust billowing behind as though it were attached to the car's rear bumper like a parachute. The Vic was going too fast, as usual, its rear tires intermittently losing purchase in the gravel.
    When Cahill was nearly past her, he stomped the brakes. The sedan skidded, spewing rocks in its wake. Tiny fragments stung Maesie's face. She held her breath and scrunched her eyes as the dust settled again on the dry, hot surface. Wild hemp shoots that choked the road's right-of-way were further dusted the color of cement mix. So was Maesie.
    Cahill backed up until he was parallel with her.
    "Almost didn't see you," he said through his open window.
    Maesie said nothing. Cahill looked rough, like he hadn't slept in days. Or if he had, it had been in his car. And his nose was puffed up like someone had recently taken a bat to it. Still, Maesie knew she had no room to talk. She imagined her hair looked as though she had recently gripped an electrified fence. That was an advantage of having no mirror around.

"Sightings of you these days are almost as rare as a virgin in my back seat," Cahill said. He grinned, but Maesie would not soften so easily.

"Where you been staying?" he asked, studying the Radio Flyer she pulled.

"Here and there. Mostly there."

"Yeah? Where you headed now?"

"Same answer."

Cahill scrunched his chin and nodded. "All right then. Be that way."

"All right then."

They looked at each other.

After a few moments of that, Maesie repeated, "All right then," and continued toward town.

Cahill backed up the car until he was even with her again.

"Hold on a sec," he said. "Get in the car and go with me."

Maesie continued walking. She did not look at Cahill. "Go where?" she asked.

"Anywhere but here. I've decided it's time to get away for good."

Maesie stopped to look at him for any telltale sign he was kidding. If he was, he had become better at it recently.

"And you're asking me to go with you?" she asked.

Cahill shrugged. "I hadn't thought about it until just now, but what the hell?"

"You'd never leave Smackdab," she said.

"Hell I wouldn't. I'm tired of this place. I intend to go somewhere where the name Renfrew ain't Chippewa for 'stupid-ass trailer trash.'"

Maesie laughed. "Don't kid a kidder," she said. "You'd never get farther than Eldora. The Vic hasn't held more than a quarter tank of gas since you've owned it."

Her doubtfulness angered Cahill. "I'm leaving right here and now. See?" he said. He pounded on the steering wheel with his fists as though that were all the proof Maesie needed.

"Yeah? How much money do you have?"

"Enough," Cahill said. "And I'll go where the wind takes me."

Maesie laughed again. Now she knew he was lying—perhaps to himself as much as her.

"Oh, Cahill," she said. "The wind's not going to take you anywhere."

She stopped walking and looked at him like he was a misguided child. "Don't you know the world's filled with disappointed people who've done the same thing? They think a change in scenery will magically make them happier. But they find out they're just as unhappy as ever. They don't realize they're the ones making themselves miserable."

"Who crowned you the expert?" Cahill asked. "You ain't never been anywhere else either."

"I've seen my dad. Why do you think he and Skunk are on the road all the time? It's not because anyone wants to hear their music. They're trying to get away from something, but it's not their families or even Smackdab. They don't like who they are, so they run all over hell chasing the idea they can like themselves better if they just find the right place. But every time, they come back exhausted, broke, defeated, and no happier than they were to start with. And they take it out on the rest of us. Then, a few weeks later, they leave again. Rinse. Repeat."

"So you think I ought to stay?"

"I'm not telling you what to do. That's your business. But if you think what's beyond the western horizon is all puppy dogs and cupcakes, you'll be in for a big letdown. You'll be the same Cahill you are now, just in a different zip code."

Cahill noticed for the first time Maesie was limping. He leaned out his window at her feet. They looked like they had become stuck in a meat grinder.

"How do you walk on those things?" he asked. "Hop in and I'll give you a ride."

Maesie continued to walk silently, her face looking down the dusty road in front of her.

"I ain't leaving out right this minute, but I'm getting tired of driving in reverse. Just get in."

"My mom always warned me not to take rides from strange men."

"Uh huh. Good one."

"I'm not getting in unless I know where you're going."

Cahill paused before answering, as though he wasn't sure he wanted to tell.

"Well," he said, "Before I leave town, I was thinking about heading over to the Klimps."

Maesie quickened her pace toward town, her limp more noticeable. The blisters, which were getting angrier, would soon force her to stop.

"Now hold on a minute," Cahill said, pushing the accelerator to keep pace. "I ain't going over there to cause mischief. Just the opposite. I kind of did a mean thing the other day, and I'm feeling bad about it. Before I leave town, I might go clean up the mess I made. I'm thinking it would be better if I didn't show up there alone."

"That's quite an offer," Maesie said. She did not know exactly what the Klimps would say if she appeared at their front door, but she imagined their response would include *get*, *hell* and *out*.

"My first thought is to say no," she said. "Come to think of it, so is my second thought. And all the other thoughts I may have on the subject."

"Well, fuck it then," Cahill said. He shoved the Vic in Drive and spewed gravel as he spun out. Maesie did not turn around. This time, rock pieces landed harmlessly in her tangled hair.

31

    Tommy's casket was still under the oak when Coach steered the Volvo into the Klimp's driveway. Someone—he guessed Patsy—had placed a rough bouquet of coneflowers on top. A signed scrawled with "SHAME" was taped to the side. An empty lawn chair sat at one end of the casket as though placed there for anyone who came to pay respects. Coach wondered if Bob or Patsy had kept watch over the casket the previous night. He could imagine Patsy sitting there, in the dark, gripping a revolver with both hands and daring anyone to come by and try something.

    Bob had heard the Volvo sputter to a stop and stepped from the garage's walk-through door. The acid left over from a second gin-filled night was roiling Coach's stomach like an angry leviathan. Before he exited the car, Coach popped a couple antacids from a bottle he kept handy on the passenger seat.

    Bob's face was sweaty, and his gray t-shirt was wet around the neck and armpits. He gazed on his visitor with a flat expression, but Coach knew he was suspicious.

    "Something I can do for you, Coach?" Bob asked.

    "Just dropping by," Coach said. He pretended not to notice the casket containing a mass murderer off to his left.

    The men stood silently until Coach asked: "Patsy doing all right?"

    Bob shrugged. "All things considered, I guess. She left the house early this morning. Didn't say where she was headed."

    The awkward silence resumed while Coach thought of something else to ask.

    "Headed back to work soon?"

    Bob shook his head. "I've been given a leave of absence," he said. His face twitched slightly, and Coach knew, even in the open air, Bob had gotten a good whiff of Coach's booze breath. Bob took a step back. "The superintendent said it would be for an 'indeterminate' length of time," he said. "I don't have a contract, so I figure I'm gone for good. The school board will make it official their next meeting."

"Sounds like you and me are in the same boat, employment-wise."

"Yeah?"

"I quit the church."

"Yeah?"

Bob was looking past Coach, at the cornfield across the road, as though he weren't listening to what his visitor had to say. Both men stood silently some more. Bob scuffed a bare spot in the dry grass with the toe of his work boot.

"If you're not a preacher anymore, you're not obligated to drop by. So, why are you here?"

Coach looked toward the casket for the first time since exiting his car. "Looks like you could use some help. Someone to keep vigil maybe?" Both men looked on the casket like they were waiting to see if it would move, levitate, or otherwise do something that revealed its power over humans.

"So?" Coach asked. "Can you use some help or not?"

Bob squinted west down the empty gravel road. "She's got her mind set on something else," he said.

"Oh?" Coach asked.

Bob continued to kick at the patch of dirt. "Never mind," he said.

"Let me help, if I can," Coach said. "Before… I don't know. I guess I just wanted to get him in the ground so we could all move forward. But now… if you'll let me help in some way… I don't mean any preacher fluff-duff, but something…"

Bob said nothing. He looked at his scuffed work boots. Meanwhile, Coach looked up. Clouds to the west weren't exactly dark but might have some rain in them. An afternoon rain shower could come through. It offered something to hope for.

"Might come up a cloud," Coach said.

Neither man spoke for minutes. Bob continued to kick at the ground like a haltered workhorse. Coach stuck his hands in his back pockets and began to whistle *Swing Low Sweet Chariot* off tune.

"All right then," Bob said. "I don't suppose you know how to swing a hammer."

Coach allowed a thin grin. "Because?"

"Because I'm going build a Viking boat and set it and Tommy on fire."

When Bob and Patsy built their house, Bob had torn down an old shed and stored some of the lumber from it. He had never known until now what to do with the ten-foot pine planks. The lumber would have stayed in the new machine shed, stacked neatly and collecting dust and cobwebs until the day of their estate sale. Now, the planks had a purpose.

The home's central air system did not include the garage, something Bob had often lamented. Despite a large box fan whirring in the back corner, the garage was a sauna. He could have set up production in the machine shed, but the heat was worse there. Another oversight: Bob should have planted trees along the west side of the building.

Bob put Coach to work measuring a plank lengthwise two inches in from its edge so it could be rip-cut. Bob hoped to cut the boards narrow enough to bend in the shape of a boat. That assumed the parched boards wouldn't snap. At Bob's instructions, Coach stacked the cut boards on a small one-axle flatbed trailer that Bob had parked in the garage. They would build the boat on the trailer so it would be ready to haul when finished.

"I never did much of this kind of work, but my dad always said to measure twice and cut once," Coach said.

"You might even measure a third time just to be sure," Bob said. In a short time, Coach had already mis-cut three boards that now would have to be used for purposes other than the long bottom of the Viking boat.

Bob liked to do jobs the right way. He believed a man should always take pride in his work, no matter how menial it might appear to others. He believed that was why he had been promoted to head custodian, though his penchant for checking the tiniest detail rankled the janitors who worked under him. However, this job needed to be finished quickly before all of Smackdab got wind of what the Klimps planned. He would do his best to overlook Coach's lack of skill in exchange for getting the project finished as soon as possible.

"How long do you think it will take us?" Coach asked.

Bob wanted to say it depended on how many more planks Coach intended to measure and cut wrong. "We can't keep him out there, obviously," he said. "If I have to, I'll work through the night."

"You mean *we* might have to work through the night," Coach said as he picked up the Makita power saw.

Bob examined a board Coach had most recently cut, sweeping the dry sawdust and flecks of faded red paint from its surface. The lumber was at least one hundred years old. Cured and seared of all moisture, Bob figured this particular piece had come from the west side of the shed where it had received the full brunt of afternoon sun and wind. "I'm obliged for the help you've given," he said, "but you don't have to stay any longer."

Coach set the saw on top of the plank he was about to cut. "You trying to get rid of me?" he asked.

"You did the burial services only out of obligation. That was obvious," Bob said. "But you don't have an obligation now. It might be easier all around if you don't stick around."

Coach pulled a clean rag from a plastic bag Bob had hung on the end of a sawhorse and used it to wipe his brow. "You think Patsy'll have a fit, huh?"

Bob said nothing.

"You're right about the burials. I was a piss-poor minister, and never more so than this past week. But I'm here right now because this is where I need to be. I believe I can convince Patsy of that, if I get the chance."

32

Patsy had driven to Eldora to search for a minimum wage job. Bob was right: The drive would eat up most of her wages, but she was tired of being stuck at the house. Tired of being around Bob. She needed to get to work doing something.

That morning, before sunlight, she had pretended to be asleep when Bob rolled up against her in bed. He flopped his arm over her neck like it was the unconscious act of a slumbered person repositioning himself. Patsy knew better; he was hard. She was already on the edge of the bed and had no more room.

She felt his stale breath on the back of her neck, his idea of waking her gently. Patsy did not move. When Bob realized that did not work, he began to grind against her. The thought of having sex now, with her son cold in a box in the front yard, nauseated her. Patsy could not imagine being intimate with her husband again, not if he thought *this* was appropriate.

She whisked out of bed and grabbed the bathrobe she had tossed on the floor.

"What's gotten into you?" she asked, her jaw set like concrete.

Bob half opened his eyes and looked up at his wife.

"Not a damn thing," he said, his nose flaring. He had slept on the left side of his face, which now looked as though it had been melted in a fire.

"What's got into *you*?" he asked.

"Oh, I don't know," she said, beginning to count off on her fingers. "Like the image of six murder victims. And our son laying on that gurney. Oh, and how about him being out there in the front yard with no place to be put permanently? And us planning to set him on fire?"

Patsy began to count on her other hand. "And how about this? How about us spending the rest of our lives in a big barrel of shit together? And never leaving this house again without everyone giving us the mean eye? Just off the top of my head, I'd say that's what's got into me. And all you want is to put your thing in me."

Bob rose up on his shoulder. "I don't just want to put my 'thing' in you. A little sex might make us both feel better. Give us a sense of normalcy."

"Normalcy? Things will never be normal again."

Bob, his mouth scrunched, said, "Just another in a long line of excuses for why you won't have anything to do with me physically."

Patsy gave a derisive laugh. "Just more proof that all Bob Klimp thinks about is Bob Klimp," she said.

Patsy had thrown on a pair of khaki pants and a pullover polo and hurried out of the house without brushing her teeth or otherwise making herself look presentable. She did not tell Bob where she was going.

Before she began her job search, she drove to Eldora's small downtown and spotted a parallel parking space across the street from Jittery Jennie's Coffee Pot. Even in the middle of a weekday, plenty of spots were available. Five minutes later, she returned with an iced coffee and an armload of empty coffee bean bags, which she tossed in the back seat. The inside of the car filled with a blended aroma of coffee and burlap.

Two blocks after pulling out of her parking spot, Patsy spotted a throwback Gulf Station, still in operation, with the original enamel logo sign and a Porte Cochere sheltering twin fuel pumps. An acne-scarred teen boy was changing oil in the sole service bay. Patsy retrieved a five-gallon red fuel can from the car's trunk and asked him to fill it with kerosene.

Before beginning her job search, she had another idea. She conducted a Google search on her phone, found what she was looking for, and drove five minutes west to a small strip shopping center on the Eldora bypass. No cars were parked in front of the small store, Scary Barry's, though an *Open* sign lighted the storefront window.

Scary Barry Zimmer, who was in his late twenties with a full brown beard and a potbelly, sat behind the front counter reading a Batman comic. He owned the store, and business was usually very slow on weekdays. He was often the only one in the store for hours. But he had nothing else to do, so he opened the store every day at ten. He sometimes didn't get his first customer until late afternoon.

Barry had recently added a small inventory of graphic novels to his business, just to try to keep things going until Halloween season. But a woman, about his mother's age, entered the store looking like her pet had just died. If she was anything like his mother, she would think comic books were a waste of time. She may have come to his store, though, because a boy or young man in her life had shown an interest. Barry pulled himself out of his comfortable seat and tried to be helpful.

"Looking for a comic book?" Barry asked.

The woman shook her head. "You wouldn't happen to have a Viking helmet?" she asked.

Another one of those.

"It depends on how many you need," Barry said.

"Just one," she said.

"You're in luck, then," Barry said. "Someone came in a couple days ago and bought me out of all the ones I had left. All five of them. But then I got one back that an earlier customer decided to return. I shouldn't have given a refund, though, because it smelled like stale beer. I think someone used it at a party."

Barry leaned in like he was taking the woman into his confidence. "It's because of the Smackdab thing and that dillweed with the Viking helmet. That's why the sudden popularity of helmets."

He paused when the woman grimaced. "Oh. Is that why you want one? I didn't figure you..."

"No," the woman said with the same terseness his mother exhibited when she was about to tell him he had a lot to learn about life.

"Well, anyway," he continued. "This guy who bought the five helmets thought it would be funny to give them out to his friends. Kind of sick, don't you think? Still, a sale's a sale."

When the customer showed no reaction, Barry went to the back of his store to find the remaining helmet.

"You sure you don't want to look around at the Halloween stuff?" Barry asked when he rang up the ten-dollar sale.

"The helmet's plenty," the woman said.

"I'll cut you a deal. I've got a feeling blood and gore's going to be bigger than ever this year. Everyone's going to dress up like a Smackdab victim. Or the killer."

Barry paused a moment. "I need to put in an order for a bunch more helmets." He believed this Halloween could turn around his business.

Patsy took the bypass around the south end of the town and stopped at the first convenience store she came to—a clean, expansive business with a dozen gas pumps that made the GasGo in Smackdab seem like a dingy mess. A red-shirted cashier, about twenty-five with a gold ring in her right nostril, was working through a Sudoku puzzle. The plastic ID pin on her shirt identified her as Kathryn. It was mid-morning, the usual lull between morning coffee/doughnut traffic and midday Cheetos/burrito business. Kathryn looked up from her puzzle and gave Patsy a smile.

"Good morning," she said.

Patsy returned the greeting. "I was wondering if you're taking applications at the moment."

Kathryn reached behind her for a blank application. "When aren't we taking applications?" she said. "Especially the late shifts." Before handing Patsy the application, she hesitated. "All the people with kids in school want to work the day shift. That's me, and it took me a year of calling the cops on drunk kleptos before I got switched off the night shift. Do you have kids in school? Because if you do, and you want to work days, don't hold your breath."

"No kids in school," Patsy said. "I'm used to working nights."

The store worker relaxed and placed the application on the counter so Patsy could complete it. She handed her a pen. "Jason, the manager, does interviews every Tuesday and Thursday afternoon around two or three," she said. "I can tell you right now, he'll offer you a job on the spot if you've got even a minute of retail experience. You're not all tatted up with spider webs on your face or anything. And you don't look like you're missing any teeth. That's really all Jason's concerned about. And that you don't rob him blind."

Patsy handed back the completed application. Kathryn gave it a quick glance. "Patsy, huh? I'm Kathryn. We won't be working together, but we'll see each other if our shifts cross." She looked again at the application. "You worked ten years at the GasGo in Smackdab? See? Jason won't let you walk out the door without getting you to fill out a W-4."

Kathryn noticed for the first time Patsy's last name. She looked at Patsy and again at the name on the application. "How are you related to…?"

Patsy cried most of the drive home. She had almost told the clerk she was not related to Tommy. Or maybe that she was a distant relative by marriage and that she didn't know him well. She couldn't believe the idea of denying Tommy had entered her thoughts, but it had been there, fighting to come out of her mouth.

She was not happy to see Coach's car in the driveway, and she did not enter the garage to say hello. From the kitchen, she could hear the two men talking over the sounds of hammering and sawing as though Tommy's casket wasn't yards away. Still, help was help, and she knew Bob needed it if the boat was to be completed any time before winter.

Patsy began fixing sandwiches for lunch. She hoped Coach liked baloney on white bread, because she wasn't going to offer a choice. She wasn't going to make one thing for Bob and another thing for Coach, although she would see if Coach liked a little iceberg lettuce on his. She was not ready to become *that* poor of a host.

At one minute past noon, both men entered the kitchen from the attached garage. They brought with them a blast of heat, combined with a sour odor of sweat, sawdust and motor oil. Bob's expression was sullen, indicating he hadn't gotten over their earlier argument.

"I guess you're in on our little secret now," Patsy said to Coach. "I hope you like baloney sandwiches."

Coach nodded. "You didn't have to go to the trouble. I could've gone into town."

"I wouldn't classify tossing a cold cut on a piece of bread as trouble."

"Just the same," Coach said, trying to smile. "I appreciate it." He kept his gaze on the tile floor.

Patsy pointed Coach in the direction of the bathroom to clean up. After Coach left the kitchen, Patsy took a package of American cheese slices from the refrigerator.

Bob leaned stiffly against the counter, his arms folded across his gut. "Where you been?" he asked.

"Out," she said. "When did he show up?"

"A while ago."

"If he's not careful, he'll be accused of giving comfort and aid to the enemy," Patsy said, putting a few slices on a small plate and setting it on the table. It was easier to talk about Coach than issues between Bob and her.

So, this was the way it would be?

"He said he quit at the church," Bob said. "He's feeling guilty, or at least he says he is. He offered to help, and I figured…"

"I'm not sure how I feel about him knowing our intentions," Patsy said.

Bob turned on the sink faucet, letting cool water wash over his wrists for a moment. "He was eager to pitch in. Hard to turn down," he said. "And I could use the help."

"But his help? He could barely stand to look at us at the cemeteries. You saw that, right? He was looking down his old crooked nose at us the whole time. And now here he is working on the boat like everything is just dandy."

Coach cleared his throat. Bob and Patsy had not heard him enter the kitchen.

"I won't stay if I'm not wanted," he said.

Patsy motioned to an empty chair at the table. "Let's eat."

33

I have plenty of time on my hands, so I've decided to name what I am. A floater. I don't really float, but nothing else comes close to describing my situation. I'm simply here, and then I'm somewhere else.

I haven't encountered any other floaters, but they have to be somewhere. I thought I would run into Tommy and the machine shop guys because we all died at the same time. I don't know what I would say to Tommy. Maybe something like, "Damn, dude. What got your panties in a wad?" And he would shrug his shoulders, if he still had them, and say, "Stupid, right?"

It would be fun to have a little machine shop reunion with the guys and laugh about it all. How we didn't see that coming. I wonder where Pink and the others are. I wonder if THIS is a space tinier than a microbe and all floaters are crammed together, but we don't know it. Or maybe this is just the space for Smackdab's dead. And other places have their own soul pods. Regional floater pods. I wonder if my grandparents are here with me. Maybe after some time we dead people start to sense and communicate with each other. Maybe Grandma Barnes is trying to talk to me.

I would like to communicate with other floaters. But more than that, I would like to communicate with the living. Maybe by slamming a door or something. Some people need waking up. But if it's possible to send a message, I haven't learned how. The first live soul I would contact is Maesie. This penitence tour she's on is getting old, and it's a waste of time.

Maesie arrived at Diane's house just as the older woman was getting in her car, which was parked in a quarter-slabbed concrete driveway on the east side of her tiny one-story house. Mammoth twin gray birches enshrouded the Olstad front yard, so much so that only a few hopeful tufts of grass sprouted in the ashy dirt beneath them. A rusting push mower parked under one birch had more potential as a trashy lawn ornament than a necessary implement.

COME UP A CLOUD

With the car door open and one foot in, Diane stopped when she heard Maesie shuffling on the graveled street.

"You remind me of a hobo," Diane said, observing the chalky filth that dusted Maesie's clothes and hair.

"That's an insult to hobos," Maesie said as she dropped her backpack at her feet. The shade of the closest birch covered her, though not enough to provide much coolness. "Anyway, I prefer *vagabond*. Sounds more adventurous."

The stench of wet sweat on top of dry carried on the hot breeze toward Diane. She leaned against her car as Maesie stood at the edge of the property. They stayed that way for a moment. Diane tapped her fingernails in the cadence of a galloping horse on the car's roof.

Finally, Maesie said, "Those food dishes you brought over the other day? I'm afraid you won't be getting them back. Unless you want to dig for them under a pile of dirt and rubble where the house used to be."

Diane nodded. "I heard Sharon ordered in a dozer."

"I'll compensate you for the dishes once I find a job and get paid," Maesie said. "I don't want you to get blamed by whoever the plates belonged to."

"Don't worry about it," Diane said. "The ones they belong to won't rush to get them back. Maybe around Thanksgiving, when they're doing a lot cooking, they'll wish they had them. Even then, they might still not come looking for them. I wouldn't blame them. It's hard to know what to say to the ones that lost their men. Folks will start to avoid us. If it was me, I would just go buy new cookware."

Maesie had nothing to say to that.

"Do you want to come in and cool off awhile?" Diane asked. "I could run your clothes through the wash."

"I appreciate the offer, but it'd take a power washer to do me much good now."

Maesie picked up her backpack as if to leave.

"Other than to tell me about the dishes, was there another reason you've come by?" Diane asked.

Maesie wavered between staying and leaving, between explaining and not.

I got your son killed, and here's how…

"I've been going around talking to some of the widows," Maesie began, her voice faltering. "Trying to get to the heart of things, but it hasn't gone very well."

"And just what is the heart of things?" Diane asked. Her voice and face were expressionless.

187

"I'm not sure. Something keeps poking at me. I thought if I talked to the ones most affected, like Jean and you, I could figure it out and move past it."

"There is no moving past *it*," Diane said. "We're all stuck with it for the rest of our lives. We're damaged goods now. Even you are. People will whisper when we're around. They'll tsk and shake their heads and say 'Poor Diane' and 'Poor old Jean.' And they don't know it yet, but those same people are damaged, too. They'll be seen differently the rest of their lives. They'll be shopping in West Fork, and someone will whisper 'there's one of those nuts from Smackdab. Be careful, because they're liable to blow you away.'"

Maesie switched her weight from one foot to the other, though both hurt equally. "All I meant was..." she began.

"I know what you meant," Diane said. She massaged her rosy nose as she studied the small woman in the road. "You're the honey that drew the fly to the trap. I get it. You feel bad about it. But I bet somewhere deep inside, you kind of liked the idea of it—that a man wanted you. *You.* Poor little unlovable Maesie Mattsen. And that man had to have you so bad that he punished us all when you denied him. That's what's really eating at you, isn't it?

"No..."

"That there might be just a tiny bit of evil in you," Diane said. "And you feel guilty because of what you're feeling. We're all capable of thinking bad things or even doing bad things, but that doesn't make us evil. It makes us human. So, my advice, which you didn't ask for, is to get over it. This apology tour or whatever it is you're on isn't doing you any good. And it sure as hell isn't doing me any good. You're just looking for sympathy."

Maesie felt anger shooting from her belly up to her throat. She limped closer. "I don't want anyone's sympathy," she said, pounding the trunk of Diane's car. "Never have. Don't go saying differently. But you know? It might feel nice to be noticed for something other than my size once in a while."

"Such as?" Diane asked, her voice flat. "What do you want to be noticed for? Hiding in your back yard? Living under your porch like a troll? Now there's a stereotype. And how about traipsing all over town like a grimy monk? Is that what you want to be noticed for?"

When Maesie said nothing, Diane pulled out a cigarette and lit it. She held the first inhalation of smoke for an extra moment before releasing it.

"I'm not looking for sympathy," Maesie said.

"Let's say, for the sake of argument, I believe you," Diane said. "So, what do you want?"

Maesie stared at the edge of the lawn where dried, gravel-dusted grass met road. Without looking up, she said: "I'm tired of being alone. Tired of feeling like I could die right here on the spot and no one would care. Except for you, because you'd have to deal with my carcass. When Luke and the others died, they had people like you who loved them and were torn up when they went. Even Tommy Klimp had his parents."

Diane shook her head and allowed a small smile on her wan face. "So I was right. You *are* searching for sympathy."

Maesie had grown tired of arguing the point. She removed her flip-flops and let her feet cool on the shaded concrete. She looked up at Diane. "I've never felt so worn out."

"There you go, still feeling sorry for yourself," Diane said. She proceeded to get in the car. "Get in. And if I hear one peep, I'll put a shoe up your butt crack."

Maesie knew their destination from the direction they were headed, though she couldn't figure why.

"Don't take this the wrong way," Maesie said. "But I'm wondering how much you've had to drink. That's the only explanation for this."

Diane said nothing.

"Their kid killed yours," Maesie said. "It's like you're going into the heart of darkness."

"This isn't about me," Diane said. "It's not about you either. But if you're really set on apologizing to someone, you could start with the Klimps."

"You're out of your pickled brain. Seriously. Just let me off here. There's no way I'm going to say anything to the Klimps. They hate me, and I'm not so fond of them either."

Diane kept her eyes on the gravel that ran south of and parallel to Route 4. "Too bad. We're about to see what we're all made of."

34

    Skunk and Rolf caught a ride north, drawing closer to Smackdab as though it were centered in a gargantuan magnetic field. For Skunk, the final destination was inexorable. He realized he didn't care about what was waiting for him in Smackdab, or whom he would have to confront. He didn't care about the Klimps. He felt no need for revenge. Hell, he thought, if Tommy hadn't killed himself, it would change nothing. Luke and the others would still be just as cold, dead and buried under six feet of prairie silt. As for Rolf's kid, no matter what her role was in making it happen, she was of even less significance to Skunk. All he wanted was to visit Luke's grave, step in on Diane if she'd let him, and then get some rest. He believed sweet sleep awaited him in Smackdab. That was what most drew him home.

    Still, there was always someone waiting for him when he returned. There would be someone who wanted to prove how tough he was by trying to pick a fight with the infamous Skunk Olstad. He wondered who it would be this time. Perhaps Cahill Renfrew thought he was tough enough now. The uninitiated did not realize fighting had nothing to do with who was bigger or faster, or who had the thickest forearms. Skunk was usually the smallest person in any fight. It didn't matter the weapon a man carried either, though Skunk always felt confident with the altered saw file he carried in his jacket. The biggest contributing factor to success was how well a man could take a blow. Skunk had seen plenty of big guys crumple quickly because they were surprised by pain. If a man could take a few punches and kicks, and not get all scared and pussy-like from the pain, he always had a chance.

    Skunk and Rolf were hitching a ride with a young family of four in an old Toyota Sienna minivan with Oklahoma plates. The interior smelled of fast food, cinnamon air freshener and body odor. The parents rode up front, the kids in the back. The two hitchers took the middle row. The kids, a boy and girl around eight and ten, played video games. They barely looked up to take note of Skunk and Rolf when the two climbed in. The boy had dishwater blond hair that jutted upward from his scalp's vertex like a vacuum had latched onto it. Luke's hair had been like that when he was young, and no amount of hair gel, spray or super glue Diane applied would make it behave.

No one in the van offered names, but the man was David. His wife validated everything he said, like she was his minion.

"That's right, David."

"You bet, David."

"It'll be good for the kids, David."

"You're speaking the gospel truth on that, David."

After picking them up north of St. Joe, and before the van accelerated to full speed, David had begun explaining in detail their plans to start a new life in St. Cloud, Minnesota. "I ain't gonna be too crazy about the weather up there, but shit, I ain't gettin' steady work in the oil fields no more. So what's a man to do? The work won't pay as good, but it'll be steady, you know?"

"You got that right, David."

"We got family up there on her side," David said, nodding toward the woman.

"Jay and his wife," the woman said.

"Her cousin says he can get me on at the car dealership where he works. Detailing cars, he says. He's a mechanic, or what they call a technician these days."

"A certified technician, David."

"I ain't sure I want to vacuum used Corollas all day. But I'll work my way up soon enough. I ain't allergic to hard work."

"You a good worker, David."

David nodded toward his spouse again. "She's gonna get on at KFC or some such. She's got all sorts of food service experience. She was working at the school cafeteria where the kids went up until the end of the last school year. She'll get on someplace quick up there and be assistant manager in no time. They'll be glad to get her."

"Count on it, David."

David drove in silence for two exits while Nintendo beeps from the back seat filled the void. Then he said to his wife as though there had been no respite, "First thing we'll have to do when we get up there is enroll the kids. I sure do hope the schools're better than the ones in Elk City."

"I sure do, too, David."

Lulled by the whine of the Sienna's tires and the drone of its driver, Rolf had fallen asleep within minutes of getting in the van. David watched

Skunk through the rear-view mirror. He liked to make eye contact when he spoke. As much as the man talked, Skunk felt he should bypass the detailing job and shoot for sales. If the Okie let customers get in a word or two, he might make some commissions. Skunk closed his eyes and rested his head in the crook between the seat and the inner side panel. Maybe David would take the hint and give the gabbing a rest.

Rolf slumped to Skunk's side and rested his head on Skunk's shoulder. Skunk wondered what to do about the man. His situation was worsening. Rolf had crapped his pants in the middle of the previous night while sleeping. Skunk was watching TV, and he knew almost immediately what had occurred when the nauseating stink filled the small room. Rolf awakened, humiliated, but he did not get up from his shit-covered bed. The food Skunk had brought back to the room the night before had not solidified in Rolf's system. It left a runny mess.

Skunk guided Rolf to the bathroom and then made him take off his soiled sleeping clothes before standing in the shower. Using the complimentary Bic pen on the nightstand, Skunk lifted Rolf's boxer shorts and dropped them into a plastic shopping bag. He employed the same delicacy a crime scene technician would use when bagging evidence. Some of the shit had gotten on Rolf's T-shirt. That went in the bag with the shorts. Skunk threw the bag in the dumpster behind the motel.

The sheets on Rolf's twin bed also were soiled. Skunk gingerly wadded and tossed them in a ball out the front door. The stink still hung in the air, though, so Skunk propped the room door open by jamming a crushed Coke can under it. Rolf exited the bathroom with a wet, yellowed towel wrapped around his waist. Looking sheepish but saying nothing, he lay down on his mattress and wrapped himself in the duvet. By morning, the odor of feces still had not completely dissipated from the small room. When he woke, Rolf wondered what had happened to his bedding and clothes.

Skunk knew Rolf could not take care of himself any longer, but it wasn't Skunk's responsibility to deal with it. Skunk no longer gave serious thought to leading Rolf to a pasture pond to drown like a feral cat. Skunk told himself it was not because he could not do it, but it was because it wasn't his decision to make. This was a family issue. Though Skunk spent more time with Rolf than anyone, they were not family. Rolf's girl would have to figure out what to do with her old man. If she asked Skunk's opinion, he might still suggest a deep pond as the most expedient option.

With that settled in his mind, Skunk thought again about the vision of Luke at the church. By the time he arrived back at the motel room that night, Skunk had convinced himself he had imagined it. He also had nearly convinced himself the minister was conjured up by his sleep-deprived brain.

However, he still had some of the cash Brother Dale had given him. He and Rolf used part of it to buy a Hardees breakfast.

Brother Dale. The way the minister had looked at him still rattled Skunk. What had that been? It wasn't judgment Skunk had seen in the other man's eyes. It had been something else. Concern? Yes, but something more. Compassion, maybe, though Skunk couldn't believe that. When was the last time anyone had looked on Skunk Olstad with compassion?

Skunk began to float into something not quite sweet sleep but less than wakefulness. Somewhere on the surface of his consciousness a memory of Luke floated up from where it had been deeply buried. They had gone hunting. Luke was about the same age as the boy in the back of the van. Yes, Skunk remembered, Luke wore a forest green knit cap that kept his rooster tail flattened. Skunk could now see clearly that he had forced Luke to go. Luke liked to hunt, but not that day. Not with his daddy. What had they gone hunting for? Quail or pheasant? No. They must have been going after rabbits, because Skunk visualized them both carrying .22 rifles.

"Don't shoot nothing unless you intend to dress and eat it," Skunk said. That outing almost made him feel fatherly. But Luke had said little. He didn't want to be there. Skunk saw it in his body language—shoulders slumped and boots dragging the ground. Skunk could see in his memory a light dusting on the leaves, so it must have been late fall. The covering had given the ground a matted coating that was more like hoarfrost than snow.

Five minutes into the hunt, Skunk spotted a rabbit about thirty yards ahead of them. It hopped away at the sound of Luke kicking through maple leaves.

"Go after it," Skunk had said.

Luke stood still, his shoulders slumping further. "It's hiding now," he said.

"Go shoot the goddamn rabbit," Skunk said.

Luke took the lead, creating as much noise as he could with his boots. He walked steadily toward the rabbit, which stopped on the edge of a fallen clump of limbs the same color as its fur. Luke eyed the rabbit, got within fifteen feet, aimed, and squeezed the trigger on the old single-shot rifle that Skunk had passed down to him. The bullet struck the animal in its hindquarters, spinning it around, but not killing it. The rabbit tried to scamper away, but its back legs were paralyzed. Luke lowered his gun to his side. Skunk was behind him and could not see his face, but he heard a weak sniffle.

"Put it out of its misery," Skunk said.

Luke hesitated.

"Kill the motherfucker," Skunk said with a growl.

Luke still hesitated, which was too much for his father. Skunk picked up the dying animal and wrenched its head from its body. He tossed the decapitated carcass at his son, who caught it automatically as though it were a football. Skunk got in his face.

"This is nothing but a goddamn little animal," Skunk said. "Someday, you might face a human with intent to do you harm. What will you do then, huh? Stand there sniveling with your thumb up your ass like you're doing now? You've got to finish the job. Finish or be finished."

Luke threw down the remains as though they were contaminated. "I'm not a son of bitch like you," he said.

"You're right," Skunk said. "But you'll goddamn wish you were some day. You can't act like a pussy if you want to amount to anything other than a Mama's boy. You think it's important to be liked? To have everyone say, 'There goes that nice Luke Olstad. He sure is good to his mama?' Shit no. It's important to be a man. A real man. And right now, I ain't so sure you're gonna make it."

Luke began to cry.

"There are two kinds of people in the world: givers and takers," Skunk said. "You can either be a taker like me, or you can get took your whole life like your mother. Now pick up that goddamn piece of meat and let's go."

Skunk did not regret his words that day in the timber.

All right, maybe a little.

Fully awake, Skunk looked at Rolf. As always, the man clutched his pillow bundle like it was a dirty teddy bear. Rolf was losing it fast, but Skunk began to wonder if he was, too. It started months earlier when he left the motel room with the cold body of the meth head Sheena still in it. But it had gotten worse in recent days. He left the GMC's owner alive in the northeast Kansas pasture. Then he allowed himself to be robbed by a minor league drug dealer. And now he was going to let Rolf live, if only for someone else to deal with. He wondered if his failure to sleep indicated something significant he couldn't identify. Old dogs often crawled off some place private when it was time to go. Why was he really going home?

35

I wish I could watch Tommy watching his boat being built. The idea of a Viking funeral ship is pretty cool. If I could go back in time, I would write a request for my mom to have me done the same way. It makes the whole dirt burial thing seem pretty lame now. Of course, if I could go back in time, I would have called in sick the day Tommy came to the shop with guns a-blazin. Beggars, choosers, etc. Anyway, the boat in the Klimp garage is taking shape, though its seaworthiness remains in doubt. Windmill Bob had to make adjustments due to inferior materials and a lack of time, so it's flat across the bow end rather than v-shaped. It looks more like a punt than a long boat you'd expect for a Viking. But Tommy should be proud to be set on fire on it, assuming it can stay above water long enough.

Patsy entered the garage through the kitchen door to check their progress.

"It only has to stay afloat for a short time as long as we apply a good amount of fuel to burn it," Bob said, watching for some indication of his wife's opinion. Her face was blank. "I think she'll be able to handle fifteen minutes at least," he said.

"So it's a 'she' already?"

Bob shrugged. "I'm not going to name it."

"I have no idea how long it takes a body to burn," Patsy said. She looked at Coach like he might know, but he studied the nail apron he wore around his waist.

"We'll coat everything real good with kerosene and whatever else we can dig up that burns fast," Bob said.

Patsy blinked. "I can't believe we're talking like this, saying these actual words like we're discussing what's for supper."

Bob set down his hammer while Coach walked to the bow of the punt like he had work to do there.

"I know," Bob said quietly. "It'll be over soon. We're doing all this because you said it's the way Tommy wanted it."

Patsy looked into her husband's gray eyes. "But what do you think?"

"I think it's the right thing to do," he said, holding her gaze. "And I think Tommy's happy. Happier than he ever was in life. We both believe that, don't we?"

Before Patsy could answer, they heard a vehicle pull into the yard. Coach, closest to the front of the garage, peeked out the window. "It's Diane Olstad. And she's got someone with her."

"I bet it's Skunk," Bob said. He took a step toward the door to the kitchen before he remembered Tommy had taken his revolver. It was now somewhere in an evidence locker along with other weapons and a bloody Viking helmet.

"I can't tell for sure, but I don't believe it's him," Coach said, straining to see through the dusty window.

"I'll go see what they want," Bob said, picking up a two-foot crowbar sitting on the edge of the boat. He held it casually at his side. The others followed him.

Maesie stayed in the car as Diane got out. Diane had turned off the engine, which meant the interior would soon smell like a rotted coyote carcass. Diane attempted a smile as the others approached from the garage, but she was out of practice. It came off looking more like she had stepped on a nail. She noticed the crowbar, though Bob had tried to partially conceal it behind him.

"You planning to smack me with that thing if I get too close, Bob?" she asked.

Bob looked at the tool like he had forgotten he carried it. "I wasn't sure who you had with you," he said.

"I've seen hide nor hair of the ex," Diane said, though she suspected Skunk was close. She could feel it. "I've got Maesie Mattsen in the car, but she's mostly harmless."

"What do you want?" Patsy asked. She held her arms folded across her midsection. Her face was hard. "And that girl with you has no business showing her face around here."

"Go easy," Bob murmured to his wife.

"Just paying a friendly visit," Diane said. "I see the preacher beat us to it."

The Klimps were confused about why *this* person had come to their house.

To pay a "friendly visit?"

"It's nice of you to think of us," Bob said to Diane, his tone a mix of bewilderment and contrition. "We're sure you've got plenty to deal with. Of our doing, of course. And we're really sorry."

"We don't need looking in on," Patsy said, her mouth pinched.

Diane peered at the casket under the tree. "I figured under the circumstances, you might need some kind of help. You're not alone, you know. Plenty of people feel heartsick for what you're going through, too."

"Are they the ones that keep driving down our road?" Patsy asked. "The ones that never stop?" She nodded toward Diane's car. "And what's her role in this benevolent jag of yours?"

"She's not necessarily a willing participant," Diane said. "I figure once it hits two hundred Fahrenheit in the car, she'll be a little more eager to step out here."

"Why are you really here?" Patsy asked.

"Just what I said. This town is too small for us to avoid each other. I'm not going anywhere. You're not going anywhere, and neither is anybody else. I'm not saying we should get together every Friday night and play bridge, but wouldn't it be best for everyone if we tried to get along?"

Bob said: "That makes some sense…"

"She's another story," Patsy said, still looking at the shadowy figure in Diane's car. "It will be the day after never before I'll ever forgive her. None of this terribleness would have occurred had she only been nice to my son."

Not wanting to take the bait and rile up Patsy further, Diane asked, "So? Can I help?" She looked past them at the garage. "With whatever you got going on in there?"

A long list of people in Smackdab passed along rumors with the zeal of the cheese dip sample lady at Wal-Mart. However, the list did not include Diane Olstad. She heard a lot, knew a lot, but she did not talk a lot. And Maesie Mattsen? No one paid her much mind.

Coach had lost patience waiting for the Klimps to answer. "We're taking the body out to Dead Lake tonight, and we're going to set it on fire if we don't run out of time," he said. "It's what Tommy would have wanted all along, Patsy says. And they won't have to worry about the casket being dug up again."

Coach paused to see if Bob or Patsy wanted to stop him or correct anything he had shared so far. Hearing no objections, he continued explaining about the punt in the garage, and how they were rushed to complete the job before Denbo found out about it.

"And Skunk, too," Diane said. "No telling what he will do. He might be all pissed at everyone, or he might pitch in and help. You never know, but I wouldn't want to bet my paycheck on option number two."

Maesie gave into the heat and her curiosity when the others, along with Diane, entered the garage to examine the boat. She followed them there. No one made mention of her arrival, though Patsy Klimp was not frugal with venomous looks. Maesie knew the Klimps would forever hold her in bad favor for turning away their son. She wondered what good an apology would do.

Oh, the hell with it.

"I'm really sorry..." she began.

"We know," Bob said, holding up his hand to stop her. "It wasn't your fault."

From the look Patsy gave her husband, Maesie could see the Klimps were not on the same page regarding fault. Still, Maesie thought, fifty percent was not a bad figure. With that out of the way, Maesie considered the roughly built wooden rig that occupied half the garage. The first image she thought of was a coffin.

"It's a funeral boat," Bob said, reading her mind. "For cremation. On Dead Lake. As you can see, it's a slapdash job. We just need to get the thing done like right now before the wrong people get wind of our efforts."

Maesie asked: "So you're going to burn..."

"Yes," Coach said.

"And how are you going to make sure the, uh, you know... the...body?" Diane asked.

"Make sure the body burns?" Bob replied. "Burlap soaked in kerosene for starters. But we're behind on that just like everything else."

"We've got to get the body prepped," Coach said, but not like he was offering to do it. It didn't seem right to ask the Klimps to do that to their son, but it didn't seem right to ask anyone else. He was worried he would be stuck with the task.

"I'll help with the body," Diane said. "But it looks like you could use another set of hands with the boat, if you truly want to get this done tonight."

"The circle of people who have knowledge of this is getting bigger by the minute," Patsy said. "Pretty soon, we'll have half the town out here. And they won't all be out here to help." She gave Maesie another hard look.

"I don't even have a phone anymore," Maesie said, "but if you need more help, you might ask Cahill. He's been out here, right?"

"Haven't seen hide nor hair of him," Bob said. "I'd be surprised if he came around here."

"He said he was headed out this way when I saw him a while ago," Maesie said. "He could use a little diversion right now. Something that will keep him out of trouble."

"This isn't a community service project," Patsy snapped. The look she gave Maesie was hot enough to melt sand, but Maesie held it long enough to show she didn't care. She borrowed Diane's phone to call Cahill.

Cahill took some convincing. "I'm not going nowhere near that cadaver," he said.

"You don't have to," Maesie said. "It's the boat you can help with. Tommy's still in his box."

"Yeah, but he's got to be put in the boat eventually." He clucked his tongue. "You people're all crazy."

"You got bigger plans?"

"Yeah. To stay away from phantoms."

"If Tommy's a phantom, do you think he'd stay in his box? Or in Smackdab? If he could go anywhere he wanted, he wouldn't stay here. He's probably half way to the Gulf by now, flying on the clouds."

Cahill didn't speak, which meant he was thinking about it.

"Get your ass out here," Maesie said. "Time's running out."

Cahill arrived thirty minutes later to help Bob and Coach in the garage. He was relieved to see the Klimps had cleaned up the muck he left near the front door. Since no one brought it up, he didn't either.

Outside, the others were preparing to open the casket.

"Why are the women stuck doing the dirty work?" Maesie whispered to Diane as they followed Patsy out to the shade tree.

"I don't know about you, but I'm not very good with a hammer," Diane said.

"I don't know about you, but I'm not very good at cremating a body either," Maesie said.

Patsy toted the crowbar her husband had used earlier to arm himself. "Let me see what I can do with this thing," she said. Then she paused. "I don't know what kind of shape he's in, what with all the tossing and turning this box has done. If you all want to go back in the garage, I understand."

Maesie was about to agree to that suggestion when Diane cut in. "We can't help you from in there," she said.

Maesie took several steps back from the casket. "Should we have masks on or something?" she asked.

Without pause, Patsy fitted the crowbar in the crack and began prying downward. The lid produced a frightening squawk of soft metal giving in to tougher metal. Maesie began to feel lightheaded. "I'm going to help with the boat," she said. She almost ran into Bob. "I should be out here," he said.

Ten minutes later, the Klimps and Diane, their faces pale, entered the garage. Diane was unfurling a hand towel, which she has used like a gas mask, from around her face. She looked like a blond Bedouin.

While they took a moment to collect themselves, Cahill hammered a piece of wood into place at the back of the boat. Coach poured the remaining drops of a gallon of black Rust-Oleum sealant on the deck of the punt. Maesie slopped the sealant across the surface with a brush.

"We used the last of the sealant," Coach said, dropping the can on the floor. He looked worse than the other two in the garage, beaten like he had wrestled a yeti and lost. His sweat-sated hair hung over his forehead in bangs, and the armpits of his beige dress shirt were drenched with sweat. Splotches of black paint accessorized his clothing from collar to cuffs. "How's it going out there?" he asked.

"We have him to where we can get him out now," Bob said. His face was grim, his demeanor reserved after what he had just done. "It wasn't too hard to get the thing open. We covered him with some plastic until we're ready in here."

To Coach: "If you're up for it, you could say a few words before we move him again."

Coach hesitated to answer.

"You don't have to if you don't want," Patsy said. "He's been prayed over quite a bit by you."

"We've done enough talking, and we're getting further behind," Bob said. "Let's get on with prepping the body."

To Diane: "We have extra burlap and kerosene in the trunk of the car. That is, if you don't mind helping with it. You've already done plenty."

"I don't mind," Diane said, already headed out the door again.

Cahill looked at the black coating on the deck and sides of the boat. "Is this going to dry in time?" he asked. "Maybe a fan or something would speed up the process."

Bob had slotted a sealant cartridge in a caulk gun, but stopped. His shoulders sank. "We have no choice," he said. "If it stays wet, so be it. Either way, we must get this done tonight."

COME UP A CLOUD

36

As the upper tip of the sun kissed the western horizon, the body was, as Cahill put it, "wrapped up like a goddamn mummy." Patsy had soaked the body with every flammable liquid they could find. Diane had just come from town with another two cans of kerosene that would be used to douse the punt.

Everyone needed a break. When Diane returned from the GasGo, she joined Cahill and Maesie on the front steps of the Klimp house, bringing them each a forty-four-ounce Coke. They could still smell the remnants of Cahill's earlier burnt cowshit stunt, but no one mentioned it.

"I'll get those cans out for you once I catch my breath," Cahill said. "That boat's gonna light up like a Roman candle. I wouldn't want to be close when it gets lit. It's liable to singe a man's nose hairs and likely his butt hairs, too, if he's standing the wrong direction."

Diane sat on the other side of Cahill from Maesie, who had slept so little in days she did not want to talk.

"Windmill Bob wants to torch the casket, too," Cahill continued. "Right there where it sits. He says he don't give one shit what people think anymore."

"That doesn't sound like the Bob I know," Diane said. She reached down and pulled a blade of fescue grass from the parched lawn. The Klimps' yard was usually one of the nicest in the area. Bob kept the grass watered and fertilized so it rivaled the nicest PGA course. "He's always been one to care too much what other people think." Diane tore the sere blade of grass into tiny sections. "This whole thing changed him. Changed us all, I guess."

For a while, the only sound was the sucking of beverages through straws. In unison, the three figures turned their heads to the west at the sound of wild turkeys crossing the road a quarter-mile away.

"It's a good thing you two are helping out." Diane said. "I know it's not easy for you to be here." She finished sectioning the grass and pulled a pack of Marlboro Lights from her jacket. Maesie gave no reaction to Diane's compliment, but Cahill broke into a grin.

"Hell. You couldn't pay me enough to be an undertaker."

"You couldn't pay an undertaker enough to do what we're doing," Diane said, tapping out a cigarette and popping it in her mouth. "This would seem unnatural in just about any situation. But the Klimps think it's necessary."

The garage door powered up. Bob and Coach exited. Each wiped sweat from his brow.

"Let's hitch the flatbed to my truck," Bob said to no one. Cahill sprung to help.

When the hitch-up was completed, Bob rested his hands against the side of the punt, bone-weary, as though the support of the makeshift craft was the only thing keeping him from falling.

"None of you need to go out to the lake," he said as everyone gathered around the punt. "Patsy and I can do it." He looked at his wife. "Are you still up for this?"

Patsy nodded, her arms still folded. "I took two of Tommy's old bed sheets," she said, "one light blue and the other white, and sewed them into a sail. It might make the thing look more like a Viking ship."

"I'll scrounge up a couple extra pieces of framing lumber," Bob said. "We can attach the sail to the boat when we have her in the water."

"I'd like to see this thing through," Coach said. "Mind if I tag along?"

Bob nodded, and Patsy shrugged.

The small group stood in the quiet of the gloaming, huddled around the trailer that was illuminated only by the tail lights on the truck.

No one spoke until Maesie said, "There's supposed to be a maiden in the boat with the body."

The others looked at her. She felt her face warming.

"We talked about it when we went to the movie," she said, the discomfort of her mentioning the ill-fated date felt by everyone. "The maiden's called a thrall, I think. I could have heard him wrong."

"You mean like a virgin?" Cahill asked. "Hell, if you want to find a virgin around here, you'd have to dip into the ninth grade."

"Maybe I should do it," Diane said. "It's been so long my virginity has grown back."

At a quarter past ten, the lake-bound two-vehicle caravan was ready to pull out onto the gravel road. Bob and Patsy would lead the way in the truck pulling the trailer. Diane volunteered to ride out with Coach in his

Volvo. Cahill knew he should volunteer, too, to help maneuver the boat into the water. He didn't mind the work, but he wanted to be nowhere near the boat when it started burning. He still feared Tommy's ghost.

Maesie knew Patsy would not want her at the lake. She had retrieved her backpack from Diane's car and was ready to make her way, exhausted, back to her camping spot.

"I'll give you a ride back to town," Cahill told her. "You don't need to be walking the roads at night. I'll make you stay at my house tonight so you can get some sleep."

Before Maesie could answer, two pickups, their headlights on bright and with several men riding in their beds, barreled along the gravel road from the direction of Smackdab. The lead truck, Denbo's, fishtailed as it reached the fence line that marked the beginning of the Klimp's property. It made a hard turn at the Klimp's yard, barely missing the parked vehicles as it careered into the open, empty casket. The front of the truck drove up on top of the container, rolling it over beneath the fat front tires. When Denbo tried to reverse off the mashed box, the casket lid tore loose and spun with the tire. It found purchase in the front wheel wells. The pickup could move no further.

The second pickup pulled up behind the first and stopped. The skulkers in the truck beds belly-laughed as Denbo put the truck alternately in First and Reverse to shake loose the casket lid. But the debris was stuck to the underside of the truck like a huge clump of duct tape.

The human water drum known as Harp Denbo exited the driver's side of his truck, leaving its lights running. He strutted around the front of his vehicle like his inauspicious arrival was by design. Jordy Wakefield hopped down from the passenger side. The men in the bed of the truck jumped out, but they stayed back in the dark.

"What do we have here?" Denbo queried, his hands behind his back like an officer inspecting his troops. He walked around the trailer. "This looks like an ungodly type of parade float. Is there some special holiday coming up I'm not aware of?"

Even with the headlights from the vehicles, which were pointed at each other and created a bright aura that extended many feet in each direction, it was difficult to make out the details of the structure on the trailer. The main sail would not be attached until the boat was in the water. It lay rolled up around two eight-foot two-by-fours in the bed of the Klimp pickup.

Denbo circumnavigated the craft again. "Smells like an oil refinery," he said. He glided his hand across the side of the boat, and then yanked his hand. "It's not even dry yet."

He studied the mummy tied to the top of the boat. If the scene had been better lighted, the realization that slowly came to Denbo would have been obvious on his face. He stood for a moment, trying to make sense of it.

"You're going to light him on fire, aren't you?"

"As long as we don't bury him around here, what does it matter to you?" Bob asked. A dim halogen glow partially lighted his face. "That's what you want, isn't it? He won't be buried anywhere. He'll be gone, like he never existed. No body, no nothing."

Coach and the other allies came closer to the Klimps by the trailer. Seeing this, Denbo's gang moved in closer, too. The groups formed two distinct sides like opposing tribes prepared for battle. But one side, the new arrivals, fidgeted with uncertainty and acted like their hearts weren't in whatever Denbo intended. They had come for a little fun.

"Harp," Coach said in a neutral voice. He nodded at the large man as though they were meeting at a Kiwanis luncheon.

"I see you made your choice," Denbo said, his voice flat.

"It wasn't difficult," Coach said. "You just have to look for the good light and head toward it."

"The good?" Denbo asked, the disgust on his face obvious in the dimness. "Take a step back and behold what you're a part of. It's evil. Every bit of it."

Coach shook his head. "What Tommy Klimp did was evil, but that does not make his family evil. They did not make him what he was, even though I'm sure they have their doubts about that. I've had mine, too, I admit. But Bob and Patsy are good people, just like these others standing here.

"I've seldom been more disappointed in another human being," Denbo said. He yelled at the men behind him: "Get a truck up here to tow this trailer and its godforsaken cargo."

Before Denbo's minions could react, Maesie stepped between Denbo and Coach. She was so much shorter than Denbo that he had not noticed her at first. He also had not noticed the long-nosed revolver pointed up at his belly. Now that he saw the gun and the tiny woman aiming at him, he grinned.

"Didn't anyone ever tell you not to point a gun unless you're prepared to use it?" he asked.

Diane put a hand on Maesie's back. "Don't do something rash, Hon," she said.

Maesie ignored Diane and stared up at Denbo. "I am quite prepared to use it," she said. She felt a malicious bile welling up from her lower gut to her throat. All her years of frustration and disappointment were now being channeled into the hand that held the cocked revolver. She wondered if this was this how Tommy had felt. Was this the only way he could find to end his dispossession?

Denbo's smile broadened so his crooked tooth could be seen in the gloom. "Even if you were stupid enough to fire, that little popgun wouldn't do much damage," he said.

Masie tried to keep the gun from shaking in her grip. "It might ruin your evening, though," she said.

Denbo spoke, but Maesie did not hear him because another voice was much louder.

Idiot, the voice said.

First, Maesie thought it was Diane who spoke, and then she suspected her dead mother. Finally, she wasn't sure she heard the voice at all. She felt the bile abating just as suddenly as it rose up. She did not want that. She wanted to savor her rage, but it was too late. Maesie knew she could no longer shoot Denbo. There had been enough stupidity the past week, and she did not want to contribute more. She uncocked the trigger, and, holding the pistol by the barrel, offered it to Denbo.

"Here. Take it if you want," she said.

The group around her sucked in their breaths, but Denbo frowned at the gun as if he was being played for a fool.

"What's your game?" he asked.

"No game," Maesie said. "Take the gun. Do what you came to do. Or if not, leave the Klimps alone. They're punishing themselves more than you ever could."

Denbo was stuck in neutral. He had not expected defiance. But even when Maesie pointed the gun at him, he hadn't looked worried. Yet, offering him the gun had thrown him off balance. Whatever he had expected to occur when he arrived at the Klimps, it was not this.

The handful of men who followed Denbo from town, including Jordy Wakefield, were not terrible people. Most of them had come along only because of the beer keg in the bed of Denbo's pickup. At the first hint of pushback, they would all disappear. Though he did not realize it yet, Denbo was alone in this.

"Dammit, Jordy," he yelled, turning toward his truck. "You got that piece of metal unstuck yet?"

37

A dusty gray Ford Falcon with Nebraska plates pulled into the one available spot in front of Snoots. Two men, gaunt and unshaven, rustled in the front seats. The man in the driver's seat stirred as though he had been asleep at the wheel. His head lolled back like he was about to pass out drunk. As if roused by an unexpected noise, he snapped back to attention. He took inventory of the other vehicles parked outside the bar.

"I don't see her car here," Skunk said. He squirmed in his seat. His rear was numb from the long drive up the highway that followed the Missouri River north before cutting across rich bottomland past mounds and hillocks built by Sauk Indians.

"Whose car?" Rolf asked.

"Never mind."

When they hit town, Skunk first drove by his old house, but Diane's car was not in the driveway. The house was dark. They next went to Snoots.

Rolf studied the cinder block exterior of the tavern, a place he no longer recognized. He scratched the salt and pepper whiskers on his neck. "We got a show here tonight?" he asked. "It don't look like much."

"It sure as hell don't. Lucky for us we ain't on the bill. Just stay put a minute, okay?"

Rolf nodded and took a sip from the icy remains of a forty-four-ounce cup of Mountain Dew that Skunk had bought him at a gas station fifty miles out. He leaned his head against the side window and closed his eyes again.

If Snoots had a piano player like in a Wild West saloon, the music would have stopped when Skunk entered the tavern. Nobody spoke. A few drinkers looked at him, but most looked away.

COME UP A CLOUD

Each time he returned to Smackdab, Skunk recognized fewer of Snoots' clientele. Some of the older ones, their livers or other organs given out, had relocated to nursing homes or cemeteries. Younger faces had taken their places. Skunk nodded at a few of the drinkers close to his age. Each nodded back, though in a way that was not too obvious.

Eladio Saurez, Snoots' part time barkeep, looked at Skunk while holding a clean pilsner glass beneath the Miller tap. Skunk waved him off.

"Just looking for my wife," he said. "Don't look like she's here."

Eladio shook his head. "I ain't seen her."

Skunk held out his hand, palm down at shoulder level. "Skinny woman? About yay high? Drinks like a fish?"

Eladio shook his head, setting the beer glass upside down on a shelf with others like it.

"Well then..." Skunk began, but the door behind him opened and Harp Denbo entered. Jordy Wakefield, Dirty Dave and Rodney Jensen followed Denbo through the door.

Like most people in Smackdab, Skunk knew little about Denbo. Unlike others, Skunk had never been anxious to learn more, because the large man was not in his orbit of interests. From what he remembered, however, Denbo had always dressed in nice clothes and kept his hair neat, like he was a little better than the locals. But the Denbo who stood before Skunk now was disheveled, sweaty, and seemed to have misplaced some of his jauntiness. A red welt, perhaps the work of a hungry mosquito, swelled on Denbo's left cheek.

Denbo's expression betrayed his surprise before he quickly collected himself. He surveyed Skunk by starting at the top: his dingy hat, wrinkled and grease-spotted jacket, soiled jeans, and finally his unpolished boots.

"Skunk Olstad, I'm assuming?"

"Last time I checked," Skunk said in flat voice.

Denbo scratched the mosquito bite. "I don't think we ever met."

They had met once, and Skunk knew Denbo remembered it.

"You look like you're about a nickel away from vagrancy," Denbo said, his mouth warped into a sneer.

"I've had better patches," Skunk said. "But I've had worse, too."

With a show of liberality, Denbo pulled a roll of paper money from his jeans. "Do us all a favor," he said, stripping five twenties from the roll and presenting them with faux ceremony to Skunk. "Get yourself a room at the motor court and take a long hot shower. I don't know if that'll make you feel better, but it would help the rest of us. You smell like the men's toilet at a beans and rice dinner."

Skunk kept his eyes on Denbo and did not look down at the money. Then he looked at the barkeep. "Good to see you, Eladio. If you see the woman before I do, tell her I'm back in town."

"I'll confess I'm a little disappointed," Denbo said as he put his free hand on Skunk's shoulder to prevent him from exiting. "The way everyone talked, I expected someone a tad more formidable."

"Sorry to disappoint," Skunk said, calmly removing the other man's hand. "I didn't get the email that me and you were to supposed to butt heads. Have your assistant call mine and maybe we can arrange something next time I come this way."

Dirty Dave and Rodney Jensen fidgeted like they wanted nothing to do with what might about to happen, but Jordy Wakefield stepped forward. "Don't get mouthy," he said, looking like he was about to piss his pants for his own audacity. "You're a washed-up, two-bit, has-been dog turd. And we'll kick your ass any time we want."

"I take some offense at the dog turd part," Skunk said, tilting his hat forward so the brim hovered at eye level. "But I don't have the energy to argue. I'm as wiped out as a one-whore brothel on payday. So, if you don't mind, I'll be on my way."

Skunk edged his way around Denbo and Wakefield and between the two other men standing behind them. Jensen smiled nervously and opened the door to allow him through. If there was to be a scrum, Skunk knew Jensen would be the first to flee. As Skunk stepped into the sultry air and let the door slam behind him, something sharp smacked into the small of his back. He fell forward into the grill of a truck parked in front of the entrance. As his face hit the truck, an upper molar loosened on the right side of his mouth. The metallic taste of blood began to coat the interior of his cheek. Skunk felt woozy and ready to topple. With his hands on the front of the truck, he kept his balance. Still facing away from his attacker, he spat a pink glob onto the gravel that edged the two-by-two cement slab at the bar's entrance.

Skunk gingerly touched the side of his face. He felt the loose molar with his tongue. He guessed he could still chew once it came out, and it felt like it would soon. But his back was his main worry. It already throbbed with a knife-sharp pain Skunk hadn't felt since a bout with a kidney stone the size of Mount Rushmore. He believed someone wearing boots with toecaps had kicked him, but he hadn't noticed Denbo or anyone else with such accouterments.

Skunk tried to catch his breath. Before he could say more, a fist the size of a large ham hock came down hard on his head, grinding the Llano into his scalp. As he buckled to his knees, Skunk hoped the crackling sound he heard was the straw in his hat breaking rather than the give of his skull.

While exiting the tavern, Skunk had nonchalantly stuck his hand inside his jacket. With a deftness accomplished through much practice, he had resituated the chainsaw file inside his right sleeve. Skunk now let the file drop so that the tape-wrapped handle rested in the hollow of his hand. He was ready to thrust the file backward and up until it met resistance with Denbo's throat. The triceps of his right arm flexed as he began the backward motion, but he abruptly halted. He realized he no longer cared, no longer felt the desire to fight. He let the file drop as though continuing to grip it would blister his palm. He would let Denbo and his crew do as they pleased. He would take whatever pain came if sleep would follow.

Skunk lowered his shoulders to the ground, rolling into a ball to better withstand the kicks and blows. Instead, he heard two impacts in quick succession. The first impact was muffled; the second a slapping sound of skin on skin. Skunk felt no pain from either blow. A nasal scream, like the trumpet of an injured elephant, arose from someone else.

Skunk had heard the same succession of sounds generated by Rolf many times. He would first attack his query with a kick to the groin. That was followed quickly by jamming the heel of his palm into the bridge of the opponent's nose as the other man bent forward to cover his groin.

Skunk rolled over to see Denbo stumble backward and fall against the bar door. The large man slumped to a seated position, his splayed knees framing his face in a V from Skunk's vantage. Denbo looked cross-eyed at his nose, which was bent to the right. Blood, the color and shape of an overripe cherry, had begun to form below his left nostril. Rolf, his arms poised in front of him like a high school wrestler, stood over Denbo. "If you try to get up, I'll knock your nose through the back of your skull," he said.

Wakefield was also lying on the ground between the tavern and the grill of another vehicle. Dirty Dave and Rodney Jensen sized up the odds and found them not in their favor. Before they could escape, however, Rolf laid a left hook into Dirty Dave's meaty jowl, only because he stood closest. The struck man crumpled on top of Wakefield, who was trying to rise to his feet.

"Let 'em go, Rolf," Skunk said.

The two men got to their feet and scurried away. Rolf kept an eye on Denbo while he picked up Skunk's hat and poked out the dented top. He placed the hat on Skunk's head, who now sat with his back against the grill of the truck.

"We ought to be gettin' while the gettin's good," Rolf said.

"Help me up, will ya?" Skunk said, reaching for Rolf. "One of 'em kicked me solid in my back."

"Lemme get a look," Rolf said, studying his partner's back as he helped him to his feet. "God Almighty, Skunk. Looks like they did more than kick you. You're bleeding like a stuck pig. Did one of 'em have a gun?"

"Not that I saw or heard."

Rolf looked at Denbo, who had yet to pick himself up. "Did you shoot my partner?" Rolf asked, stomping on the man's quadriceps.

"Let him go," Skunk growled as an order.

Rolf complied and turned his attention back to Skunk. He picked up the chainsaw file and placed it back in Skunk's jacket pocket.

"I think maybe we ought to get you to a hospital," he said.

slow his breathing. "It won't take long."

38

Midnight. The offload of the funeral boat was taking longer than Bob had expected. He wished he had persuaded Cahill and Maesie to join the rest of them at the lake. The extra muscle, though it was not much, would have helped. However, Cahill refused to be present at the immolation, and Maesie had become morose after Denbo and his crew returned to town. She would not look at or speak to anyone. Diane had put a hand on her shoulder to console her, but Maesie had shaken it off. Even Patsy had made an effort.

"You stood up for us," Patsy said. "I won't forget it."

Cahill drove her back to town when the two-vehicle cortege left for Dead Lake.

After they assembled and erected the makeshift sail, Bob had backed the trailer to the edge of the water where it became bogged in mire. Drought had lowered the lake's volume and widened its mucky shore. The trailer sank into the ooze several feet from where the water was deep enough to float the punt. Though the replica of a long ship wasn't much to look at it, it was built sturdy. With the mummy of Tommy already affixed to the bier, it had become much heavier than the original casket. Four bearers middle-aged and older could not easily move it off the trailer and through the mud into the water.

While mosquitoes feasted on them, the four inched the boat closer to navigable water. Their feet sunk into the putrid ooze, which smelled like a backed-up sewer in which someone had tossed a case of rotten eggs. Only Bob wore gumboots. Patsy wore an old pair of running shoes, which she didn't mind getting grimy. Diane wore flats, which she had taken off on the shore when she rolled up her slacks. Coach wore an old pair of loafers, which he would have to toss away after this night.

Diane and Coach pushed from the bow, which was positioned at the front of the trailer. The Klimps, stronger than the other two, lifted and pulled the stern. The crew stopped every few feet to rest. With each break, Coach bent over with his hands on his knees. The others leaned against the boat, all breathing heavily and slapping at voracious mosquitoes that swarmed to their necks like Dobermans to a T-bone. The air felt and smelled like a wet, rotted blanket.

"Should've built her out of balsa wood," Bob said, breathing heavily. No one responded. The moon was full, the sky clear, which enabled Bob to see everyone as though it were late evening. Flashlights and vehicle headlights were unnecessary. The lakeshore would have made a pleasant setting if not for the eye-watering stench, mosquitoes, and the task still to be done. As everyone caught a breath, Bob thought of ways to make the job easier. As it was now, he didn't believe the four of them had the muscle to get the boat in the water.

Bob wondered if Diane, in the early stages of alcohol withdrawal, was doing them any good. Coach worried Bob, too. The old man seemed to have shrunk since the morning. The events of this marathon day had eaten away at him.

"You okay, Coach?" Bob asked.

"As good as ever," Coach said. His front shirttail had pulled out during the lifting and pulling. He pulled it up to wipe his face.

"How do you figure the Vikings did it?" Diane asked. Everyone had been asking themselves the same question.

"Tree trunks," Coach said. "They would've rolled the boat on poles."

No one spoke until Patsy asked, "Anyone got some poles in their back pocket?"

Since they had finished the boat, Patsy seemed to have loosened up a little. Bob had begun to transition from wondering how long his marriage would last to thinking it still had a small chance. He wasn't convinced it was worth the trouble, but they would see how it went. He wasn't sure how Patsy felt.

No one spoke as they listened to the synchronization of their panting, which had slowed and quieted. An occasional slap at a mosquito interrupted the calm.

"I'm sorry for not thinking this through," Bob said.

"Didn't there used to be a boat dock on the other side?" Coach asked. "I was thinking it fell apart."

Nobody knew. None of them had been to the prairie in years.

"Are you thinking about using the stanchions?" Bob asked.

Coach stood straighter, somewhat revitalized. "Assuming they're still around and we can get at them. I'll run over there and have a look," he said, taking off around the edge of the lake in the direction of the old pier. "Back in a minute."

"You want a flashlight?" Bob called after the old man.

Coach waved off the offer as he walked into the gloom.

"If he finds anything, we'll need to haul them over here," Patsy said. She started unhitching the trailer. They found the old man two hundred yards around the lake, standing where the old dock used to be. It was the first bit of good news of the night. Two stanchions, each about ten feet long and eight inches in diameter, lay along the shore, half in the water and half out. In a wetter summer, they would have been submerged. In the glare of the truck's headlights, three more stanchions were visible in the water, still upright, at various angles like straws in a cup. Bob quickly pulled a log chain from the pickup bed and wrapped it around the first log. Within ten minutes, they had the two stanchions chained together and dragged behind the truck back to the funeral boat. After the poles were under the boat, the process was still slow going, still exhausting. But everyone could now envision the possibility of success. After much grunting and panting, they pulled the boat far enough into the lake that it began to wobble and float just above the bottom of the lake. The water came up to their knees.

"I don't suppose anybody's a champion swimmer," Bob said, leaning against the boat.

"What's your plan?" Patsy asked.

No one had thought this far ahead. Just getting the boat in the water had been a major accomplishment. As his adrenaline began to wane again, Bob felt a bone-tiredness that surpassed his roughest days as a janitor. Yet, he knew he had to be the one to navigate the boat farther into the water, and then to swim back to shore.

"I'll pole the boat out and set her afire," he said.

Patsy took two additional containers of kerosene and a box of matches and loaded them on the boat. She then brought a plastic bag and handed it to her husband. Bob pulled the Viking helmet from the bag and placed it atop his son's wrapped body. He then began to push the boat away from shore. The chore could be handled by him alone now that the craft was in deeper water. When the lake was waist-high, he climbed on and used a ten-foot two-by-four as a push pole.

The going was slow at first. With no wind, the sail proved worthless. Each time Bob shoved the board in the water at the punt's stern, it stuck into the mushy bottom of the lake. In freeing the board from the mud, the force would take the boat back toward to the shore. After several efforts, the water deepened, and the punt began to move more easily toward the center of the lake. A small breeze arose and helped draw the craft farther. Bob switched to a second, shorter two-by-four that Coach had fashioned as an oar with a section of barn plank tacked on the end.

Fifty feet from the shore, Bob emptied the rest of the kerosene on the remains of Tommy and the boat's tacky surface. He balanced on the edge of the boat, ready to strike and toss the match on the freshly poured kerosene. He would jump in the water as close as possible to simultaneously lighting the pyre.

Standing on the edge of the craft, he thought of an old poem, which he had memorized as a boy. His mother had it published in the death and remembrance section of the West Fork paper on the first anniversary of the death of Bob's father. Bob had never liked the poem for its nostalgic hopefulness—the belief that loved ones would reunite someday "on the other side." For the rest of her short life, Bob's mother spoke nearly every day of such an ideal. She never questioned it. Bob did, but that mattered none now. He began to recite the poem, which he knew as though he had written it himself:

> *It was just a year ago today*
> *They took my darling man away.*
> *And never more will I hear the sound,*
> *Of his steps around the old home ground.*
> *But when I cross to the other shore,*
> *I hope to meet him as in days of yore.*
> *And together travel the streets of gold,*
> *And share our joys as we did of old.*
> *For there is no sorrow there I'm told.*

Bob wondered if his parents were getting to know the grandson they never knew in life. Perhaps that wasn't such a bad thought.

Bob lighted the match and threw it atop the pyre. The kerosene and other combustibles immediately did as they were designed. Bob paused for a moment to watch, and then he heard Patsy's panicked voice calling to him from the shore. He dived in the water and swam toward the bank.

In his exhaustion, Bob began to labor quickly. He wasn't sure he could make it back to shore. He treaded water, just enough to keep his mouth above the line. He wondered what the rest of his life would hold for him other than shame and regret. What was the point? It would be so much easier to let go.

A ferocious whoosh of oxygen and other chemicals being sucked from the air by fire brought Bob out of his reverie. He turned back to the punt and watched. As he dogpaddled, a fireball hurled into the darkness above the lake as it was fed by the sulfurous vapors that hovered over the water. Tommy's body burned quickly.

COME UP A CLOUD

Bob was about to let his body sink into a watery sleep when he heard his wife's voice again, this time even more panicked and closer than the first time. She was trying to swim out to him.

He swam to her.

39

I have discovered that floaters have feelings, and they can be mixed. I believe my mini microcosmic floater pod is about to acquire another tenant, and, damned if it isn't an Olstad. I won't have to interact with him, but just knowing he is occupying the same floater pod unsettles me. Human Skunk negatively changed the atmosphere of any space he occupied. I fear Floater Skunk will do likewise to my pod. Damn, afterlife is going to suck. But, as I said, I have mixed feelings. He won't be bothering anyone else again.

Cahill pulled to a stop by the croquet court. A lone utility pole light coated the court in pale blue. The rest of the park was cave-dark. He kept the Vic running; the AC fan spun noisily but could not keep the cabin cool. Cahill did not want to let out Maesie at the park should Denbo come looking for her. But she had refused his offer again to come to his house.

As she reached for the door latch to get out of the Vic, Cahill said, "That was a ballsy move back there."

"I wish everyone would quit acting like I did something good," she said. "It doesn't take balls if you have a gun and the other guy doesn't." She couldn't get rid of the image of her holding the metal barrel within an inch of Denbo's massive gut. "I can't believe I almost shot him," she said.

"You've been through a lot lately," Cahill said.

"Who hasn't?" She stared out her window at the inky gloom and thought about Diane. The woman had suffered more than Maesie, but she had refused to pity herself.

Maesie began to cry. A strangling sorrow expelled her anger, which had replaced her fear. Agony had begun to wrap itself around her, and it squeezed more tightly any feeling she ever had. She welcomed it, however, no matter how much of it was self-pity. She had been waiting for this since her mother died.

COME UP A CLOUD

Uncomfortable with her weeping, Cahill began to fidget in his seat. He looked out his window, but there was nothing to see in the blackness but the fuzzy shapes of white pines along the other side of the street.

"Maybe I'm looking at this wrong," Maesie said, wiping snot from her upper lip. "I don't have to worry about the house anymore. And I don't have bills and all that fun stuff. In a way, I've never been so free. Maybe I'll see what the world is like outside of Smackdab. Maybe I'll find out what my dad's world is like."

"Wasn't you the one who told me you can't solve your problems by leaving?" Cahill asked. He still faced away from her.

"This is different," Maesie said.

"Not so," Cahill said, looking at her and smacking the steering wheel with both palms. "You said I was a fool to want to leave town." He shook his head. "I don't get you sometimes."

"Maybe I was being a bit of a hypocrite, but I meant a change in location does no good if you don't change yourself, too."

Cahill stewed for a minute and then asked: "So, where do you plan to go? Out west like Rolf?"

Maesie wasn't sure, but she knew Cahill would want to go with her. Neither of them had anyone else. However, she wondered if bringing Cahill would be like bringing all of Smackdab, too.

"I have tonight to think about it," she said. "And I'll do it by Mom's grave. It's been awhile since I've been to see her."

Cahill locked her door from his side. "I ain't letting you out. It's as dark as a bear's ass out there. The only people in graveyards this time of night are dead ones. Or live ones praying to Satan."

Maesie unlocked the door. "I'll give Charmin your regards," she said.

Maesie had nearly reached the cemetery when a specter walked toward her out of the haze.

"Daddy?"

As she hurried toward her father, Maesie saw dark stains that blotched much of his shirt. Though it was too dark to see, she could smell blood. She began looking for the source.

"Are you hurt?"

"Who's that?" Rolf asked, affronted that the small stranger accosted him.

"It's me, Maesie."

"Maesie?"

"Are you okay?" She furiously ran her hands over his clothes. She confirmed it was blood, which was tacky to the touch, and there was a lot of it.

"Your shirt's all bloody, but I can't find where you're hurt," she said. "What happened to you, Daddy?"

Rolf looked dazed, out of sorts, but not like he was drunk. More like he had been conked on the head with a metal pipe, she thought. His eyes marginally focused, and she thought he now recognized her.

"What're you out so late for?" he asked.

"On my way to visit Mom," she said. "Are you hurt somewhere?"

Rolf thought for a moment. "No, I don't believe so." He looked around him. He had two bags at his side. "Where's my guitar?"

"I was about to ask the same question. Did you leave it in the truck?"

Rolf's eyes turned glassy before quickly regaining some focus. "I don't think I own a truck no more. Might not have the guitar no more neither. Goddamn, Skunk."

"Speaking of which, where is your partner in grime?"

"Skunk?"

"Yeah, Skunk. You just damned him. Are you all right, Daddy? Maybe you were popped in the noggin. Bend over and tilt your head toward the street light so I can look better."

Rolf complied. Maesie ran her fingers over his greasy scalp. "I don't feel a thing. No bumps. Nothing."

Still at a forty-five-degree angle, Rolf said, "I think Skunk and me got in a fight. That's right. It was that new guy Denbo." He stood up and smiled. "I still got what it takes."

"That might explain at least some of the blood," Maesie said.

Rolf stood and looked behind him. "Where'd I put my guitar?" Nodding, he said: "Must've left it at the cemetery with Skunk."

"This cemetery?"

"Where all the dead people are."

"Is Skunk hurt?" Maesie asked.

Rolf did not speak, but he looked worried.

"Maybe he's just visiting Luke's grave," she said.

Rolf furrowed his brow. "Luke passed?"

"Forget it. We'll talk about it later."

Rolf already had forgotten it, but he had remembered something else. He picked up one of his bags, which Maesie could see was two dirty pillows tied together. He began trying to unhook the bungee cords, but he had trouble.

"You need some help?" she offered.

"No," Rolf said, turning away from her. "This is for my daughter."

"Dad… it's me. I'm your daughter. Maesie. Are you sure you didn't get clocked in the head?"

Her father's shoulders slackened as he looked at her. This time he offered the bundle to her. "I can't get the damn thing loose."

Maesie unhooked the cord and removed a Stentor violin and bow from between the pillows. She let the pillows drop to the ground as she gawked at the instrument.

"Dad…"

"I couldn't afford the case," Rolf said, looking sheepish. "The old Jew tried to get me good on that, but I said he could take his overpriced case and shove it."

"It's okay. I'm sure I could find a used one someplace."

Rolf plopped to the pavement and sat with his legs crossed, the same way he sat when he used to play dominos with Maesie. She had forgotten about that. Her father had not completely ignored her. He had not been as terrible as she often thought she remembered.

Maesie sat next to her dad, cradling the violin in her lap as she watched him. He looked like he could fall asleep at any moment. Maesie now saw changes in her father were deep and, perhaps, permanent. Now that she thought about it, he had been slightly addled his last return to Smackdab. She had forgotten that, too. Everyone forgot names occasionally, but Rolf had fumbled for simple words like "mayonnaise" and "dandelion." It frustrated and angered him. When he couldn't remember "jelly," he had thrown a jar of peach jam out the back door so hard it hit and shattered against the base of a cedar tree twenty yards away. It took Maesie time to recover from that. Not because she loved preserves, but because it was from the last batch her mother had made. Rolf's memory had now deteriorated so much it no longer bothered him.

Everyone in Smackdab, those who slept peaceably and those who sought to, would envy Rolf Mattsen's knack for sluicing his brain of all unwanted thoughts. He had always wanted to be admired for something. Now that he was, he could not enjoy it. He lay down on his side and curled into a fetal position. Father and daughter occupied the middle of the road, but no traffic had come by. Likely none would until the morning.

"It's been a hard road here lately," Rolf said.

"I'd take you home," Maesie said. "Except we don't have one anymore."

Rolf nodded as though he expected to hear such news.

"You got that new fiddle?" he asked, unsure if he had given it to her.

"Yes. Thank you. This means so much to me."

"Why don't you play me a song? Just this once."

Maesie hesitated, and then she plinked the strings and tuned the instrument. If Rolf did not like her playing, he would forget it quickly. She began to play a few bars in A minor, but she already felt so sad about her father the music only made her feel worse. She stopped, laying the fiddle across her legs.

"That's a pretty tune," Rolf said. He took one of the pillows and put it under his head. He looked comfortable. "Kind've sad though."

"I can't help it," Maesie said. "I have nothing in me but sad music."

"Your mama always said you was a good player," he said, closing his eyes. "She was real proud."

"Maybe I should try my hand at making a living at it," Maesie said, leaning back on her elbows and looking where stars pricked light in the charcoal sky. She had never told anyone of her dream before. She wasn't sure it had been a dream until just then.

"I'd like to try your life for a while, she said. "Except for some parts of it."

Rolf mumbled something unintelligible.

"Against my better judgment, I may ask Cahill to drive me. He can be my combo chauffeur and roadie."

She continued to study the sky as she began to add meat to her plans, talking more to herself to than to her father. "Maybe I'll go to Branson. There's some band out there that would take a chance on a midget fiddler," she said. "Might be just the gimmick someone's looking for. You know?"

Maesie studied her father. He wore baggy gray cotton sweat pants like the ones that seemed de rigueur at nursing homes. He wasn't so old—still in his fifties—but Rolf Mattsen looked ancient, withered, and worn down.

"What are we going to do with you, Daddy?"

Rolf was asleep.

Unless a family had purchased their plot many years earlier, new burials in the Smackdab cemetery occurred in the annex on the eastern edge of the cemetery. That's where Charmin Mattsen was buried, near a sugar maple that also shaded Luke Olstad's site. As Maesie approached, she saw a car parked nearby with its driver and passenger doors open. The key-in-ignition warning dinged.

Maesie saw a body lying near the fresh plot.

"Skunk?"

The figure moaned.

"I expected to find a dead body," she said, kneeling down beside him.

"Well, shit, this is a graveyard after all," Skunk said. His voice was weak. It was difficult to tell in the dark what shape he was in, but Maesie could smell blood.

"We need to get you some help."

"It don't matter."

"I don't have a phone. Let me use yours. It won't take long to get someone here."

Skunk mumbled something Maesie could not discern. If he was dying, she needed to say something.

"I'm sorry," she said. "This whole thing was my fault. I got Tommy all wound up. I knew what he was going to do. I could have stopped him if I'd tried harder. Do you still have that chainsaw file? I could let you jab me with it."

Skunk again said something she could not understand.

"What was that again?"

Skunk grabbed her hand; his had tacky blood on it.

"Shut up," he said.

He tried to prop himself up on his elbow, but he gave up and lay down. "You need to take care of your daddy. He's not in good shape," he said.

"I know. He's sleeping in the middle of Pitchfork Road. I don't know what to do with him."

"My Martin's in the car," Skunk said. "Give it to him. He can play it wherever you put him. Tell him I'm sorry for taking his Taylor." He laughed, which was more like a weak gurgle. "Funny. I don't think I ever said sorry before. Not when I meant it anyway. I'm a late bloomer."

Maesie didn't know what to say. Skunk lay back down; he moaned.

"I failed him."

"My dad?"

"Luke."

"Luke was good. You and Diane did okay."

Maesie thought Skunk had died, but then he said, "Mostly Diane."

Maesie nodded. Skunk's eyes closed.

"Take care of your daddy," Skunk said.

"He adores you."

"Yeah."

Maesie watched a jet streak across the blackness two miles above her. Something lower, along the tree line, caught her eye. A column of blue-edged fire, incongruous with the rest of the dark firmament, hurdled above the horizon in the direction of Dead Lake.

ACKNOWLEDGEMENTS

    I give my warm gratitude to MJ Franklin, who slogged through an early version of this novel and encouraged me to continue, though she diplomatically informed me that some characters left her cold. I tried to warm up ones who could be salvaged and excised others. Also, I thank Craig Layne who provided editing tips and for giving me confidence that I had not wasted my time writing this book. Finally, I thank my wife, Michele, who always likes my writing even when she doesn't.

> Chapter 9: Lamentations 5:15 taken from the English Standard Version of the Bible
> Chapter 11: President Ronald Reagan spoke to the nation on January 28, 1986 following the *Challenger* shuttle disaster.
> Chapter 18: "I Wonder as I Wander," by John Jacob Niles, 1933

ABOUT THE AUTHOR

Ron D Smith is the author of two other novels: *The Savior of Turk* and *The Night Budda Got Deep in It*. He is also the author of a biography: *The Storm Before the Calm: The Early Lives of Venus and Hiro*. Ron would love to hear from you at www.smithdeville.com or on Twitter @smitrond.